Louisa Heaton live with her husband, f... has worked in vario... most recently four y... Responder, answering 999 calls. When not writing Louisa enjoys other creative pursuits, including reading, quilting and patchwork—usually instead of the things she *ought* to be doing!

Three-times Golden Heart® finalist **Tina Beckett** learned to pack her suitcases almost before she learned to read. Born to a military family, she has lived in the United States, Puerto Rico, Portugal and Brazil. In addition to travelling, Tina loves to cuddle with her pug, Alex, spend time with her family, and hit the trails on her horse. Learn more about Tina from her website, or 'friend' her on Facebook.

THEIR MARRIAGE WORTH FIGHTING FOR

LOUISA HEATON

FROM WEDDING GUEST TO BRIDE?

TINA BECKETT

MILLS & BOON

First published in Great Britain 2022
by Mills & Boon, an imprint of HarperCollins*Publishers* Ltd,
1 London Bridge Street, London, SE1 9GF

www.harpercollins.co.uk

HarperCollins*Publishers*
1st Floor, Watermarque Building,
Ringsend Road, Dublin 4, Ireland

Their Marriage Worth Fighting For © 2022 Harlequin Enterprises ULC

Special thanks and acknowledgement are given to Louisa Heaton
for her contribution to the Night Shift in Barcelona miniseries.

From Wedding Guest to Bride? © 2022 Harlequin Enterprises ULC

Special thanks and acknowledgement are given to Tina Beckett
for her contribution to the Night Shift in Barcelona miniseries.

ISBN: 978-0-263-30131-1

07/22

MIX
Paper from
responsible sources
FSC™ C007454

This book is produced from independently certified FSC™ paper
to ensure responsible forest management.
For more information visit www.harpercollins.co.uk/green.

Printed and Bound in Spain using 100% Renewable Electricity
at CPI Black Print, Barcelona

THEIR MARRIAGE WORTH FIGHTING FOR

LOUISA HEATON

MILLS & BOON

For a baby I never got to meet. xxx

CHAPTER ONE

THE ORANGE-PINK GLOW of the setting sun glided across the façade of the beautiful St Aelina's Hospital as Grace Rivas let out a deep, pent-up breath. A breath that was meant to steady her. To help her try to contain her nerves. A breath that was supposed to make her gird her loins, to prepare her for what waited inside.

Who waited inside.

She'd not called Diego to say she was back. It didn't feel right with the way things had been left. What were they? Husband and wife legally, yes, but *friends*? People who called one another up just to say hi? People who would rush into each other's arms, the way they'd used to? No. They were nothing that even came *close* to that.

That last argument before she'd left to visit her Aunt Felicity in Cornwall had been Heart-rending. The kind of argument that signalled the end of a relationship. And when you ended a relationship and then went away you didn't call that person when you got back home, because technically they weren't in your life any more.

She was not proud of the way she'd behaved. The lengths she had gone to in her desperation. The way she'd shouted. Ranted. Raved. Desperate for him to *say* something. To *do* something. To *react* to anything. Hoping beyond hope that somehow her words would get through that thick, impenetrable skull of his and he would call her *mi amor*, pull her close, kiss the top of her head and whisper into her hair that they would be okay. That he understood. That they would get through this. That they could deal with all the crap that life had thrown at them and come out on the other side somehow better, stronger than they'd been before.

Only he hadn't done any of that. He'd just stood there. Listening. Looking sad. Looking like a berated child. Looking sorry, but not actually saying it, his lips pressed together so tightly, so grimly, it had almost been as if he was biting them. Stopping himself from speaking. He'd just stood there and taken the full force, the full brunt of her fury and her rage.

Oh, how she wished he'd said something! *Anything!* To show her that there was still some chance they could pull themselves through that quagmire of anger.

But his silence, his inability to salvage anything from their relationship, had caused her to throw her hands up in frustration and storm past him, slamming the bedroom door behind her so that she could check her luggage one last time, knowing she couldn't miss her flight back to England. Especially because she'd be going *alone* now.

She hadn't heard him leave. Maybe because she'd been too busy muffling her sobs. But when she'd finally emerged, pulling her luggage behind her, expecting one last tearful goodbye, maybe even a last attempt to turn things around and save their relationship, she'd found a note on the kitchen counter.

I think it's best if I move into staff accommodation at the hospital.
For now.
D

Just *D*.
No kisses.
No, *let's talk when you get back.* Nothing. Grace had scrunched the note up in anger and tossed it into the bin.

Now, even thinking about that night caused a sour sensation in her stomach, and she had to swallow hard and look up at St Aelina's and try to remember the joy of this place.

The way it was lit up at night was particularly beautiful. Like another world. Which it was. A world in which Grace had always been able to find joy. Happiness. Refuge from her own heartbreak. Working as a midwife in the maternity unit of St Aelina's hadn't been just a job for her. It had been a way of life. She'd adopted this country and its people and given them her heart. Before meeting Diego she'd thought she'd never leave the hospital in London. Never leave her country except for holidays. But Spain—Barcelona, St Aelina's—had become home. More than she'd ever thought possible.

The people, the weather, the historic beautiful buildings, the language… They had all made their way into her heart just as Diego had left it.

No. That wasn't true. He was still in her heart. He

was her husband and, no matter what had happened between them, he would always have a place in her heart. Especially because of all that they had gone through. But she hadn't been able to keep him. He had walked away. Had not fought for them the way she'd hoped he would. And if he didn't want to fight…? Well, then. What was the point?

But as she stood there, looking at the hospital she'd thought she'd work in for the rest of her days, she knew she would have to tell her boss that she couldn't stay any more. That with her marriage over, with the way her life had crumbled, this place that had once given her such joy could only now cause her pain, if she stayed.

But she had more self-respect than that. She wouldn't linger in the hope that Diego would offer some small crumb of comfort, like friendship. That would be pathetic. It was love, or nothing, and he'd made it quite clear that he couldn't love her in the way she needed him to.

No. It was best to make a clean break.

Squaring her shoulders, she walked inside, ready to say hello to the many friends she hadn't seen for two weeks.

'Buenas noches.'

She said good evening to the night cleaners, the porters. She waved at Jorge, who ran the hospital café, as he left to get a good night's sleep.

Working the night shift was perfect for Grace. She had been unable to sleep for so long now that she might as well be working anyway. And, to be honest, it took her mind off her own problems. In every ward, every room of this hospital, stories were being played out. Some ended. Some became difficult roads to travel. But in Maternity new adventures began.

Families expanded. Miracles happened. People experienced joy and happiness and love such as they had never experienced before. Hearts expanded. Grew. Enveloped new faces and new lives. Sometimes there was grief. Sometimes there was pain and loss and despair. and Grace felt those keenly, tried vainly not to let them destroy her, considering her own past, but happiness outweighed those moments, and the thing about joy and happiness was that it was catching. All those in the department—the midwives, the doctors, the care assistants—got to share in a piece of those miracles. The IVF babies. The rainbow babies. The twins and triplets and multiples.

It was a special place to be.

She climbed the stairs to the first-floor maternity wing, rather than take the lift and risk running into Diego. He worked nights, too, but hopefully she wouldn't run into him just yet. Diego was a neonatal surgeon and worked on the second floor. Technically, she could get through a whole shift without seeing him if he wasn't needed. She hoped he wouldn't be. Crossed her fingers that all her mothers-to-be sailed through as normal, full-term cases.

Was she ready?

Could she ever be?

They would meet at some point, but she wanted a dose of happiness first, and so she greeted her friends and colleagues, and listened in to the hand-over, and then went to find her first labouring mother, who she was extremely pleased to discover would not need a neonatologist.

Alejandra de Leon was at term, fully dilated, and waiting for the urge to push. This was her first child with her husband Matteo, and up until this point she'd been cared for by Grace's friend and colleague Nena.

Grace introduced herself to Alejandra and Matteo. He looked excited and nervous as he set up cameras and recording devices from different viewpoints around the room—including one attached to the bedframe near his wife's head.

'Don't want to miss any of it?' she asked in Spanish, amused.

'We have a video channel.'

'You do?'

'Nearly a hundred thousand subscribers,' he said proudly.

'Wow. Your views are about to go way up, aren't they? Do you know what you're having? Did you do a gender reveal?'

'It's a surprise.' said Alejandra, rubbing her abdomen. 'Oh, another one's coming…should I push?'

Grace nodded. 'Take a deep breath and bear down, like you're having a bowel movement.'

She began coaching her. It was difficult sometimes for first-time mothers to know how to push. Some were afraid. Which was understandable. But that was why Grace was there. To encourage. To help. To motivate. She wanted to see those babies born just as much as the parents did. There was nothing quite like that moment when the baby emerged, was draped on its mum's tummy and let out that first cry...

Matteo clutched his wife's hand, whispering words of encouragement. 'You're doing brilliantly. I love you. I love you so much!'

Alejandra turned and smiled and kissed him, but it wasn't long before another contraction began.

Grace counted to ten. She could see the baby's head. It had a lot of thick dark hair. 'Alejandra? Reach down and touch. The head's right there.'

She reached down. 'Oh!' She turned to look at her husband, her face a mix of surprise, love and awe.

Matteo kissed her on the forehead. 'You can do this! You good?'

Alejandra nodded and began to bear down with her next contraction. With each contraction that came the head emerged a little more, disappearing again as each pain ended.

'This is the hard part, but you can do it!' Grace told her. She didn't think that Alejandra needed an episiotomy—a small cut to help the baby pass through. And she'd only been pushing for about half an hour, so actually she was doing really well. And this was just what Grace needed. A straightforward birth. She had missed this.

Getting away for a couple of weeks and visiting Aunt Felicity had been wonderful, even if she had gone alone, her marriage in tatters. They'd had so many lovely walks along the beach, and hot chocolates in cafés, and fish and chips out of paper bags as they'd sat shivering on the blustery seafront, the British weather not providing them with the expected sunny weather despite it being July.

It had been great to see her aunt again, even though there'd been questions. Difficult questions. About what her future held. What decisions she needed to make. And about all the things she yearned for—like a baby of her own.

Not all her aunt's questions had had definitive answers, and a lot of the time all Grace kept hearing herself say was, *I don't know.*

Even when she'd come back to their home, here in Spain, she'd not found any answers. Just an empty flat. Lifeless. A pile of post on the mat. Nothing much in it except for a wedding invitation. Javier and Caitlin, their colleagues and friends, were getting married on the estate at Maravilla. The invitation should have made her happy, but it had just reinforced the fact that she had no idea if she would be attending that wedding. No idea at all. And what would she say to them if she saw them at the hospital? Because they'd expect her to say she'd be coming. With Diego.

It was all too much. Too complicated.

But *this* couple were about to become a family. Their lives were changing for evermore. Alejandra and Matteo were going to experience the one thing that Grace had yearned for, for years. She'd had no problem with getting pregnant. It was just the *staying* pregnant part that had eluded her.

But she refused to focus on that pain again. This wasn't about her. It was about this couple.

Alejandra screamed with the force of her latest contraction. *'Duele!' It hurts.*

'I know it does…it's just the baby's head, stretching everything. One more push and your baby's head will be out!'

Alejandra nodded and took a sip of water from the cup that Matteo held to her mouth. He grabbed a facecloth and dabbed at her forehead. 'You're beautiful. I love you so much!'

Grace smiled at them both. It was so lovely to see it almost made her ache. She and Diego had been that much in love once. How had it gone so wrong?

Alejandra began to bear down again.

'That's it! Exactly right. Push harder! Harder! Okay, pant…'

The baby's head emerged, turning to face its mother's right thigh.

'Head's out! One last contraction, Alejandra, and you'll have your baby in your arms.'

Alejandra gasped, nodded, and squeezed her eyes shut as she pushed.

The shoulders emerged and Grace supported the baby. 'Open your eyes, Mummy, and reach down.'

She helped place the baby on her mother's stomach. Alejandra was crying with gratitude and relief, and Matteo's eyes wet with tears as the baby cried out. Suddenly everyone was laughing and cheering as Grace let Matteo cut the cord and draped a small blue towel around the baby.

Alejandra held her baby and cried happy tears.

'Want to see what you've had?' Grace asked.

Matteo reached forward, his hand gentle, as if touching the baby would somehow break it, his already radiant face breaking out into a bigger smile when he declared to his wife, 'It's a girl!'

Grace smiled for them both as she awaited the delivery of the placenta. Alejandra had only a small tear, and it was something that would heal on its own—she didn't need sutures. 'Have you chosen a name?'

'Eliana Maria.'

'That's a beautiful name. Happy birthday, Eliana.'

Grace checked the placenta, which was all fine, and the mum's blood loss was normal. Now was the time when she'd clean up, as unobtrusively as she could, so that this new family could have some privacy for a short time, before coming back to carry out the postnatal checks and Apgar score.

She wondered, as she always did at this moment, looking down on such a happy new family, if *she'd* ever get to experience this for herself. They looked so ecstatic in their little joyous bubble. Mum cradling baby in her arms... Dad half perched on the bed, his arm around his wife. Now that Eliana was here it was as if Grace wasn't even in the room any more.

'I'll be back in a few minutes.'

She backed away to the door. As much as Grace loved it when a baby was born, and everyone's faces erupted into smiles, she hated *this* moment. When she was forgotten, and yet again came the stark reminder that this happiness was not hers and she was not part of this family. They might remember her in the future, when they told the story of their child's birth. They might mention the lovely midwife who'd helped them get through it all, but that was all.

Grace silently closed the door behind her and let out a breath. As always, she felt the white-hot pain of her own empty arms, but she forced back the tears threatening to fall and headed to the board to update it, sniffing determinedly as she wrote up Alejandra's details. Next she stood up and went to the small kitchenette, knowing that Alejandra and Matteo would probably appreciate a nice cup of coffee each.

She poured the drinks into a couple of mugs and was just walking down to Alejandra's room when in her peripheral vision she caught movement off to her left. She glanced over with a smile, expecting to see Ana or Gabbi or Mira.

Only it wasn't.

Grace froze as her gaze met her husband's.

Diego.

Her smile, meant for one of her colleagues, faltered as he stared back at her. She felt sick as her mouth dried out and her heart pounded furiously behind her ribcage. Why was he here? Who had called him down to this floor? She'd not heard of any early labourers in the hand-over when she'd arrived and she'd thought she'd have more time before she saw him. Time so that she could micromanage their first meeting, so that she'd be prepared, so that she'd know what to say and how to act. But to be caught off-guard like this...

He looked good—but of course he did. He was Diego! And apart from being tall and ripped and disturbingly sexy, the man saved babies' lives. Premature babies' lives. What *wasn't* there to drool over? Even from this distance his dark brown eyes bored into hers with an intensity that ought to come with a blood pressure warning, and he looked like he was growing a beard. The dark, stubble emphasising his jawline.

He wasn't smiling. In fact, he looked shocked to see her there. Just as unprepared as she was. And that made her feel a little bit better—because she'd been fighting to get some reaction out of him before he left and now she had one.

'Diego…'

She saw him swallow. Saw him look down at the blue file in his hand for an interminably long time. And then he turned and walked away without saying a word.

The second he was out of sight she realised how much she'd been sweating, how much tension she'd held in her chest and stomach and legs. Now it was as if she'd become boneless and weak, and she needed to sag against the wall for a moment, just to catch her breath and to stop the tears. Because, despite everything that they had gone through, she'd hoped that somehow, no matter how unexpected their meeting, that he would at least have said hello. That he might even have looked happy to see that she was back. Maybe even smiled. Only he hadn't.

He didn't even say hi.

Was she not worthy of acknowledgement? Not even a nod of the head? Did he hate her so much that he couldn't even bear to look at her? That he'd walk away without saying a word? She knew that the last time they'd been together she'd stormed away from him and slammed the bedroom door, but... Surely they could be adult about this? They were going to have to work together, and they didn't need to transform this place, this hospital which had so very quickly become like home, into a place where she felt uncomfortable. Where their colleagues had to tread on eggshells around them. Where—God forbid—their friends felt they had to take sides.

It's a good thing, then, that I'm going to be leaving.

Grace squared her shoulders, stood up straight and rapped her knuckles gently on Alejandra and Matteo's door before going in with their coffees. She placed the drinks on a side cabinet and smiled at them. 'I just need to perform some newborn baby checks on Eliana and then I'll have her right back with you, okay?'

Alejandra nodded and placed the baby in Grace's arms. She looked down at the chubby little baby, admiring her thick dark hair, clenched tight fists and tiny button nose, and then laid her down in a bassinet.

One day she might be lucky enough to be a mother, but she very much doubted that it would happen any time soon. And it certainly wouldn't happen whilst she stayed married to Diego.

He clearly wanted nothing to do with her.

The sooner she went back home to Cornwall, the better.

Her marriage was over.

He'd been working non-stop whilst she was away—that was what he blamed it on. Being blindsided by the sight of his wife, back at work in St Aelina's. He'd been so busy bringing some medical notes down for tomorrow's day shift that he'd not even thought to remember that today was the night shift when Grace was due back.

And she'd looked…beautiful. She'd always had the power to grab his attention. The warm caramel of her hair had been twisted up into a bun, loose tendrils framing her heart-shaped face. And those startlingly blue eyes of hers—not pale, but richly blue, like the domed roofs in Santorini. To be caught in their gaze just now…

These last two weeks had been interminable. They were meant to have gone away together, to Cornwall, to visit her aunt. He liked Felicity. Loved her little seaside cottage. Liked the people there. They'd all made him so welcome—though her aunt hadn't been too impressed that she'd not been invited to their wedding.

He and Grace had married in London—a civil ceremony, near work, with two colleagues as witnesses. Not the big white beach wedding he'd later learned that Grace had always dreamed of, but they'd been so keen to get married. Grace had yearned to travel back to Barcelona with him, settle down and begin a family together. At the time it had seemed time was ticking away too fast, and their love for one another had been so all-consuming it had seemed the right thing to do. Just get married as fast as they could, leave London, come to Spain, then have fun trying to start that family.

The world had been at their feet and they'd thought anything was possible.

Now look at us.

It had hurt to see her. Physically hurt. As if someone had pounded him in the chest and then his gut, just to doubly make sure that he was winded enough to be unable to speak. His gaze had caught in hers and it had been like being caught in a beam of light…just like in those sci-fi shows he loved so much. Unable to move. Unable to breathe. Unable to *think*.

He'd wanted more than anything to run to her, to pull her into his embrace and hold her tight and never let her go. To say sorry over and over again. They'd only been apart these last two weeks, but before that they'd argued so badly and he'd moved out, feeling he had no other choice.

Since bringing her here to his home in Barcelona all he had caused her was pain. Grief. Loss. Upset. Heartbreak. Their hopes and dreams had been destroyed.

He'd wanted to run to her. Wanted to hold her in his arms. To say sorry. But the shock of seeing her… He'd clenched his jaw, looked down at the paperwork in his hands as if to remind himself of why he was there, and then, grounding himself somehow, he had found the strength to walk away from his wife.

He told himself he would talk to her later.

Maybe he would find the right words then?

Maybe in the future they would be able to talk without causing each other upset? Perhaps time would heal all wounds, as people said it did. That was what they needed. More time.

But for now those things didn't seem possible. And each step that took him further and further away from her orbit just made him heartsick. Just like when he'd packed his things a few weeks ago. He'd hated doing so. Almost hadn't been able to believe he was! But he'd done it for her. She didn't understand. Hadn't understood his silence or why he'd not said anything.

Maybe she would never understand that.

For now, though, he could soften the blow, knowing that she was back. They'd have time to sort through their problems. There would be no more breaks. No more going away. It might take a few weeks, or maybe even months, but they would be able to talk again.

But for now it's for the best. For both of us.

Grace had just finished escorting Alejandra and baby Eliana to the postnatal ward when her pager sounded. She checked the display and saw that she was urgently needed down in the ER.

She dialled from the midwives' station. 'I've been paged?'

'We've an urgent case coming in and you've been requested by name.'

That was odd. 'Who by?'

'The paramedic.'

The only paramedic who really knew her name was Isabella. *Diego's older sister.*

'I'll be right down. Do we know who they're bringing in?'

'We've only got vague details. But it's a young female in premature labour.'

Oh.

Grace was used to being called down to the ER. The midwives were often paged to consult on a woman who was in labour. But if *Isabella* was bringing someone in… If her sister-in-law had time, would she want to take her to one side and talk about what was happening between Grace and her brother? Did she even know? Would she say something to her? And if this was a preemie then that would mean they would also need the help of a neonatologist at some point, and the only one she'd seen on the night shift, too, was her husband.

Diego.

The two of them.

Together.

That's going to be awkward.

She almost—*almost*—considered getting one of the others to go and meet the ambulance. But Grace had never been a coward—and anyway, maybe Issy would be rushed off her feet and unable to stay once she'd dropped off her patient. And maybe, if the gods were kind, this young lady might not even be in premature labour at all. Her dates could be wrong.

Maybe.

Am I ever that lucky?

She didn't want to think about the answer to that much.

'I'll be right down.'

Grace replaced the receiver of the phone and stared at it, her stomach churning slightly. She looked up as Ana approached. 'I've got to head down to the ER. Possible preemie. Can you alert upstairs for me? Check they've got a spare incubator?'

'Sure.' Ana smiled.

Grace headed to the lifts and bypassed them, opening the door to the stairs and trotting down them, her mind awhirl with possibilities. What if Isabella had heard about Diego moving out? What if her sister-in-law was angry with her? Isabella and Diego didn't seem all that close, but would that matter? She wasn't sure she'd be able to stand up to a fiery Spaniard right now.

When she made it to the ER, she saw Issy wheeling her patient into cubicle three. The patient looked as if she was in pain.

Grace smiled, hesitant. 'Hi. What have we got?'

'This is Zara. She's eighteen years old, complaining of abdominal pains that come and go, and estimates that she's about eight months pregnant.'

Grace looked at Issy. 'Estimates?'

'She's been living on the streets. No scans. No healthcare.' Isabella sounded concerned. As if she couldn't quite believe it. 'She doesn't even know how many babies are in there.'

Right.

'Hi, Zara. My name's Grace,' she said in Spanish. 'I'm a midwife and I'm going to be looking after you.' She smiled, before turning back to Isabella. 'Where did you find her?'

'In St Aelina's Park. She's been sleeping in the folly.'

Poor girl. 'Okay, Zara, tell me about these abdominal pains. Can you describe them for me?'

Zara began to give a description, but it didn't sound like labour to Grace.

'Can I have a feel of your tummy?'

Zara nodded.

'I'll leave you to it.' said Isabella, almost sharply.

Grace turned to thank her, expecting a glare, or something, but her sister-in-law didn't even look at her.

She seemed distracted. As if she just wanted to get out of the ER as quickly as possible.

Grace watched her go, pushing away the trolley that they'd wheeled Zara in on. It was weird, but Grace was thankful. Isabella hadn't said a word about her and Diego! Perhaps she didn't know that they'd split up yet.

She concentrated on palpating Zara's abdomen, then used her tape to measure the height of the fundus—the top part of the womb. Thirty-six centimetres. 'You're right. You're nearly full-term and baby is head-down, which is good. I'm going to put you on a trace machine, if that's okay? It will allow us to monitor the baby's heartbeat and check for contractions.'

Zara nodded.

She was eighteen. She must be terrified.

'Anyone we can call for you? Friends? Family?' Grace couldn't imagine being this young and this pregnant, in pain and alone.

This time Zara shook her head and looked away from her.

'What about the baby's father?'

Another head-shake, and this time the welling of tears.

Grace's heart ached for the young girl and she placed a hand on Zara's arm. 'That's all right. You're safe now. I'm going to look after you, okay?'

Zara nodded.

'To make sure I can do that properly, I need to gather some information. I'll need to take some blood from you and ask you about your medical history. Is that all right?'

'I guess…'

'And maybe get you to do a wee sample, too?'

Again, the girl nodded.

'One last question?'

Zara looked at her, uncertain. Almost angry 'What?'

Grace smiled. 'Would you like a drink?'

It was the first time she'd seen even the hint of a smile.

Whilst Zara was having a scan, Grace took the opportunity to create a new patient record for her on the computer. They were on a maternity ward now. It seemed a better place for Zara to be—away from the chaos and noise of the ER. The emergency room could be a frightening place, and Zara was already scared.

Grace couldn't imagine being in the young girl's position. Eighteen and pregnant and living on the street. It was no place to be—not for anyone. And yet she still found herself envying the young girl, because despite her situation Zara was about to do something that Grace had been unable to achieve—she was about to become a mother.

Life very often played games like that, Grace thought. There were many people in the world like her—hard-working, honest, kind. People who had a decent home, who were law-abiding, who had never done anything wrong in their lives. And some of them were desperate to start a family and couldn't. Either the women couldn't get pregnant at all, or they were couples like Grace and Diego. The women could get pregnant, but they lost their babies—every single time.

And then there were other kinds of people. The women who abused their bodies for years with alcohol or drugs, or committed crimes, did terrible things. And they seemed to get pregnant at the drop of a hat. Grace wasn't saying that they didn't deserve to be parents... just that it seemed unfair. Sometimes you could do everything right in life and yet...

Poor Zara. What had happened to her? Where were her family? She must have some—somewhere. Even if she'd have to go and live with an aunt, the way Grace had when she'd lost her parents.

It had happened when she was so young. Grace's parents had been crazy in love and had wanted to live life to the full by travelling around the world. And yet their promise, their lives, had been cut short by a tragic car accident that had killed them both almost instantly. That was when Grace had been taken in by Aunt Felicity. Dear, quiet, reserved Aunt Felicity, who'd worked as a nurse and inspired Grace to join the medical profession, thrilled to discover her niece wanted to train as a midwife.

And although Grace had missed out on having a large family, living in a home filled with noise and laughter, she'd always thought she could build one of her own by marrying a man she fell in love with and having plenty of babies.

But she'd not been able to do even that simple task.

She'd fallen in love. She'd found the man. She'd got pregnant. And then her body had failed her. Time after time after time. And with each loss her husband had spent more and more time away from her. Almost as if he couldn't bear to be with her.

He'd clearly thought he'd made a terrible mistake. Because Diego came from a huge family. Six siblings! Isabella was the oldest, then Diego, then Eduardo, Frida, Luis and Paola. All grown-up now, but Diego had lain in her arms when she was pregnant with their first child and told her that he would love to have lots of babies with her. That he wanted the kind of big family that he was used to. And she had laughed with him, agreed with him, and told him that she wanted that too. That she would have as many of his babies as she could.

Grace let out a sigh, not wanting to dwell on her pain and grief, and luckily she didn't have to as Zara was wheeled back to the ward. Grace gave her a little wave from the desk, and then got up to go and talk to her patient.

'I've got some of your results back. The pains you were having earlier…you have a urinary tract infection. They can happen to anybody, so I don't want you worrying about that. We'll start you on a course of antibiotics and keep you here, so we can maintain your hydration and feed you up a bit before you go into labour fully.'

'My baby is all right?'

'I'm just waiting for your scan results to come through, but you've been feeling the baby kick and move?'

Zara nodded.

'Then those are good signs. Let's start you on the antibiotics and wait for your scan result. One thing at a time, okay?'

'Okay. Thank you.'

Grace stroked her arm. 'No problem. I'll leave you to get settled, but I'll be right outside if you need anything. Press this button here, okay?' She passed Zara the patient remote control and then headed back to the desk. But suddenly right there—right in front of her— was her husband. Diego. Her gaze locked with his and her breath caught in her throat. She swallowed hard.

He looked past her with regret, and his gaze was full of apology as he locked eyes with Zara. 'I have your scan results.'

CHAPTER TWO

GRACE.

He'd not expected her to be right there! She was so close to him. Close enough to reach out and touch. And by God he wanted to! But he couldn't do that any more, seeing as he'd walked away—and besides, he was here to give Zara the results of her scan. He was here for the patient and her baby—not, unfortunately, for Grace. He knew they needed to talk, but he couldn't imagine that that would be easy.

Nor was the news that he was about to deliver to Grace's patient.

'My name is Dr Diego Rivas. I'm a neonatal surgeon and I'll be in charge of your case.'

He saw Zara glance at Grace, and watched as Grace went to her and took hold of her hand.

'It's okay. Just listen.'

Grace was smiling at Zara. Her smile telling Zara that she could trust him. Clearly they had developed a bond. He and Grace had once had a bond, but now that was a broken and ragged thing. Torn. Weak. In tatters.

'We noticed during the scan that the level of your

amniotic fluid is quite low, but also that your baby has a condition called exomphalos.' Diego risked a quick glance at Grace. She would know what that was, and what exactly Zara would be facing over the next few weeks.

Grace squeezed Zara's hand.

'What the hell is that?' Zara asked, her voice full of fear and panic.

He was about to answer, but Grace got there first.

'It means that as your baby developed in your womb, the baby's intestines didn't relocate as they should have from the umbilical cord, so remain in a sac outside of the abdomen.'

'Ay, Dios mio!' Zara swung her legs off the bed. 'No. No, I'm not doing this! Let me go!'

Diego took a few steps back. He could tell this young girl was incredibly frightened. 'Please,' he said in a low, urgent voice. 'We need you to stay.'

Zara glanced at Grace.

'Your baby needs looking after. You need to stay here,' she told her.

'Did I do this?' Zara asked. 'Because I didn't get checked?'

She was like a cornered animal. Glancing from Grace to Diego and back again. He felt she might bolt at any moment unless they played this right, and he couldn't afford for that to happen. Because if this young girl went into labour on the streets with a baby with exomphalos... Well, it wouldn't have a great ending.

Diego shook his head. 'No. No one knows what

causes this to happen. But we know about it now and we can be prepared for it when he's born.'

Zara stared at him. 'He?'

He smiled and nodded.

'He. A little boy.' That seemed to really sink in. Made Zara think.

Diego glanced at his wife. They needed to persuade this young girl to stay. 'We'll need to perform a more detailed scan, so we'd like to keep you in and I need to devise a plan for after he is born. He's going to need surgery to put his intestines back inside his abdominal cavity.'

Zara's eyes welled up with tears. 'Could he die?'

Diego paused. He hated this question. All parents wanted to hear that their baby would be fine, and he could never promise that. But if he didn't promise would she run?

'All surgeries carry risk, Zara. But he has a good chance here—better than if you were back on the street. And we will do our very best to get both him and you through this.'

'Will I have to have a caesarean?'

'No. You can give birth normally. But we would like to monitor you both closely.'

Zara crumpled and began to sob. Loud cries of pain and anguish. It was terrible to hear, and all he could do was reach for tissues and pass them to her, one hand rubbing her back as he tried to calm her and reassure her.

He was acutely aware that his wife was on the opposite side of Zara, doing the same thing, and he wanted nothing more than to look at her and acknowledge her help, or smile at her, or *something*. But Grace wasn't looking at him. Her full attention was on their patient.

Grace was smiling, whispering comforting words. 'We'll get you a private room, okay? But I need you to promise us that you'll stay here until both you and the baby are well?'

Zara sniffed, wiping her nose on her sleeve. She looked up at him, her gaze assessing, checking, trying to see if she could trust him. Then she glanced at Grace—who, he had to admit, was being amazing.

But then again, she always was.

Finally, Zara nodded. 'Fine. But I'm only going to deal with you two. No one else.'

He nodded. That was fine. It might give him the opportunity to smooth things over with Grace, too. 'Agreed.'

After Diego left the ward Grace let out a breath, releasing the strain she'd been under in his presence. She wasn't looking forward to having to work closely with him over the next few weeks, but she would do so for the sake of her patient, who she already felt a kinship with.

Zara had no one fighting for her. No one in her corner. At least, no one she knew about. So, in lieu of family, Grace was happy to do whatever was needed to get this girl and her baby good care. Something they would both need a lot of.

'When did you last eat something?' she asked.

Zara looked embarrassed. 'I can't remember. Yesterday? Maybe...'

She nodded. 'I'll see what I can rustle up. And I'll bring you a menu later, so you can order your meals for tomorrow.'

'Thank you.'

Grace smiled. 'It's no problem. And I'll try and organise that private room for you—unless you'd like to stay on the ward? It's just that you'll see a lot of people come and go...it might be quite noisy for you, and you need to build yourself up and rest.'

'A room of my own?' Zara seemed to think about that. 'I've never had one.'

'Then let's find you one. I'll be back soon, okay?'

Zara nodded.

Grace headed out of the ward, squirting her hands with antibacterial gel and rubbing them together, hoping that the midwife in charge would agree to a private room. But as she approached the desk she could already see Diego talking to her, and assumed that he was arguing Zara's case for one. She didn't want to talk to him right now, so she walked past him and headed to the small kitchenette, to see if she could find a sandwich, or something she could make for Zara.

She'd only been in there for a few minutes when she heard the door open. When she turned, expecting to see one of the other midwives, the smile on her face froze, then disappeared when she saw Diego standing there.

Grace's heart began to thud, but she turned away from him and began making a sandwich, glad to have something for her hands to do.

'You're back.'

She wished her hands would stop shaking. It was

hard to put butter on the bread and spread it evenly with him standing behind her.

'It's good to see you.'

Ham. Cheese. Salad. Maybe a yoghurt? Grace tried to focus on Zara's food. Tried to ignore her husband behind her.

And then he said, 'I missed you.'

He was kidding, right? After everything that had happened. After letting her get so wound up that she'd ranted and raved, hoping that he would tell her that they still had something to fight for.

Grace turned and looked at him incredulously. 'Are you kidding me?' She pointed at him with the butter knife.

'I just thought that—'

'No! You don't get to think *anything*, Diego!' She threw the knife down into the sink and leaned against it, breathing heavily, trying to calm herself, trying to keep her voice down. Their colleagues and patients didn't need to hear them arguing. 'You moved out. You left. You ignored me in corridors. You hardly spoke to me for weeks. Avoided me. And now, when I've been away for two weeks, you have the audacity to tell me that you've *missed* me?' She laughed. '*You* made the choice to leave. Mentally, emotionally and physically. Do you know what that did to me? At all?'

He stared back at her.

'Those weeks in Cornwall were hell for me, knowing my marriage was over. *Over!* I've spent the last two weeks getting used to that fact and telling myself that there's nothing between us any more, and now, when

I come back to work, you tell me you've missed me? What? Do you think I'm some sort of plaything that you can toy with? Do you enjoy torturing me? Is that it?'

'Of course not,' he said quietly, looking suitably apologetic.

'Then don't say things like that to me. We talk about work. Nothing else. We talk about that young girl who's depending on both of us? We need to be professional for her sake. I will work with you, and I will be polite and considerate, but all I can be to you right now is your colleague and nothing else. Because I need to work on mending the heart that *you broke.* And you telling me that you miss me…? That just opens up old wounds.'

She stared hard at him. Hoping and praying that he would understand, that he wouldn't push for more. Not that she thought he would. He was probably keen to know where they stood with each other, too. Keen to hear that she didn't expect anything of him. Because he had made his choice clear.

'I'm sorry, and of course I shall abide by your wishes.'

She'd expected that. But to actually hear him agree with her that it was over… That hurt all over again. Some small part of her must have still wanted to hear him say *It's not over. Not yet. I love you. Let's fight for us.* Only he didn't. He agreed with her.

She turned away to hide her tears, angrily grabbing another knife from the drawer and cutting up the sandwich, placing it on a plate and then pushing past him and heading towards Zara's room.

Grace couldn't mend them, but she could help Zara.

And this place—St Aelina's maternity unit—had always brought her calm and happiness. Even on the worst days.

She needed it to work its magic once again.

The hospital rooftop had always been a haven for Diego. It wasn't pretty, by any means. Air-conditioning vents, chimneys, wires—it was all very industrial. But it had become a place for him to think. A sanctuary that only he seemed to know about or access. From here he could look out to the blue sea, focus on the horizon and take a few deep, steadying breaths. Sometimes, if he couldn't make it all the way to the beach, he would stand here and watch the sun rise.

He'd come here whenever there had been a Covid surge. Every break that he could manage he'd come up here—just to take the mask off his face and breathe. To steady his nerves, to gird himself for the battle that was being waged below, in almost every room, of life over death. Too often they'd lost that battle, and he'd lost count of the number of times he'd had to ring a family member to tell them of a loss. And each loss had been another stab to the heart. As if it was personal. Despite their vast knowledge, their years of training, their science, their medicines, they were losing the battle. Each death had told Diego that they weren't good enough. They weren't clever enough.

They simply weren't *enough*.

He wasn't enough.

As always, his thoughts drifted to the joy he had experienced at discovering Grace was pregnant. A smile crept across his face as he remembered how happy she'd been to tell him! He could see her face now. The brightness of her eyes. The wideness of her smile. They'd both wanted to start a family. They'd both dreamed of having a big one—a house filled with love and laughter and joy.

And then she'd lost the baby. Just a few weeks after discovering she was pregnant. Grace had lain curled up in bed, her face drawn and pale, her cheeks tear-stained, crying for hours until the bleeding had stopped.

He'd done what he could. Tried to reassure her that these things often happened with first pregnancies. That it had never been meant to be. That there must have been a developmental abnormality or something like that. He'd spoken to her like a medic to make her see that it wasn't her fault, that there was nothing either of them could have done, trying to be a calm port in a storm as she'd grieved for the baby she'd loved and lost.

He'd hurt, too. Of course he had. He'd had so many plans in his head. He'd wondered what type of father he would be. Thought of the games he would play. The bonding moments with his son or daughter. To lose that possibility…to lose that wish had been devastating. All he'd wanted to do was curl into a ball himself and grieve for the child that would never be born. Never have a name.

But his wife hadn't needed him to be falling apart when she was, and he'd wanted back the woman he loved, and so he'd been her shoulder to cry on. Her listening ear. The rock that she'd needed. Swallowing down his own pain to deal with hers.

Eventually they'd decided to try again, when she'd

felt ready, and they'd allowed the hope and the excitement of trying to conceive to fill their lives with joy and laughter as Grace had quickly fallen pregnant a second time.

They'd both been thrilled, and optimistically cautious, and when Grace had made it past the first trimester they'd gone out and finally told everyone. Their colleagues. Their friends. Isabella. The rest of his siblings. Aunt Felicity. With each new person they'd told it had made the reality of the baby even more official. The world had finally seemed back on its axis once again, and at the first scan they'd both cried to see the baby's heart beating so fast and so strong!

They'd begun making plans. Grace had bought some maternity outfits. They'd begun working on the spare room to make it into a nursery. Having conversations about paint colours. Names. Feeling nothing could go wrong this time. They'd had their bad luck.

So when tragedy had struck a second time, six months in, and Grace had had to give birth to a stillborn baby, they had been broken. Torn apart. His stoicism and wise words had meant nothing to her and she'd lashed out in her grief and anger at the world.

He'd tried. He'd really tried to be there for her. But her pain had been such that he hadn't been able to handle seeing her broken that way. When he had tried to comfort her it had done nothing, and so he'd begun to look for excuses to stay at work, knowing he shouldn't, but also knowing he needed time for himself, to grieve in private.

He would never forget what it had felt like to look

down at his stillborn son. They'd taken a long time to heal from that second loss. Their relationship had not the same feel as before Grace had tried to get pregnant. Their freedom, their happiness at life in general being good, was gone. They'd both been tempered by loss. They'd sniped at one another without thinking. They'd felt wary of ever trying again. They'd been nervous. Anxious even to suggest it—even though it was all they could think about…having a child.

When she'd got pregnant a third time, unexpectedly, neither of them had felt happy. Neither of them had been carefree. Grace had panicked over every twinge. Every symptom. His wife had changed from the woman she'd once been to a woman who was nervous, fidgety, who chewed on her lip constantly, who kept going to the toilet to look for blood, who barely wanted to move, just in case…

They made it to the thirteen-week scan.

But the baby had not.

The third loss was the thing that had totally destroyed them.

He'd had no words for her. Nothing at all. And she'd just seemed so lost in her own pain and grief that she'd hardly noticed that he was grieving too. With nothing to say to her he'd stayed at work, taking on extra shifts, giving his all to his patients because his wife wouldn't let him take care of her.

His patients had salved his pain somewhat. Here at St Aelina's he could help. He could make a difference. He could be the puppet master for happy outcomes. They weren't his, exactly, but he felt triumph with every baby he saved. Every baby he saw go home the way his own babies never had.

Here on the rooftop he could breathe.

Here on the rooftop he could tell himself that what he did mattered.

Here on the rooftop he could tell himself that somehow, someday, he and Grace might work things out.

Zara lay on the bed, about to have a more detailed scan of her baby. Grace sat to one side of her, holding her hand, whilst Diego performed the ultrasound himself. They already knew this baby had exomphalos, but he knew that babies with that condition often had comorbidities—other conditions alongside it—and he wanted to be informed before the baby was born.

Pre-warned was pre-armed.

This second scan would give them that knowledge and allow them to be ready for when the baby arrived, and if it needed emergency surgery straight after it was born, to ensure its survival, then so be it.

'The gel might feel a little cold,' he said.

He placed the transducer onto her abdomen and began to move it around to get the basic picture of how the baby was lying, before he could look for more markers.

'What exactly are you looking for?' asked Zara. 'You already know what's wrong with him.'

'We're just checking to make sure there's nothing else. Dr Rivas will also get a chance to have a more detailed look at the exomphalos, as he will be operating,' Grace said in a soft, low voice.

It was the one she used so as not to frighten her patients. He'd heard her use it before. But this was the first time he'd heard her refer to him as *Dr Rivas*. What? Couldn't she even call him Diego any more? Was this her way of trying to create distance between them?

He'd had plenty of time to stew on his decision to move out, to walk away, and for most of the time he believed he'd made the right choice. It had become unbearable to witness his wife's pain whilst trying to work through his own privately. But in moments like this, when she couldn't even refer to him by his first name, he began to see the extra damage he might have caused her.

And he'd never wanted to do that.

The exomphalos was sizeable. In the pouch he could see the intestines, and a small portion of the baby's liver. A silo pouch would be the best option for reduction, he thought, as he moved the transducer to look for any other abnormalities. He began at the head and moved down, then paused, hovering around the throat and upper chest area.

'What is it?' Zara asked. 'What's wrong now?'

He zoomed in, tried to see more clearly. 'I think I can see an atresia.'

'What's that?'

He could hear the panic in her voice.

'An atresia is a condition in which a passage or orifice in the body is closed or completely absent,' Grace said calmly.

'It looks like an oesophageal atresia, Zara,' he confirmed, moving the transducer this way and that to get a proper look. 'The oesophagus is your baby's food pipe.

If it is indeed closed, and it looks like it is, it means your baby won't be able to feed normally. The milk won't make it to baby's stomach.'

'Oh, my God!' Zara began to cry. 'Does that mean he's going to die if he can't eat?'

He shook his head. 'No, no. Not at all. We can perform surgery to reconnect the two pouch ends. It looks like your baby has developed a tracheoesophageal fistula. That sounds scary, but what it means is that when your baby was developing the body created an abnormal junction. We can sort this out with surgery after he's born, at the same time as we work on his exomphalos.'

But Zara was crying heavily now. 'Is it my fault? It's my fault, isn't it?'

'Hey, now, no…it's not your fault. No one knows what causes these things to happen. They just do.' Grace stood and grasped Zara's hand more tightly and made the young girl look at her. 'Listen to me. We know now. We can help him. We can do this.'

Grace was so good with patients. It was what had initially made him fall in love with her. She just got it. She knew how to relate to them. She knew how scared they could be and she knew the right words and the right tone to use. She gave them strength. Strength they'd never known they had. When a woman in the final stages of labour felt she had nothing left to give, no more strength to push, Grace could help her dig down deep and find it.

He wished he could have done the same for her when she'd needed strength.

Guilt flooded him and he looked away, unable to bear witness any more. He focused on checking the rest of

Zara's baby. He clenched his jaw and concentrated hard on the scan images, remembering to print a couple off so Zara could look at them.

'We're all done. I couldn't see anything else.'

Grace didn't look at him. She just looked at her patient. 'That's great news. All you need to focus on now, Zara, is growing your little boy so he comes out big and strong and ready for his surgery.'

'Promise me he won't die.'

He looked at Grace again. They couldn't promise that.

'Everything will be just fine.' His wife smiled.

Zara was settled back in her private room, and Grace was about to go and check on another patient, when Diego stopped her in the corridor. She could see him standing there. Waiting for her. Hands on hips, looking incredibly fed up.

Sucking in a deep breath, she went to pass him, but he stepped in front of her. 'You shouldn't have told her that everything would be fine. You don't know that.'

'She needed to hear something positive. All you've done since getting on this case is give her bad news.'

'I told her the truth. She needs to know that.'

'And the truth of those surgeries is that they usually go well.'

'Usually. But you know that every surgery carries a risk, and we have no idea how Zara's baby will react to being under anaesthetic. There could be complications. She needed to hear the reality of the situation.'

'Which you're so good at delivering.' She could feel

anger and hurt rising over his criticism of how she was handling Zara's case. She pushed past him, rage flaring, and before she knew it turned to face him again. 'Would it hurt you to show some compassion? To stop being a doctor and for once—*just once*—show that you're a human being?'

Before he could answer, she pushed open her next patient's door and went inside, forcing a smile, knowing she had to leave her private feelings outside. Right now this couple, Carlita and Emilio, needed calm, confident vibes.

'How are we doing?' she asked.

Carlita was still only four centimetres dilated with her first baby, so she had a few hours to go yet.

Grace checked the trace of the baby's heartbeat and noted that Carlita seemed to be contracting every five to six minutes. Then she settled herself into a corner of the room and noted down other observations—temperature, blood pressure, blood sugar. Carlita was suffering from gestational diabetes and was being induced at thirty-seven weeks, because her baby was already registering at around nine pounds.

'You're doing great. How do you feel?'

Carlita smiled nervously. 'I'm okay so far. Nervous of what's to come.'

'That's understandable. But what you've got to remember is that no matter what happened to other women in labour, no matter what horror stories you might have been told by well-meaning friends and family, your labour and your birth will be your own experience. Some women sail through without making a sound. A couple of pushes and the baby is out. No one ever tells those stories, do they?'

She smiled, thinking back to when she'd lost her first baby. How so many women had told her that they'd also experienced a miscarriage the first time they'd got pregnant. That it was normal. Natural. And that they'd gone on to have four kids. Five. Twins. Triplets. It had seemed that everyone had a success story to tell her.

When she'd lost the second baby they'd had less to say. When she'd lost the third it had felt as if women looked at her differently. They'd hidden their own pregnancies, hadn't told her until they absolutely had to, thinking that she was going to get upset.

She *had* been upset. Of course she had! It had seemed all the women in the whole world could get pregnant and deliver safe, happy, healthy babies except for her. Coming into work each day had been painful. Each birth a stark reminder of what she had lost. What she and Diego were missing. But eventually these births had become comforting. Each baby in its mother's arms a victory.

Maybe they weren't hers, but she lived vicariously through them.

Grace had come to accept that she would never have children. Never have the large family that she'd always craved. Something was wrong with her. It was no wonder that Diego had left. He wanted a large family, too. He'd grown up in one. Five siblings! She couldn't even begin to imagine what that must have been like, having grown up an only child herself.

He'd tried to tell her once. Told her about how Isabella had looked after them all after their mother had passed away when baby Paola was only one year old. Isabella had been thirteen—much too young to take on such a responsibility—but as the eldest she had done so. And then his father had become ill a few years later, and she'd taken on more, becoming his carer too.

They'd all tried their best to be good, and not cause her too much work, but there had been six of them and Isabella had lost her teenage years—Diego, too, as he'd become the man of the house. They'd tried to instil fun and laughter into their lives, but it had been hard, and as soon as they could they'd all flown the nest, spreading out across Spain, though he and Isabella both still lived in Barcelona.

Diego didn't seem all that close to his sister. They stayed out of each other's way, mostly, but Grace knew there must be love there. Appreciation.

Diego had looked for his freedom before.

Now he was free to find someone who could give him a family.

The thought saddened her. Made tears sting the backs of her eyes. She blinked them away rapidly. Maybe once she got back to the UK she should start divorce proceedings. There would be no point in hanging on to a relationship that had fizzled out, despite how strongly it had started.

Warmth spread through her at the thought of happier times long past. How she'd been working in that hospital in London and looked up at the sound of footsteps coming down the long corridor and seen him— Diego—for the first time.

Had it been love at first sight?

Lust at first sight?

All she knew was that her heart had begun to pound, her mouth had gone dry, and she'd felt like a silly teenage girl with an immediate crush. That hair, those beautiful dark brown eyes, so full of exotic spirit. His gaze had met hers and for just a moment time had stood still and the rest of the world had faded away. She'd been rushed off her feet at work. The ward had been full of new mothers that day. Grace had struggled to find time for a decent break, and she'd felt exhausted, but in that one moment as their eyes had met all that had fallen away.

Tiredness—gone.

Aching legs—gone.

The desire for a cup of tea and a sit-down—gone.

And then time had begun again, and he'd smiled at her and nodded, and her cheeks had flushed, and that had been that. Hook, line and sinker. When he'd found her at the end of his shift and asked her out of course she'd said yes! Despite the fact that only hours before all she'd wanted from her evening was to lie in the bath with a good book and have a soak before falling into bed.

Instead, she'd ended up dancing the night away in some club, with Diego teaching her how to salsa. And when they'd gone back to his home she'd ended up in his shower with him, and there had been no reading done, no standing there letting the spray from the water refresh her body.

Diego had done all that. And more. And afterwards

they had fallen into bed and carried on enjoying and exploring each other.

She'd fallen hard and fast. They'd had a whirlwind romance and when Diego had proposed she'd thought nothing in the world could ever make her happier.

Where had all that excitement gone?

Where had the love gone?

Grace knew she should never have said what she had just now. Diego had actually been very good at explaining to Zara what would need to happen, and he'd been absolutely right that she shouldn't have told her that everything would be all right when she had no way of knowing for sure.

But it was just...

Whenever she'd needed him to say some encouraging words, or soothe her soul, he had always just stuck to the facts. Been clinical. Been Dr Rivas rather than Diego, her loving husband.

She'd wanted a sign that her loving husband was still there somewhere.

But all he continued to show her was that he was nowhere to be seen.

CHAPTER THREE

'GRACE? COULD I have a word with you before you go?'

Her supervisor and chief midwife, Renata, stood in the doorway to her office. Grace had been about to go home. To get some much-needed sleep, if she could, in the cold and empty apartment that had once felt like home.

'Sure.' She followed Renata into her office. 'What's up?'

'Olivia has been called away to Andalusia, to look after her mother who's had a stroke, so I'm going to be short on night staff for a while. Could you cover her night shifts for the next few weeks? I appreciate it's a pain, but you're the most senior midwife amongst everyone, and I need to know I have someone I can trust on nights.'

Oh. Grace hadn't been expecting this. She'd been hoping to speak to Renata about giving her notice and leaving… But their patients meant more to her than any personal requirements right now—plus, that would allow her to follow through on Zara's baby. She had promised, after all.

'All right. That seems okay. Do we know how long Olivia might be in Andalusia?'

'Long enough for her to make sure her mum's okay. I think she wants to see her through the beginning of her physio and then get help arranged before she can come back.'

Grace nodded. 'Keep me informed.'

'I will. Did you have a nice break back home?'

She thought of her time in Cornwall. Alone. 'It was different. Cold.'

'Once you get used to the Spanish sun…' Renata smiled.

'Exactly.' She stood to go, said goodbye, and headed out of the hospital.

It had been a crazy first shift back. Running into Diego like that when she'd not expected it. Then his rather distracted sister. Realising she'd have to work with Diego on Zara, and now she was going to be on nights for a while. Maybe Diego would be on day shifts? Maybe he could keep an eye on Zara during the day, whilst she looked out for her at night? That seemed sensible. Perhaps she should suggest it to him. Tell him it was in their patient's best interests, rather than mention the fact that she didn't want to argue with him all the time and running into him each night would be incredibly distracting.

Night shifts were crazy. The hospital was a different world at night. It was more intimate. And did she want intimacy with Diego?

Physically, she missed him. He'd been gone from her bed for a long time now. She missed the feel of him in her arms. The way it had felt to wake in the morning and see him lying beside her, his face in soft repose. The way she would often lean over and touch him, watching his face, waiting for him to wake up and smile at her, reach for her, pull her close so they could lose themselves in each other.

She couldn't remember the last time they'd done that. She couldn't remember the last time they had laughed with one another. Couldn't remember the last time they had simply sat on the sofa, watching a movie, sharing a bowl of popcorn.

When had it gone so wrong?

After the first miscarriage? Or the second? Or the third? Or had it been when Diego had realised that her empty, barren womb would not give him what he wanted? When he'd realised that if he were to have the family he wanted he would have to find it elsewhere? When he'd begun to pull away from her and retreat into medicine? Into work? Taking extra shifts in a bid not to be near her? When she had started doing the same?

I'm hungry.

She hadn't eaten all night. She'd been with Zara and then with Carlita for most of it—Carlita having given birth to a bouncing baby boy just before Grace's shift had ended. It was always nice to leave on a high. But she'd been denied even that. The baby's blood sugar had been low and he'd been taken to the NICU as a precaution, until he could be stabilised.

Grace knew she had to think of her own blood sugar. As she walked through the streets she thought about going to La Casa. It was a nice little traditional Catalan breakfast place that she and Diego knew. A place they'd often gone to for breakfast after sharing a night shift. The idea of sinking her teeth into their delicious *torrada amb tomàquet* or their deliciously thick *punxo de truita* made her mouth water. The owner, Felipe, knew exactly how she liked it.

But the idea of walking into La Casa alone, sitting at a table by the window alone, forcing a smile for Felipe, pretending that everything was all right, facing his questions...

No. I can't do it.

Instead, she allowed herself to enter a fast-food joint that was open twenty-four hours and picked up a hot chocolate and a rather lacklustre breakfast sandwich that was thin and simply filled a hole.

The owner there didn't know her name. The staff didn't know her or greet her or say goodbye. They simply moved on to the next customer. It was almost as if she wasn't there.

She'd known coming back to Barcelona would be difficult.

She just hadn't realised how lonely she would feel.

Diego lay in bed in the hospital's staff accommodation, staring up at the ceiling. He couldn't sleep. Couldn't lie still. Grace's last words to him were burning into his brain.

'Would it hurt you to show some compassion? To stop being a doctor and for once—just once—show that you're a human being?'

Frustration forced him to his feet, and he pulled on

a tee shirt and some trainers before grabbing his phone and earbuds and heading out on a fast run.

The sun was beginning its slow journey across the sky and already the temperature was in the late twenties and promising mid to late thirties. It was July. The middle of summer. Already the streets of Barcelona were filled with natives and tourists. Normally, they didn't bother him, but today he took a thin alley between a couple of whitewashed buildings adorned with hanging baskets and cracked blue mosaic tiles, that took him away from the crowds perusing the shops and storefronts towards the seafront, where he could run on the promenade. The sea air always made him feel good. There was nothing quite like fresh air mixed with the scent of the sea.

'Would it hurt you to show some compassion?' The words echoed in his head.

Was that how she viewed him? A compassionless monster? He thought he had shown her how much he cared. He had been there for her, holding her hand, mopping her tears in the beginning. Had she forgotten those days? The days when he'd listened to her cry, when she'd doubled over sobbing, almost as if her grief were cutting her in two and she was trying to hold her broken pieces together?

He hadn't cried with her—had that been his mistake? He'd thought he was doing the right thing. That by staying strong he would allow her the room to fall apart. He'd understood her grief, her pain—he'd felt it too. But what would have been the point of both of them collapsing under the weight of their sorrow?

She'd needed him to be strong. She'd needed him to be factual. And, yes, maybe he had brought out the side of him that he used to cope with the families of sick babies in the neonatal unit. Maybe he was guilty of distancing himself. But it had been for *her*! Because he'd loved her and had wanted to be strong for her!

And now that strength was being used as a weapon to bash him with.

He wished he could tell her…let out all the pain that the loss of their three babies had caused him, too. The pain of the dreams that had been taken from him. His own childhood had been difficult—there'd been almost no time to be a child himself. So when he'd pictured himself as a father he'd told himself he would always be there for his children. Love them. Care for them. Have fun with them and show them the world. He'd dreamed of raising those children with Grace. Bilingually, if they could. They would have the brightest, most beautiful children together!

His chest began to burn as he ran harder and faster. The air was thick with heat, rather than oxygen, but he didn't care. He needed to run, needed to burn, needed to feel the pain of the muscles in his legs protesting, his lungs straining, his blood pumping. Needed to punish himself.

And that was when he saw her—Grace—sitting on a low wall, looking out to sea.

His steps slowed and he stopped a few metres short of her, panting heavily.

She must have sensed him, or something, because

suddenly she turned, and when she saw him she quickly looked away and wiped at her eyes.

Had she been crying?

It was as if someone had punched him in the gut. Just the thought that she was in pain again broke him. So instead of challenging her and telling her that he wasn't a monster, that he *did* care, that he *did* feel compassion and that she had no right to accuse him of not having any, he pulled his earbuds out and walked over to her. Putting his own pain to one side yet again to put hers first.

Sitting down on the wall with his back to the sea, he waited for her to gather herself. Waited for her to be able to speak. He knew in that moment he would take the verbal bashing, whatever she needed, just as long as she stopped crying. That was something he couldn't bear to see. That was something he couldn't bear to be the cause of.

When he realised she had composed herself, he offered an olive branch. 'Carlita's baby was doing well when I left.'

He saw her nod in his peripheral vision.

'Good. I'm glad.'

He could hear her trying to be strong. To steady her voice.

'It's always a tricky thing when the mother has gestational diabetes. We'll keep an eye on him for a while. Make sure he doesn't get too jaundiced.'

'That's good.'

He thought about the next thing he wanted to say. Whether it would upset her or not. But he decided she might actually find comfort in it. 'They decided to call him Luca.'

She turned to look at him, then, her eyes searching his. Luca was the name they'd picked for their second baby, if he was a boy. It had always been a favourite name of Grace's. He hoped that she would view this piece of news as a good thing.

It seemed she did. Grace smiled. Then looked away to the sea again. He understood the peace it brought. He often came here to look out to sea. Mostly at sunrise.

The promenade was filled with people. Most of them headed to the beach, to fry themselves beneath the sun's strong rays.

'Couldn't sleep?' she asked him.

'No. You?'

'I haven't been back to the apartment yet.'

He liked this. Talking to her again without it being a battle. Okay, it wasn't as comfortable as he would have liked. He would have loved to have one of their usual conversations, where they told each other about their day, laughing over silly things, or sympathising over some of their harder cases. But this would do for now. This…ceasefire. Maybe they were able to talk like this because they weren't at home or at the hospital.

'You should try and get some rest,' he suggested.

'So should you.'

He smiled. She was right. And maybe he would be able to sleep now. Now that they'd spoken and now that her last words to him weren't accusatory ones.

She stood up from the wall, slung her bag over her

shoulder. 'Aunt Felicity sends her love. She missed you. You always could wrap her around your little finger.'

'I missed seeing her, too.'

Grace folded her arms. 'We…er…we need to work out what we're going to tell people.'

He was confused. 'About what?'

'About us. And we'll need ground rules for when we see each other at work. No over-familiarity. No personal stuff. Let's just keep it professional, yes?'

He sucked in a breath, realising that her walls were going up again. He didn't like what she was saying, but what had he been expecting? He was the one who had moved out. He was the one who had stayed here whilst she went to Cornwall alone.

They had both agreed that their relationship was over. But he guessed knowing it and actually acting on it were two different things.

Grace was being sensible, that was all, and he would have to agree. Especially when it came to telling Isabella, his sister. He didn't want her rushing in and mothering him all over again, thinking that he needed it the way he had when they'd been children. Not now. Not when Isabella had other concerns on her mind. Concerns he'd not yet been able to tell Grace about.

How to tell Grace?

The guilt of knowing Isabella's big news when Grace didn't, and knowing it would hurt her when she did find out, made him agreeable. 'Sure. We can do that.'

'So, if anyone asks about us, what do I tell them? Just that we're over? That it didn't work out? Keep it simple and not embellish?'

He figured most of them would guess why. They all knew about the lost pregnancies. And who would want to probe into that mess? He didn't, so why would other people?

'Whatever you want.'

'I'm going to take you up to see your baby now.' Grace smiled as she went into her patient's room, pushing a wheelchair before her.

Amelia Lopez nodded and swung her legs out of bed, one hand holding her belly, where her caesarean incision was. Earlier that evening Amelia had been rushed into Theatre after suffering an early placenta praevia at just thirty-two weeks' gestation, and when her daughter had been born she'd been blue and floppy. Diego and his team had worked quickly to oxygenate Amelia's baby, and had whisked her away whilst the rest of the surgical team had continued to try to prevent Amelia haemorrhaging. It had been difficult, but they'd managed to staunch the blood before the decision to perform a hysterectomy had been made.

Since then Amelia had been recovering on the postnatal ward, hooked up to a blood transfusion, and her husband Joseph had gone home to shower and change, once he knew his wife and daughter were safe.

Grace set the brake on the wheelchair and then gently helped Amelia lower herself into it. She grabbed a blanket from the bed and draped it over Amelia's legs, because she felt a little cold still.

'How is she doing?' Amelia asked.

'As good as can be expected. When we get up there

I'll get the doctor to come and talk to you. Explain what they've been doing and how they expect her to proceed.'

Amelia nodded.

'Have you thought of a name for her yet?'

'I'm not sure. I think I need to see her. I've not seen her face. I need to look at her and see what suits her.'

'Good idea.'

Grace began to push her out of the room and towards the lifts that would take them up another floor to the NICU. She felt great empathy with Amelia. How scared she must have been to feel that she was losing her child. And poor Joseph, her husband, who must have feared he was losing them both! But she was envious, too. Amelia and Joseph had been scared to death, terrified, fearful, and yet they'd still got their daughter. She was alive. Upstairs in a neonatal incubator. She had people fighting for her. Rooting for her. For these two, there was still the hope of a future with their child.

The lift doors pinged open and Grace wheeled Amelia inside, steeling herself for meeting Diego again.

Seeing him in Theatre earlier, those dark brown eyes of his smouldering above the surgical mask, she'd had to force herself to look away. To concentrate on what she was doing. Because when she looked at him, dressed in his scrubs, saving a baby, it did strange things to her insides.

He had skills she didn't understand. Knew how to do things she would never be able to get her head around. He could keep a steady hand when operating on a tiny baby, navigating his way around tiny organs, tiny hearts. He could go into a zone and somehow forget the tiny human on the table and just concentrate on fixing the problem, whatever it was. He could distance himself so that he could do his job, and it was something she both admired and feared. Because when she saw him doing that—doing the very best he could for his tiny patients and their families—it simply reminded her of why she'd fallen in love with him in the first place, and right now she didn't need to be reminded of why she loved him.

I need to remind myself of why I'm walking away.

She tried to steel herself as the lift doors pinged again and she wheeled Amelia out and headed for the NICU. She knew Diego would be there. Focused and sure and confident in his surroundings. This place was his castle and he ruled here. He was the king, and she had once loved to see him in his element here. Diego was intensely passionate about what he could do, and he had to be one of the best neonatal surgeons in the country. People came for miles, sometimes even from other countries, just to have him consult on their case. He was wanted. Desired. And not just by her.

As they got closer to the unit and she saw him there, his hands inside an incubator, listening to a baby's chest with a stethoscope, she gritted her teeth and wheeled Amelia in.

She felt his gaze upon her as soon as she came in. Like a warmth, an intensity washing over her. She glanced in his direction and met his eyes with her own. 'The Lopez baby?'

She watched as he looked at Amelia, then back up at Grace. 'She's over there in the far corner. Why don't you take Amelia over and I'll be there in just one moment to explain everything?'

'Thanks.' She tried to sound businesslike. Professional. Not sad or wistful. But it was hard. Now that she was back, she knew she would have to start taking the steps to walk away, and at some point actually *tell* Diego that she would be leaving. That would be much harder. Nerve-racking. She hadn't even told Renata yet. No one knew. Except her and Aunt Felicity.

She wheeled Amelia over to the incubator and set the brake once again. 'Here she is.'

Amelia peered through the side and tears welled up in her eyes. 'She's so tiny! Like a little bird!'

The baby was covered in wires and tubes. And although Grace knew what most of them were for, and what they did, she also knew that to Amelia they were strange and frightful things. Alien, almost. She was just about to start explaining what all of them were for, when she sensed Diego arriving beside them. She straightened up, nodded at him in acknowledgement.

'Mrs Lopez? I'm Dr Rivas, and I've been in charge of your daughter since you gave birth to her in Theatre.'

Grace stood back and let him take the lead. Allowing herself to listen and watch as he explained the condition of Amelia's daughter and what assistance she'd needed since being born. Apparently she had fluid in her lungs and needed a respirator, so that explained the tube down her throat. She also had wires monitoring her heart and her temperature. The little red light strapped to her big toe measured her oxygen saturations, and the tiny wrap around her arm measured blood pressure.

She was holding steady. Doing as well as could be expected. They were monitoring her closely and she had a dedicated nurse, just for her.

Grace noted how his voice softened when he was talking to Amelia. How his eyes bloomed with a kindness and a sympathy that she loved—that she wished she'd seen and heard when they'd lost their own babies. It had been there at the beginning, but after that... He'd retreated from her.

Diego was talking to Amelia on her level, so that she would understand. He didn't use big, complicated medical terms; he kept it simple without being patronising. It was a difficult line to walk, but she could see that he was making Amelia feel confident that her baby was in good, strong and secure hands.

'Thank you, Dr Rivas. I appreciate everything you're doing for her. Can I touch her?'

He smiled broadly, the smile lighting up his eyes, and for Grace it was like a punch in the gut. 'Of course you can. There's a sink over there, where you can wash your hands first. Let me take you.'

Grace stepped back, clasping her hands behind her back so that she didn't touch Diego's accidentally on the handles of the wheelchair. Her heart was thudding hard in her chest and she was beginning to realise how hard it was going to be, keeping herself from him.

But I have to do it. There is no other way.

She looked at his broad back, at the shoulders she knew so well, and at the narrow waist around which she'd often draped an arm, resting her hand on his hip or caressing his bottom, the way she'd used to when they hadn't been able to keep their hands off one another. She missed that casual touching they had once done at work. Little ways in which they'd let the other know *I'm here... I love you.*

How long did it take for love to stop?

'I'll be doing night shifts exclusively for the next few weeks, so maybe it'll be good if—'

Diego bit his lip, hands on his hips, as they stood on the other side of the NICU while Amelia visited her daughter. 'Ah...'

She frowned, looking up at him, and he couldn't help but be mesmerised, as he usually was, by her beauty.

'What do you mean by *ah*?'

He grimaced. 'You're going to suggest I do days, so that we can stay out of each other's way, aren't you?'

'No,' she answered, quietly but brusquely. 'I was thinking about Zara. If she's only wanting to deal with us, what if she needs one of us during the day? I thought it would make sense, if I'm doing nights, for you to do days.'

'Right. Only I'm already signed up to cover nights for the next month or so.'

'Oh.'

He couldn't read the expression on her face. Was it disappointment? Discomfort? Awkwardness? He'd hoped for something better than that. He wasn't sure why after that chat on the promenade, when she'd discussed with him different ways to tell people they'd broken up. He knew he'd been the one to move out, but that had been to give her space, to give her...

Who am I kidding? I did that for me! Because I couldn't bear to see her pain any more. Because I couldn't bear to feel so helpless.

But to actually start telling people they were over...? That was a different kettle of fish. It was like telling people you were expecting a baby. The more people you told, the more real it became.

He didn't want to think that he and Grace were over. He'd hoped that somehow, somewhere, there was still a little love left to salvage.

But how can there be? All I do is cause her pain by giving her babies she can't keep, and then I have to watch the fallout! I'm bad for her. I always have been. Dragging her away from the home she knew to this place. Putting her through what I have and somehow expecting her to still love me. Loco.

'I'll try to stay out of your way—except for when we're with Zara, of course. If that will make it better for you.' It pained him to offer this, but what else could he do? He had to let go of the woman he loved. Give her the chance to find happiness elsewhere. Even if it killed him to see her with someone else.

He instantly felt sick at the thought.

She nodded, not meeting his gaze. 'Fine.'

And then she went back over to Amelia, a bright smile pasted on her face, and it physically pained him to watch her walk away.

He knew it was something he would have to get used to. But at least she was still here. At least he could see her for now.

It wasn't as if she was about to leave Spain and return home, never to be seen again.

At the end of her shift Grace didn't feel tired at all, so she headed for the staff swimming pool.

St Aelina's was a modern hospital, designed by a very sought-after architect who had blended the building itself into the local area, artfully hiding the solar panels among the rooftops and cultivating St Aelina's Park behind it, which was filled with sculptures and water features created by local artists.

The hospital itself had obviously been designed to cater for its patients with the best technology and equipment, but it also prided itself on looking after its staff's physical and mental wellbeing. Apart from the pool, with its low dive board, there was a sauna, a steam room, a gymnasium, a juice bar, and also a quiet library, a sensory room and a staff counsellor on site.

Although Grace loved the peacefulness and quiet of the library, today she felt the need to be in the water. Hopefully no one else would be there, and she would be able to swim a few lengths and then relax by just floating on her back for a while and closing her eyes.

She got her wish. No one was there at this time of the morning, and as the early sun beamed through the floor-to-ceiling windows, she dived in, swimming for a few metres underwater, before surfacing and performing a powerful front crawl from one end of the twenty-five-metre pool to the other.

For a moment the exercise did what it was meant to do. She forgot everything. Diego. Their both being on nights for the foreseeable future. And the fact that at some point she would have to tell him she was leaving.

She would have to tell Renata, her boss, too. She didn't want to let her down, but what else could she do? She couldn't stay and see Diego every day.

The water soothed her. She'd grown acclimatised to the chemical tang of chlorine in the air and she powered through the water as if all that mattered was getting from one end to the other. As her lungs began to burn and her muscles protested she slowed, flipped onto her back, and let her residual energy float her gently into the heart of the pool.

She closed her eyes and gently began to paddle her arms to stay afloat. She heard the door at the poolside open, but ignored it. All that mattered was the floating. The feeling of being in warm water and all her cares floating away...

She heard a splash. Someone diving into the water. She heard them swimming, but paid no more attention.

Just float. That's all you have to do...

When she finally began to feel hungry, and knew she ought to get dressed, go home and try to get some rest, she straightened and swam breaststroke to the edge of the pool, hauling herself onto the side and wrapping her towel around her. When she turned, she stopped, her breath suddenly caught in her throat.

It was Diego. He was the person who had been swimming. He was the person even now up on the dive board, adjusting his footing preparing to dive in.

Her gaze hungrily raked over his body. This was an unexpected gift. The body she knew intimately. And the sudden, gut-wrenching yearning she felt for him almost left her breathless.

But she knew she couldn't stay and stare at him when he suddenly locked eyes with her. She saw a range of emotions cross his face, but the one that was strongest was regret. He looked down at the water, took a breath, and dived in.

She knew she couldn't dive back into the water and swim into his arms, the way she once might have done. Instead, sadly, she turned away and headed back to the changing room, unaware that he watched her go.

CHAPTER FOUR

'How are things going for you back there? Have you seen Diego?' asked Aunt Felicity over the phone.

Grace had been honest with her aunt when she'd visited. Told her everything that she and Diego had been through. And, bless her, her aunt had sat and listened and had not been judgmental about either of them.

'We've spoken.'

'How did he take the news that you're coming home?'

Grace shifted in her seat. 'I haven't told him yet.'

'What? Grace, you have to tell him. He deserves to know. Unless…'

As her aunt trailed off, Grace sipped at her coffee. 'Unless what?'

'Unless you're having second thoughts. I'd understand if so. You've made a life over there. A commitment. It will be hard for you to leave that—especially if you still have feelings for him.'

Grace shook her head. 'There are no second thoughts.'

'But there *are* feelings?'

Grace paused to think. Of course there were. You didn't marry someone and move to a whole other country and try to have three babies with him and not have feelings. But… 'Not like that.'

'Oh, Grace, honey… You know you can be honest with me.'

'I am! He left me feeling alone, remember? He could barely look at me. Once he realised I was faulty goods, he couldn't get away fast enough.'

'People deal with grief in different ways.'

'So, I'm just supposed to accept abandonment and carry on like nothing ever happened?'

'No, I'm not saying that. I'm saying that maybe you need to tell him how you feel.'

'I did. And he moved out. Remember?' Grace shook her head. 'You always did have a soft spot for Diego, like he could do no wrong.'

'That's not fair, honey, and you know that. I love you, and I have raised you to be a strong woman, I think. It's just that sometimes you…'

'What?'

'Sometimes you don't always give people a chance to explain.'

'I begged him to tell me what he was feeling. I begged him to show me some kind of emotion, and he walked away.'

'Maybe he found it difficult. Maybe he was trying so hard to be strong for you that he forgot he also needed to share his feelings.'

'No. No, Diego isn't like that.' She felt sure of it. *Didn't she?* This conversation wasn't going the way she'd expected it to. 'Anyway, I haven't told anyone

I'm leaving yet. We're short-staffed, and I've offered to cover nights for the next few weeks.'

There was a sigh at the other end. 'You need to tell Renata if you're planning to leave.'

'I will. When I'm ready.'

'Maybe Diego will talk to you when *he's* ready, too.'

Everywhere he looked, it seemed Grace was there. At the hospital, in the pool, on the wards, in the hospital cafeteria, on the promenade...and now the operating room. His wife stood opposite him, waiting to collect the baby after he'd finished its surgery in utero.

The baby was at thirty-eight weeks and had been developing a small, non-cancerous growth on its neck over the last couple of weeks that, on ultrasound, looked like a cyst. He'd decided to perform a caesarean section and operate on the baby before cutting the cord, so that the cord could continue to supply blood and oxygen until the cyst was excised, the wound stitched. Then he would complete the caesarean and deliver the baby.

Normally in Theatre he felt as if he could do anything. This was where he excelled—this was where he thrived. But since moving out of his home with Grace even the happiness he got from being in Theatre was dampened.

He should be feeling happy. The cyst excision had gone perfectly. And yet when he'd looked up to meet Grace's eyes and smile at his success she hadn't been looking at him. Instead she'd just stood there, eyes cast downwards, with a sterile cloth draped over her hands, waiting to receive the baby.

It was like being stabbed in the heart. This had been one of their things. Operating together and on a successful outcome meeting each other's eyes and smiling.

He'd felt her dismissal at the pool, too. Up on that diving board, ready to slice through the water, he had known she was looking at him and he'd met her gaze. But he'd realised all too quickly that they could never be what they'd been before. He'd seen it in her eyes. She blamed him for everything. For leaving her. For treating her badly, as she saw it, and being the one who'd caused her all that pain in the first place.

He'd not been able to stay on that board a moment longer under her accusatory glare, so he'd dived into the water. And when he'd surfaced she'd been leaving, and he'd had to stop swimming, feeling all the air gone from his body as he ached for her so badly it had physically pained him. So much so that he'd pulled himself from the water and sat on the poolside, struggling to control his breathing.

It was like losing a piece of himself. As if someone had chopped off a limb. No, not that. As if someone had dug out his heart and left a gaping, bloody hole in his chest.

He missed her so much. Missed her smile when she looked at him. Missed the sound of her laughter. The feel of her at his side.

The better part of him was gone and it was all his fault.

Diego clamped the cord and passed her the baby. She turned away to take it to the Resuscitaire, and he returned to finish off the section.

Had she told anyone yet? That they were over? He'd told Isabella that they were having problems, but he'd kept it vague and hadn't even mentioned that the marriage was probably over. He'd made it sound as if they'd had a bit of a tiff and it would all blow over.

Perhaps he needed to face facts. Instead of looking at his wife with regret and longing, he should just accept the truth. Did he really want to be a man who walked around the hospital pining for his wife?

They'd been through too much.

It was too late for them.

What they'd had was lost.

After the surgery Grace was having a well-earned rest. It was just after two o'clock in the morning and all was quiet on the wards. Today she was looking after the postnatal ward, and most of the mothers and their babies were asleep. All the lights were down except for the ones at the midwives' desk, and so she sat there, holding one of the babies, appreciating the quiet and the solitude.

To her there was something special about the night shift. It was weird, because when she'd first started doing shift work she'd hated nights. Hated the disruption it caused in her life, playing around with her sleep schedule. But now that she was an experienced midwife she actually preferred them. The phones didn't ring constantly, upper management weren't always walking around, and she didn't have to cope with streams of visitors coming and going.

Night shifts were quiet. Just the sound of soft shoes

on tiles, the occasional cry of a baby, the gentle murmuring of mother's voices as they tried to soothe or feed their newborns. And if she needed to help anyone—help a mother breastfeed, show her how to latch the baby on so that she didn't get pain—then there was an intimacy to doing that in the middle of the night. Mothers who had just given birth were tired and happy and grateful, and Grace was always ready to go and make an exhausted mother a hot chocolate, or some toast, or even take a baby for a little while and give it a cuddle, just so its mum could get some sleep.

And that was what she was doing now.

In her arms she held baby Arlo. His mum Emilia had been in labour all day yesterday and she'd only given birth a few hours ago. The poor woman was exhausted, but once she'd fed her son he hadn't seemed to want to settle in his cot. Grace had offered to take him for a while, so that Emilia could sleep.

Gazing down at the baby now, she couldn't help but smile and stroke his fat cheek, and marvel at the wonder that was a newborn child.

'That suits you.'

Diego.

She looked up. How had she not heard him approach? Her cheeks flushed, but she looked down at Arlo and continued to rock him. She was not sure what she could say to this man she was trying her hardest not to be around.

'I can't do this, Grace.'

She heard the upset in his voice and it pulled at her. Pulled at her heartstrings. She heard real angst there, real emotion—and, damn it, wasn't that what she'd begged him to show her? She couldn't ignore it now.

'Can't do what?'

Arlo grizzled slightly at the sound of her voice, but then settled down again.

Diego stared down at her from the other side of the desk. 'I can't do my job with you ignoring me. With you not even able to look at me. We used to be close…we used to be…' He stopped and bit his lip before changing tack. 'I need to be able to talk to you. We need to be civil.'

'You're talking about what happened in Theatre?'

He nodded.

She thought about his words. About how hard it had been in Theatre for her to ignore him. Not to look at him in his scrubs, not to remind herself that this gorgeous, amazing man was no longer hers, not to fall in love again with his skills and abilities and talent.

Talent and intelligence. Two things that Grace found incredibly attractive and sexy. And Diego had both of those and much more. Today this man in front of her had performed surgery on a baby in utero! If people knew how much study that took—how much training, how many hours of education and learning had to go into something like that—they'd be amazed. And yet Diego had done so easily and without breaking a sweat. She might not have watched his face, but she had watched his hands. His fingers. How skilfully and surely they had manipulated the instruments. No shaking. No nerves. Just precision. Skill. Talent. The irrefutable knowledge that what he was doing was right. It had been powerful and dizzying stuff.

'This isn't easy for me either, Diego.'

'You think it is for me?'

She met his gaze, shocked, hearing again a little surge of frustration in his voice. She'd thought it *was* easy for him. He was the one who had walked away!

'We work together, Grace. And we've got to work together on Zara. If that girl is going to trust us, then we've at least got to show that we're partners. In work, if nothing else.'

He was right. She knew it.

'You ignoring me, not looking at me, refusing to speak to me, even to acknowledge that I'm in the same room as you…' He stared at her as if he couldn't quite believe she had acted in such a way. 'It's disrespectful. But more than that it's hurtful.'

So he *was* capable of feeling hurt? Grace gazed at her husband, then looked down at the baby in her arms. If only she'd been able to have one of her own then they wouldn't be in this mess. Her husband wouldn't be on the other side of a desk, telling her that she was hurting him. She wouldn't have failed him. That was why he was angry now. She had failed him and she was failing him again.

He had married her, thinking that she would give him the huge family that he had dreamed of. And she'd failed him. Over and over again.

Her aunt's voice came back to her *'Maybe Diego will talk to you when he's ready.'*

Maybe he was ready now?

'You're right. I apologise. From now on I will be perfectly civil.'

He stared at her, almost as if he were checking to make sure that she wasn't playing with him. But she stared back at him, determined and sincere.

'All right. Thank you.'

She saw his gaze drop to the baby in her arms again and his face filled with sorrow.

'It really does suit you, you know.'

Then he was gone, disappearing from the light and into the shadows of the corridor.

Diego knocked on Zara's door and went in when he heard her say that he could. 'Hi. Just thought I'd see how you are. You've had a lot of information to take in over the last few days.'

She must have just woken up. It was early. Seven a.m. Her hair was all mussed, her face swollen with sleep.

'I'm okay. It's weird sleeping inside.' She glanced at the window. The sun was beginning to stream in through the blinds.

'But better than sleeping on the ground?' He grabbed her notes from the end of the bed and sat on the chair beside her. 'Any more pains?' He flicked through her notes, noting that she seemed stable. Her blood pressure was good and the traces she'd had showed that her baby was doing well.

'No. I think the antibiotics are working.'

'That's good. I thought I'd let you know that Grace and I will be working nights, if you need us. But I can pop in during the day, too. I often work overtime or stay late. Just ask one of the midwives to page me.'

She looked at him curiously. 'When do you sleep?'

He smiled. 'Not often these days. And mostly in on-call rooms. It just seems easier, if there's an emergency I need to rush to.'

She tucked a strand of hair behind her ears. 'Is my baby going to be okay? He's got a lot wrong with him.'

'I know it's scary to have to sit and listen to doctors using all these medical terms, when your expectation is that your baby will be healthy and like everybody else's, but it's a good thing, Zara. We know what he needs, so that when he's born there's no complications. No panic. We know what we're doing and we'll look after him.'

She bit her lip and he saw her glance at the door. Was this girl a flight risk?

'I don't want you to run,' he said. 'Think about what will happen if you do. You'll go back into the world—an *uncaring* world that will see you back on the street. And if you give birth out there, to a baby that needs medical intervention to survive, you could lose him. But here… with us…' He implored her with his eyes. 'We can give him the very best start, with your help.'

She nodded. 'Okay. Thank you.'

Diego stood and smiled down at her. 'I'll leave you be. No doubt breakfast will be here soon. I just wanted to pop in and let you know that if you don't see us around too much during the day it doesn't mean we've forgotten you.'

He needed the save on this one. He didn't want her running away with fear. They had every chance to help this baby and, having lost three of his own, every save gave him back hope. Every save made him extremely happy indeed. Made him feel useful.

'And I can page you whenever I need to?'

He nodded. 'Whenever you need to you can have them call me. Night *or* day.'

He hoped that now he'd talked to Grace, and she'd promised to be civil, working together on Zara from now on would be a lot more pleasant.

He liked spending time with her, and had missed her like crazy when she was gone. Part of him had feared she would never return, and if that had happened he didn't know what he would have done. Gone after her? Begged her to come back?

But she had come back, and when he'd seen her in that corridor the first time he had felt such relief! Such joy. Along with the realisation that they still had so much to say to one another. So much to sort out. He wasn't ready to lose her. All of this didn't seem real, and he was actually thankful that he had Zara as a patient, to work on with Grace. It would give them plenty of opportunity to talk—professionally and, he hoped, privately.

Persuading Zara to stay was one thing.

Persuading Grace might be another thing entirely.

And what would I be asking her to stay for?

Grace was being paged to the ER. As senior midwife during the night shift the onus was on her, but she was happy enough to leave the maternity floor in the capable hands of her colleagues. They weren't too busy that night. Zara was fast asleep, and the two labouring mums they had in were still at their early stages—only three to four centimetres dilated and contracting irregularly.

Carlos, a nurse in the ER, had asked for her after a woman had been brought in with a pelvic bleed. She was eighteen weeks pregnant.

Hearing the symptoms made her heart almost stop. Instantly she knew what this woman must be feeling. What she must be fearing was happening. Was she losing her baby?

Grace put down the phone and stared at it for a moment. She wondered if she was strong enough for this. Would she be able to get through it without becoming emotional herself? Eighteen weeks was too soon to deliver. The baby would not survive. This bleed the patient was experiencing might be nothing, but what if it was something terrible? What if she had to sit with this woman whilst she lost her baby?

Could I handle that?

She picked up the phone again, dialled the number that would ring the doctors' line in Neonatal.

'Dr Rivas, neonatal surgeon.'

'It's me.'

'Grace? What's wrong?'

She could hear the concern in his voice, and it was almost like the time when she'd had to ring him after she'd begun to miscarry their second baby.

She'd been at home, folding laundry, getting ready to put the clothes away, when she'd experienced sharp, stabbing pains in her womb that had made her double over. She'd sat down on the edge of their bed and taken a few deep breaths, thinking it was over, that it hadn't been anything serious. Then the pains had come back. Fiercer. Stronger. So much so she'd cried out and scrambled for her mobile phone on the bedside cabinet.

She'd somehow made it to the bathroom, pulled down her clothes and seen the first signs of blood. She'd tried to dial his number, her trembling fingers misdialling at first, and by the time she had rung the blood had been flowing.

'Hey?'

'Diego...'

'Grace? What's wrong?'

He'd heard it. In her voice. The upset, the terror. The tears. It all came back to her now.

She swallowed hard. 'I need you to meet me in the ER.'

'Okay. Why?'

'I've been paged for a woman with a pelvic bleed. She's eighteen weeks.' She knew she didn't have to say any more. Knew that he would understand her trepidation about going down there and facing this alone.

'I'll be right down.'

She nodded and put down the phone, hearing her pulse thrumming in her ears, feeling light-headed, weak. If Diego was there, perhaps he would be able to speak and offer comfort when she couldn't? This was going to be hard. A real test for her. She'd not been called down for a bleed as early as this since her own losses. Now she would be on the other side, and she had no idea how helpful she'd be.

Ana, busy scribbling notes into a patient record, asked her if she was okay? 'Do you want me to go instead?'

'No. I should do it. I have to do it sometime.'

Ana nodded. 'Okay. But I'm here if you want me to take over at any point.'

She appreciated that. 'I won't be long.'

Grace headed down to the ER, thanking whatever gods might be listening for the lift that took ages to arrive, for the slow ride down, giving her the time to steel herself, to prepare, to try to be strong.

The patient was going to need her strength. Her comfort. Her reassurances. Her patient was going to need a professional—not a bumbling mess.

As she got down to the ER she saw that Diego was already there, chatting to a male nurse. The one who'd called her? And that he'd seen her arrive.

He came straight over to her. She was instantly taken by the way he looked. The determined stride, his face sincere, yet with that professional distance. Clearly he was more ready for this patient than she was.

'Grace, thanks for calling me.'

She shrugged, so nervous it was almost as if her teeth were about to start chattering. 'I just thought that together we'd be able to—'

He shook his head. 'No. I think I should see her alone.'

'But I was the one paged. I know how she's feeling!'

'I know. I can see it in your eyes. And you cannot go in there looking and feeling the way you do.'

'Diego, I—'

He placed his hand on her shoulder and his touch

did remarkable things. Her voice stopped working, her body came alive and her heart, which had already been thrumming hard, seemed suddenly able to jump out of her body and go hopping along down the corridor with every beat.

'Let me take this. Let me perform a scan. Then, and only then, I will decide whether you should be involved.'

She knew what he was doing. He was trying to protect her. She got that. She really did! But all she heard was Diego telling her what to do and deciding what was best for her. When really those decisions were her own to make.

'*I* was paged. *I* was called. This is my patient. I called you to *assist*. We go in together.' She didn't mean to sound so harsh with him, but she couldn't help it. He'd actually infuriated her.

He stared hard into her eyes, looking exasperated, and then nodded with reluctance. 'Okay.'

He stepped back and let her lead the way.

Grace dropped her shoulders, lifted her chin, took a deep breath and asked the nurse which cubicle their patient was in.

'Cubicle five. She was here earlier today.'

'Thank you.'

She led the way, her stomach in turmoil, her mouth dry. She hoped beyond hope that this was just a benign bleed. That this was not going to be a loss. She wasn't sure if she could watch the same thing she had experienced happen to another woman. She knew it was part of the job, and that this kind of thing happened, but it had more impact when you'd been through it yourself.

Grace had lain in an ER bed. She'd been the patient.

She'd been the one who had had a midwife called down to her. It had been Renata. Her boss. And although she'd always viewed Renata as a woman who could be firm, yet fair, on that occasion, with Grace crying in the bed, Renata had been wonderfully kind. Sympathetic. Honest. And yet also the kind of professional that Grace had needed. She might have been among her colleagues and her friends, but that day they had been her medical team, more than anything else. They had found the distance they'd needed to treat her and care for her.

Grace pulled open the curtain and saw a woman curled up on the bed. She looked to be in her thirties, wearing a set of pyjamas. Her heart ached for her. This woman must have gone to bed thinking it was just another day. That everything was normal. Before her world came crashing down.

'Hi. My name's Grace and I'm a midwife, and this is Diego Rivas, a doctor.' She didn't want to say neonatal surgeon. Didn't want this woman instantly thinking of surgery and blood and emergencies. Not yet. Not whilst there was still hope. 'What's your name?'

'Mia. Mia Fernandez'

'Tell us what's happening, Mia,' she said gently.

'There was a car accident. This afternoon. Nothing huge. Just someone rear-ended me whilst I was stationary, waiting for some kids to cross the road. No damage to the cars. Nothing. I just had a little backache. A small pain in my neck. I came to the ER this afternoon and got checked out. Everything was fine.'

'Okay.' Grace nodded. Smiled. Encouraging her. Not rushing her. She picked up the patient notes at the end of the bed, opened them, began reading today's earlier admittance information. Mia was right. Everything had checked out. Baby and mum had seemed fine.

'I went home. Had a bath. Then I went to bed and fell asleep. But I woke around midnight with pains, and then I noticed the bleeding and I...' Mia began crying again. 'Please... I don't want to lose my baby!'

Grace's blood ran cold. They were the same words that she had cried out. She remembered pleading with Renata. With the ER doctor who had been attending her at the time. The memories it brought back were sharp and painful. Like a knife cutting open an old wound.

Suddenly she couldn't speak, and she looked imploringly to Diego.

He stepped forward. 'We're going to do an ultrasound, Mia, is that okay? And we may have to examine you...make sure you're not dilating.'

Mia nodded quickly, her long hair obscuring her face as she sobbed.

Grace was grateful that Diego had stepped in when she couldn't speak. She offered to fetch the ultrasound machine. It would give her time to gather herself. Catch her breath. Get control of all the memories that were flooding in.

As she began to wheel the machine back towards cubicle five Diego met her, his face full of concern. 'Maybe you should sit this out?'

'I'm fine.'

'The hell you are. Look at you—your hands are shaking.'

She stopped pushing the ultrasound and folded her

arms, hating it that he had seen that. 'I need to see this through.'

'Why?'

'Because I'm a professional and this is my job.'

'You lost three babies, Grace. No one would blame you if you sat this out.'

She looked up at him. Frowned. 'You mean *we* lost three babies. And if you can be in there, then so can I.'

She began to push the machine again, furious that he had implied that she somehow couldn't do her job because of her loss. Only it hadn't just been *her* loss, but theirs. Or had he already moved on? If he had, she envied him that ability. She had no idea how he could even be in that cubicle with Mia and not feel *something*.

But that had been the problem all along, hadn't it?

'I'm just going to scan you, Mia, okay? You'll feel the cold gel and then I'll use this wand to take a look inside. It shouldn't hurt, but if it does you tell me, okay?'

Mia nodded, lying back and lifting up her pyjama top.

Grace eyed her small bump. 'Is this your first?'

Mia nodded again.

'And do you have someone we can call?'

She shook her head. 'No. I have no family and the father is away. He works on an oil rig.'

Grace hoped her hand was no longer trembling now that she was using the ultrasound wand, and as she moved it over Mia's abdomen she began to see the baby. It was moving. Its heart was beating. She smiled, feeling relief flood through her.

'Look.'

Mia peered at the screen, frowning, then a hesitant smile crept onto her face. 'It's okay?'

'It is. And the placenta looks fine, too.' She measured the heart rate. It was perfect. Exactly as they'd expect. The bleeding wasn't happening because the placenta was separating. At least not from what she could see. 'We'll need to run some more tests, and we'll want to keep you in for rest and observation—is that okay?'

Mia beamed, nodding. 'Absolutely. Do what you have to. Whatever keeps my baby safe.'

Grace removed the probe. 'I'll order those tests.' She wheeled the machine away, returning it to his place, and let out a heavy sigh. So far it was looking good for Mia's baby. She was glad. And envious. She couldn't help it.

'Baby's okay—that's good.' Diego was at her side.

She glanced at him, straightening the cable and the plug. 'It is.'

'She'll need to stay in for a while. Observation.'

Grace nodded. 'I've told her that already. And that we'll probably run some tests to check where the bleeding is coming from.'

'It might just be her cervix. Sometimes it gets—'

'I *do* know, Diego. I'm a qualified midwife, remember?'

He looked about them. One or two people had looked their way when she'd raised her voice.

She blushed, annoyed that she'd drawn attention to them. 'Sorry. I didn't mean to...' She sighed. 'I guess this has just got to me a little bit.'

He nodded. 'I understand.'

'*Do* you, Diego?' She stared at him, curious. Did he truly understand just how this had affected her?

He met her gaze. 'I always have.'

CHAPTER FIVE

THE NEXT FEW night shifts passed in a blur. Grace was present for her patients, helping them welcome their babies into the world, celebrating with them, rejoicing, admiring their newborns and genuinely telling each of them how precious and how beautiful they were. But each morning when she got home again, back to her empty flat, she felt as if she'd been working on automatic.

Something was missing. Whether it was from the job, or just something at St Aelina's, or whether it was to do with Diego she wasn't sure. She just knew she didn't feel as fulfilled as she normally did after a shift.

When Diego had told her that he'd always understood how she felt after seeing Mia Fernandez, who was now safely at home, still pregnant—it had been a bleed from a lesion on her cervix—she'd found herself looking for him, wondering, wanting to ask more, but the last few nights she'd hardly seen him.

'I've heard one of the paramedics is seeing a nurse in the ER,' said Gabbi, as she and Mira and Grace had sat together, sharing a rare moment and enjoying a cup of coffee together.

Grace shrugged. 'It's not surprising.'

'Don't you know?'

'Know what?'

'I'm talking about Carlos.'

Carlos. The nurse she'd spoken to when she went down to see Mia. 'Oh. Well, good for him. He's a good-looking guy.'

'He's going out with your sister-in-law! Hasn't Diego said?' Mira asked in surprise.

Isabella? 'No, he…er…'

'Is everything okay between you two?'

Grace felt her cheeks colour, having hoped to avoid this conversation entirely. 'Things have been…difficult lately.'

Mira and Gabbi exchanged glances. 'Sorry, we didn't mean to interfere. You don't have to say if you don't want to.'

'No, it's fine. It's just…it's been difficult since the miscarriages, you know?'

'We get it.' They shared another look, and Mira mouthed something to Gabbi. Then Gabbi was shaking her head as if to say, *No, not right now.*

'What is it?' asked Grace.

Gabbi looked at her wide-eyed. Innocent. 'Nothing.'

'Tell me, Gabs.'

Gabbi looked at Mira once more, then turned to face Grace. 'It's just that there's rumours that…'

'What?'

'That Isabella's pregnant.'

Grace felt as if she'd been punched in the gut. Her mind whirled with thoughts and emotions, none of them pleasant, or feelings that made her feel particularly proud. Jealousy was the main one.

But then she focused on her friend's words. 'Rumours. Not fact?'

Gabbi and Mira nodded. 'Just hearsay.'

Grace sipped her coffee. It had to be hearsay. Diego would have told her if that was the truth, surely? He had seemed distracted lately. They were getting used to working together in a new way now, but it was difficult being thrown together to work on a case when they couldn't be the people they used to be—husband and wife.

He would have told me.

Wouldn't he? Or did he feel that he couldn't? That by telling her he would somehow be rubbing salt into the wounds of their still raw losses?

No. He would have said. This had to be a rumour. It couldn't be anything else. If Isabella was pregnant, then... A wave of sadness washed over her and she suddenly felt as if she could cry. Was that why Isabella hadn't stayed to talk to her the night she'd brought in Zara? Was that why Isabella had hardly looked her in the eye? Was that why Diego looked at her as if he was frightened of how she might react after her outburst before she went to Cornwall?

'Excuse me.' Grace took her mug to the privacy of the small kitchenette, tipping the rest of her suddenly bitter drink into the sink and taking a deep breath before washing cold water over her face.

Rumours in hospitals spread like wildfire.

They weren't always true.

She had to believe that if this one was, then Diego would have had the good grace and the respect to inform her.

She would ask him to tell her the truth the next time she saw him.

'I thought I'd let you know that you are no longer showing any signs of infection.' Diego smiled at Zara as he scribbled a note into her medical file.

'So I'm healthy?'

'At the moment.'

'Are you going to put me back on the streets?'

He met her gaze, shocked that she'd ask. 'No, of course not. Why would you even think that?'

Zara shrugged. 'I guess I'm just not used to people looking out for me. They normally can't wait to get rid of me.'

He put her notes back in the slot at the end of her bed and then sat down on the chair beside her. 'We're not going to do that. You're vulnerable. Young. Your baby is going to need attention when he's born and we're going to keep you here until you're both fit and well. Okay?'

'And after that?'

He didn't know. Though he'd like to try and help her out. Maybe find her some accommodation for her and her son.

'And what if he doesn't make it? He's safe right now, inside me. I can look after him. But when he's born he's going to have all those problems and...' Zara began to cry.

Diego passed her a box of tissues and waited. 'I know you're scared. It's normal to feel that way. But he can't stay inside you for ever, and when he's born you'll have a crack team of specialists to support both of you.'

'You'll perform his surgery?'

He nodded. 'I will.'

'And you'll be honest with me? I don't want you to lie to me. I know I'm only eighteen, but I am going to be his mother and so I'll deserve to know the truth!'

'I will be honest with you.'

'You promise?'

He nodded again. 'I promise. Now, how about we get you in a wheelchair and I take you for a bit of fresh air in the park?'

It was the middle of the day and Diego felt the need for some sunshine. He loved nights, he really did, but he just needed to bask in the warm rays of the sunshine on occasion.

Zara smiled. 'Deal.'

Grace hadn't slept very well, and she had a headache because of it as she went in for her next night shift. She kept alert, looking for Diego, needing to talk to him about Isabella. He'd know for sure if his sister was pregnant or not, and although Grace didn't want to let hospital gossip fuel her fears and worries, this one struck quite close to home.

She knew she could call Isabella and ask her herself, but she didn't know how she would react if Isabella confirmed the news. False cheer? Pretending to be thrilled for her whilst being swamped with jealousy? And if Isabella just laughed and told her it was gossip it would make Grace look as if she was someone who avidly listened to the hospital grapevine. Was nosy.

No. It was Diego she needed to talk to.

She placed her bag and jacket in her locker and headed onto the ward for the hand-over.

Renata stood at the front of the small room and gave them the information. Three labouring mothers currently on the labour ward. A first-time mother at forty-one weeks, who'd come in that morning to be induced and was currently at five centimetres, a second-time mother who was labouring with a twin pregnancy, currently at four centimetres, and a mother who was labouring with her first, at seven centimetres dilated.

'Grace? I'd like you to take her, if you don't mind? She's in room six. Sofia Grayson. She's only thirty-six weeks, so I've notified Neonatal and they're sending down your husband.'

Grace nodded. 'Okay.'

So she would get to see Diego tonight. Speak to him quietly about this ridiculous rumour that was going around. Set things straight. Because he wouldn't have kept something like that from her, would he?

But have I really given him the opportunity to tell me?

She pushed that thought to one side. She was not going to take the blame for that. Diego had had plenty of opportunity to tell her anything. On the promenade that morning a few days ago. Down in the ER when they'd met over Mia's case. They'd chatted privately then. He would have said, surely?

No. He wouldn't have said, because it's not true!

That was why Diego hadn't said anything.

Grace put her notes into her pocket and headed down to room six. She said hello to Sofia and her English husband, Henry, then caught up on the case from the day-shift midwife, who updated her. Sofia was contracting well and regularly and making good progress.

Henry stood to one side of his wife's bed, holding her hand.

'So, how did you two meet?' Grace asked.

She liked to ask a couple of questions to her labouring mothers and parents-to-be. It helped establish a bond of trust and allowed each of them to get to know one another a little better. Sometimes it relaxed the mum-to-be to talk about something other than the human about to exit her body in a painful way.

Henry smiled at his wife. 'She was an air hostess on my flight from London to Barcelona. She charmed me with her offers of coffee and snacks.'

Sofia smiled too. 'The way to a man's heart is through his stomach.' Then she sucked on her gas and air as another contraction came. She was coping quite well with them and hadn't had any other form of pain relief.

'What do you do, Henry?'

'I'm a chef.'

'Interesting! And you live here in Barcelona?'

He nodded. 'To be with this woman, I'd live anywhere.' Henry smiled at her. 'You're English. How come you work here?'

'Similar thing. My husband is Spanish. I came out here to live.'

'Oh? And what does he do?'

At that moment there was a knock on the door.

Grace smiled, feeling her heart suddenly pound. 'If this is who I think it is, then I'll let him tell you himself. Come in!'

The door opened and there he was. Looking fresh and perfect and just as handsome as he always did. Those dark chocolate eyes of his were intense and yet dreamy. He was in his scrubs already, soft curls of hair at the nape of his neck, his four o'clock shadow stumbling his jaw. His dark olive skin was perfect, his biceps strong and delicious.

Just the sight of him standing there, with his stethoscope casually draped around his neck, and the way his gaze instantly went to her before turning to the parents-to-be in the room, and the way he was giving them the benefit of that charming, attractive, *you-can-trust-me-I'm-a-professional* smile… Would she ever stop physically reacting to the sight of him?

'I'm Dr Rivas and I'm a neonatal surgeon. I thought I'd come down to introduce myself. Nothing to worry about. I'm just here because you're with us a few weeks earlier than expected.'

Sofia and Henry said hello.

Then Diego came towards Grace.

He smiled at her—a soft smile, a *hello* smile—and

picked up Sofia's trace to take a look at how she and the baby were doing.

Grace knew he'd find nothing wrong with it. Baby Grayson was doing well. Tolerating the contractions and without decels. She gazed up at Diego, wishing she could ask him right now about Isabella, but now was not the time. Instead, she took a moment to study his profile, to take in those lips she knew so well, the prominent cheekbones, the roman nose that had been broken when he was a teenager, the thick dark lashes around those eyes of his...

'This all looks good. How are you feeling, Sofia?'

Sofia nodded, completely under Diego's spell. 'I'm feeling good.'

'Excellent.' Diego beamed. 'That's what we like to hear.'

Grace wished she could ask him to step outside, so she could ask about Isabella, but she knew that if she did Sofia and Henry might think the conversation was about them and that something was wrong. She didn't want her patients to think she was keeping secrets from them. This job was all about patients being able to put their trust in the professionals.

'How are you?' she whispered to her husband.

He looked at her, as if surprised that she'd asked.

'I'm good,' he said in a low voice. 'You?'

'Good.' She nodded, itching to ask. But this was not the place. 'I'd like to speak to you when you have a moment free.'

Now he turned the full force of his gaze upon her. 'Is something wrong?'

'No. Just something I need to ask you.'

Diego nodded. 'Okay. When I get a free moment I'll page you.'

'Sounds good.'

He *smelled* good. She could smell that bodywash that he liked to use in the shower. It was doing dizzying things to her brain. Scent could be such a powerful thing when it came to memories, and she recalled the time when she'd joined him in the shower and helped lather him up. That scent had been ingrained into her memories as part of a very happy erotic, moment. Just inhaling it now was making her tingle in places that hadn't seen any action for quite a while now.

Which wasn't helpful.

Which was extremely frustrating!

'Call me when she starts to push,' he said.

'I will.' She watched him say goodbye to Sofia and Henry and then he was gone again. God, she missed that man! Missed being held by him, touched by him. Loved by him.

'That was your husband?' Sofia asked.

Grace nodded.

'Wow.'

Had he stopped loving her? Because she wasn't sure she'd ever stopped loving him, despite everything. Despite all the pain and the upset and the grief. Diego was going to be a hard habit to break. Would it get easier when she'd left Barcelona to go back home to England? Easier to know that he wouldn't be on the floor above her at work? Wouldn't be the on-call neonatologist?

Wouldn't come swooping in to rescue other people's babies?

If she didn't see him every day—if they had distance between them and all that had happened—would that be simpler? They said absence made the heart grow fonder. She hoped that wasn't true. And when she'd been in Cornwall with Aunt Felicity she'd thought about Diego non-stop. Would he ever leave her heart?

She spent the next couple of hours concentrating on her patient, and when Sofia started to feel the urge to push she called Diego down.

He stood off to one side, just monitoring, waiting for Grace to deliver the baby.

Sofia pushed really well, and her husband Henry was a great coach.

'Come on, Sofia, you can do it! That's it! Yes! I can see the head!'

Sofia pushed with all her might, and after forty-five minutes of doing so baby Andrea burst into the world with a cry.

'Congratulations!' Grace said, clamping the cord as Andrea got his first cuddle with his mum. She looked up at Diego, smiling, happy. She couldn't help it. Every birth was special. Every healthy baby and healthy mother was a victory to her, and she wanted him to share her joy.

Eventually Diego took the baby to assess him, check his breathing, his reflexes, and pronounced him a healthy boy as he handed him back to his mother.

'No stitches!' said Grace. 'You're all good. Can I get you both anything? A drink?'

'Thank you,' Henry said, nodding.

'I'll just be a moment.'

Grace headed to the kitchenette, made them both a drink and some toast, took it to them and left the new parents to it.

Back at the midwives' desk, Diego waited for her. 'Do you want to get a coffee with me? I'm free now, if you want that chat.'

She nodded, suddenly nervous once again. 'I'll just tell Gabbi I'm going on my break.'

It felt strange to sit down with Grace at a table again. It had been a long time. When they'd lived together they'd tried to sit down and have meals with each other often, whether at home or at the hospital, snatched between shifts. It had been important to them that they stayed connected. Stayed present with one another.

He'd missed that. Having to sit in the hospital cafeteria alone felt awful, so Diego had often found himself dropping in on Zara if he stayed late at work and carried on into the morning. Zara seemed to like him dropping in at breakfast time to check on her.

'That was a good delivery,' he said, stirring milk into his coffee.

The cafeteria was mostly empty at night, and they sat alone in a booth by the back wall.

'Yes. It was. Sofia and Henry are lovely people. I really like them as a couple.'

'He's English?'

'Yes. A chef. He works here now.'

Diego nodded. 'But I don't think you asked to speak

to me to talk about Henry's work. Is there something on your mind?'

He was dreading whatever it might be. Was this the point where she told him she was going to leave Spain? Or ask for a divorce? Neither of those was he ready for—though he assumed they were inevitable, after all the pain he'd caused her.

'There is.'

'Okay.' He tried to steel himself for it.

I want a divorce. I'm leaving.

'I've heard a rumour.'

'Oh?' That wasn't where he'd thought this conversation was going.

'About Isabella.'

Ah. Now he knew what this was about. He felt the muscles in his jaw tighten.

'She's seeing someone—an ER nurse?'

He nodded. 'Carlos.'

Now Grace nodded. 'I've met him a couple of times. He seems nice.'

Diego said nothing. Waiting.

'Is she pregnant, Diego?'

He looked away, down at his coffee, stirred it one more time even though he didn't need to. He'd dreaded this coming up, and knew he ought to have told her— but when could he have done so? When the words he was about to say would rip out her heart and cause her even more pain?

'Yes. She is.'

There was a terrible, dreadful pause as he saw all manner of emotions cross his wife's face.

'Why didn't you tell me?' she asked him, sounding hurt and betrayed.

The pain in her eyes tore through him and he felt ashamed and guilty. All he'd ever done was cause this woman pain, and here he was causing even more. He'd thought keeping the news from her was wrong, but he'd simply not known how to say anything.

'How could I? When would there have been a good time to say it? Tell me.' He looked at her imploringly. 'I wanted to tell you. Believe me, this is not news I wanted to keep from you. But I didn't know what to say.'

'How long have you known?'

He sighed, knowing this would hurt her, too. 'Isabella told me when you were in Cornwall.'

Grace gasped, shocked.

Diego lowered his eyes, staring at his cup, unsure of what else to say. No matter what he did, no matter what he said, he always seemed to be in the wrong.

'Has it come to this? That we've ruined things between us so much we can't even tell each other the truth? That we walk on eggshells around each other?'

'I'm sorry. I've never meant to hurt you, Grace. Never.'

She stared back at him and took a big breath before sighing. 'Well, I hope it goes well for her. And maybe… just maybe…this can be a new beginning for the two of you. You've never seemed all that close. You have this great, huge family—you're so lucky—and yet you all seem so distant. Maybe this baby will bring you and Isabella closer.'

He wanted to reach out for her hand then. To lay his

hand upon hers and thank her for being so…well, so graceful about all this. For thinking of him. For thinking of his relationship with his older sister when he knew that this news had to be hurting her.

'I can be happy for other women being pregnant, Diego. I can. I'm only hurt when people think they have to keep such good news from me. Am I so fragile that I have to be protected? Is that what people think?'

'You're the strongest woman I know,' he said, with an encouraging smile. 'After all that you've been through… you deserve your own happiness.'

He remembered when they'd met. How quickly he'd fallen in love with this remarkable woman who sat before him now. How Grace had accepted his proposal of marriage and how excited she'd been about the idea of a beach wedding in Spain with all his brothers and sisters. She'd been so excited to meet them and become a part of the Rivas family.

How disappointed she'd been to find out that they were not close, and when he'd managed to steer her towards a more sensible, more logical ceremony in London, with just a couple of colleagues as witnesses.

Was he fated always to disappoint her? To quash her dreams?

She smiled back. 'You're going to be an uncle.'

He nodded. Isabella would be the first of them to have a child, if all went well. 'And you're going to be an aunt.'

A strange look that he couldn't read passed over her face. There for a second, then gone.

'It's probably the closest I'll ever come to being a parent if...' Her voice trailed off.

'If what?'

'If we stay married.'

She was talking about them splitting up. Had she thought of that, then? Of leaving? Of divorcing him? He hoped not. He wasn't ready.

'What are you saying?' he asked.

'I'm just trying to be sensible, Diego. You left me. You moved out. We've agreed to tell people that it's over... Have you told anyone yet?'

He shook his head. 'No. Have you?'

'No.'

Well, that was good, at least. Or was it? Why exactly was he hanging on to this relationship when he knew in his heart of hearts that he had to let her go? When he had to give her the opportunity to find someone she could have babies with?

Because I still love her.

At that moment he wanted to take hold of her and hug her and kiss her, hold her tight and never let go! Show her just how much she still meant to him. But he knew he couldn't. It would be cruel. And so he sat with the pain and the discomfort of not being able to hold his wife. Of not being able to show her just how much she was still in his heart.

'I don't see how I will have any part in that child's life. I'm just trying to be sensible,' she said.

'You're its aunt. You will always be its aunt.'

At that moment her pager went off, and with reluctance he saw her look down at it.

'It's the ward. I'm being paged.' She pulled her mobile phone from her uniform pocket and called. 'It's Grace. What's up?'

He watched her face as she listened. Saw her go into work mode.

She put her phone away. 'It's the Garcia-Hernandez baby.'

'The spina bifida case?'

She nodded. 'It's here.'

Felicia Garcia-Hernandez and her husband Marco had been coming into the hospital for regular scans ever since her baby's spina bifida was diagnosed. Grace had met with the couple numerous times before, and had even sat in on a consult with the couple, when they'd met Diego to discuss what treatment options their baby would need when he was born. She'd asked to be paged when they came in, and to be allowed in Theatre. As she stood scrubbing her hands and arms in the scrub room next to Diego she filled him in on what she'd been told.

'Apparently she went into labour just a couple of hours ago and gave birth in the car outside.'

'In the car park outside the hospital?' Diego asked.

She nodded. 'Ana was called out to the car. Felicia must have been terrified.'

'I'll bet.'

It felt good to be scrubbing in next to Diego. She had a focus—something else to think about after Diego's revelation about Isabella. She'd not been that surprised by the news. Rumours spread fast in hospitals, and they usually had an element of the truth to them. It was just the fact that he hadn't told her that upset her. But she had to be realistic. She had not made it easy for Diego to tell her about his sister. They'd hardly been talking to one another. They'd certainly not been having idle conversations allowing him to just drop it in casually.

Yet standing here now, side by side with him, something felt right, and she briefly wondered how many more of these occasions she would have with him. The thought made her sad. It felt wrong. They'd always made such a good team, and the thought of losing him completely...

I don't have to leave. I could stay.

But would that cause more issues in the long run?

If I stayed, would I have to watch Diego fall in love with someone else? Start a family with someone else?

She knew she would never be able to bear that. Despite everything that had happened she loved him. Deeply.

As they both walked through into Theatre nurses helped them don gloves and gowns, and they saw that baby Garcia-Hernandez was already prepped and anaesthetised on the table, face down, with only a small square of his lower back exposed, revealing the defect of an opening at the base of his spine, and a small sac containing nerves and membranes within.

Diego would operate to put the spinal cord and any exposed tissues and nerves back into the correct position and then close the gap, sealing the hole with muscle and skin. It wouldn't reverse any nerve damage. All he would be doing was repair work.

'Scalpel.' Diego held out his hand and the theatre nurse placed the blade in his hand so he could start.

Grace looked at Diego as he concentrated hard on the task at hand. His gaze was focused, determined. He worked methodically and carefully. Watching him was like watching the conductor of an orchestra. His movements were so sure and exact. Perfectly in control. The melody was of instruments and the procedure an exquisite choreography. The team knew what he needed even before he had to ask for it.

Diego was able to make such delicate surgery look easy. And watching him do the thing he'd been born to do…watching an expert—a maestro—at work… She could feel herself falling in love with him all over again.

Behind her mask she smiled as she looked at him, and in that exact moment he looked up and caught her doing so. He smiled back, his eyes creasing at the corners, and something between them changed in that moment. She wasn't sure what it was. Whether it was herself withdrawing from the battle lines, or whether it was something else. She didn't know, but she did know she didn't want to keep on fighting this man.

'Closing the dura now.'

The surgery had gone smoothly, as expected. She remembered something Diego had said to her when they'd first started going out. He'd come out of the theatre after performing a difficult foetal surgery, come over to her, smiling, and said, 'Every baby saved is a lifetime saved.' The words had struck her then, and they did so now.

Baby Garcia-Hernandez might still have a difficult road ahead of him, but at least he had a road. Her and

Diego's babies had never had that chance. There had been no road, no path, not even a tiny muddy trail for them to go down. There had been no chance of a life-time ahead of them. No going to school, no relation-ships, no finding their special someone. They'd had no idea how much they'd been loved and wanted and cher-ished. They'd never known. All that love only lived in her heart. And Diego's.

As they came out of surgery she looked at him and shook her head, smiling.

'What is it?' He smiled back, hands on hips, look-ing delicious and scrumptious, his hair slightly mussed from his scrub cap.

'You're amazing. I don't know if I ever told you enough, but…you are. What you're able to do in that room is unbelievable.'

Diego could do a great many things in many differ-ent rooms. The operating theatre was one. In the bed-room he was just as skilled, and by God she missed the feeling of his hands upon her body!

He looked down at the floor, still smiling, as if over-whelmed by her kind compliment. 'Thank you. I ap-preciate that.'

'It's the truth.' She laughed, suddenly feeling shy, suddenly feeling that this conversation would go in a direction that neither of them was ready for if she al-lowed it. Blushing, and feeling the heat in her cheeks, she decided that the best thing would be to create some space between them. At least for now.

'I…er… I'd better get back.' She met his gaze.

He was staring at her as if he was also fighting an internal battle. 'Okay.'

'I'll see you around.'

He nodded, backing away in the other direction, seeming reluctant to tear his gaze from hers. 'You most certainly will.'

Grace forced herself to turn and walk away—but, oh, goodness, it was so difficult!

What's happening? Were we flirting? We were flirting! We're not meant to be doing that!

But she couldn't stop smiling. Couldn't stop a small chuckle escaping. And when she allowed herself one last look over her shoulder as she reached the corner she saw that Diego was watching her go.

He smiled.

And her heart began to pound…

CHAPTER SIX

'Why the frown, Santiago?' Grace had stopped off at the cafeteria to grab a bowl of cereal for a patient when she'd seen him at one of the tables near the exit. Santiago was a paediatrician here at the hospital and one of Grace's good friends. 'Anything I can help with?'

He looked up at her and smiled. 'You're back! Did you have a good time in Cornwall?'

It had hardly been a good time. But she didn't want to tell him that. Especially since her relationship with Diego was now at a new and unknown stage, after they'd been in surgery with the Garcia-Hernandez baby.

'It was great. How are things with you?'

He shrugged. 'Frustrating. I've got a patient I'm having problems diagnosing. Her test results are mostly clear, but she's ill and I'm not sure what's wrong with her.'

At that moment another member of staff—Caitlin, the cardiothoracic surgeon who had sent Grace and Diego an invitation to their wedding in Maravilla—appeared beside them. 'Apologies, I don't mean to butt in, but I couldn't help but overhear what you said to

Grace. I know an absolutely fabulous diagnostician called Elena who might be able to help you?'

Santiago looked up at her. 'Is she in this hospital?'

Caitlin shook her head. 'No. She's in Mallorca. But she's advised me on a couple of difficult cases before. I have her number, if you want it?'

He took a moment to consider it. 'Sounds great. All help is welcome on this one.'

Grace frowned. 'Do you mean Elena Solis? I think she's the lady who helped out with one of our patients, too.' She looked at Santiago. 'She's good. You ought to call her if you're stuck.'

Santiago smiled at both of them. 'I know when I'm beaten. Text me her number, Cait, when you have a spare moment.'

'I will. It's nice to have you back, Grace. We missed you!' And Caitlin went on her way.

Grace watched her go. Caitlin was at the beginning of all the fabulous adventures her life would hold. She was about to get married to Javier Torres, another cardiothoracic surgeon. They'd been reunited after Caitlin had been tasked to operate on Javier's sister. Quite the romance! And now their future was ahead of them.

Grace recalled how she'd missed out on the chance to plan her own wedding and make it the spectacular beach wedding she'd always wanted, whereas Caitlin was going to be married in the beautiful sprawling ancestral estate Maravilla, which belonged to Javier's family. She could only imagine how much fun Caitlin had had planning that...

There was much that Grace wished she had done

differently. Even the happiness of having her big day had been denied her. But she'd been so keen to marry Diego and then fly with him to Barcelona to live and find work.

Why did it sometimes feel that life was happening to everyone else except for her? Why did she feel as if she was standing still?

'You okay?' Santiago asked.

She blinked, pulled back to the present, and smiled at Santiago. 'I'm fine.'

Diego had stopped by Grace's department. 'I've got an inguinal hernia to operate on. Want to join me?'

He looked down at her, once again taken by how much this woman was still a part of his life and how much she still meant to him. He was probably torturing himself by asking her, but he was still running on the high of their last conversation, when everything had gone so well and, like an addict, he needed more.

She nodded and said, 'Sounds great.'

He grinned. 'Ten minutes. Theatre two? It's Emilio Perez.'

'I'll be there. I'll just let Ana know where I'm heading.'

'Okay.'

He was inordinately thrilled that she'd agreed to join him. Something had changed in the last day or two between them. He didn't know when, exactly, or how—he just knew that he liked it. He liked the way she'd complimented him that day, and how she'd blushed when they'd flirted with one another. There was nothing he liked more than to see her smile at him like that. He'd missed it. And now, incredibly, she was doing it again.

He wanted her back by his side in Theatre. Not so that she could admire him again, but because he *wanted* her there! Right now, they were getting on. The battle lines had been withdrawn and they were being friendly again—and by God he was grateful for that! At one point he'd thought he'd never be able to make her smile again. He'd never thought he had the right even to *try*. But she was smiling, and it was because of him, and he wanted to capture that feeling and hold it tight against him and never let it go.

So now she'd agreed to be with him in Theatre he almost skipped into the scrub room, and he still had a smile on his face when she joined him, to scrub in too.

'Hi.'

'Hi.'

She was already in scrubs, and was busy tying her hair up in a scrub cap decorated with unicorns. It was her favourite one.

She saw him look at it. 'You bought me this, remember?'

Of course he did. 'I do.'

She hit the water tap to get the water to the right temperature and then opened up the small package from the dispenser that contained a nail brush, scrub sponge and nail pick. She laid it on the back of the sink, still in its packet, as she began to wet her hands and arms.

'Fill me in on the case?' she asked.

He liked this. They were good together. Not just at work, either.

'Baby Perez, born at thirty-nine weeks and two days,

diagnosed with an inguinal hernia at birth. It was some-how missed on the ultrasound.'

'Was the baby born here? I don't recall seeing the name.'

'No. He was born at another local hospital but I've known the father of the baby for many years and he wanted me to do the surgery, so he brought the baby here.'

'Oh, okay... How old is he now?'

'A week.'

'And no other issues?'

'No, it should be relatively straightforward. And I thought after this maybe we could go and see Zara together?'

She smiled and nodded. 'Sounds good.'

'I've been checking in on her during the day when I can, and she seems to be bearing up well.'

'You're not tired?'

'You know me.'

He winked at her without thinking, enjoying this simple conversation. This *ease* of conversation. The ability to just talk to Grace again as if the past hadn't happened. Could they carry on like this? Ignore the past and pretend that everything was all right? How long would that last?

The urge to take advantage of this moment and just lean in and kiss her was strong, and it physically pained him not to be able to do so. Instead, he concentrated on scrubbing, making sure he was thorough.

'Ready?'

She nodded. 'Ready.'

* * *

Grace watched him make a small incision so he could visualise the hernia. He easily separated the tissue sac containing the hernia from the cord structures, then opened it to look at the contents. Thankfully, it was empty. No bowel had slipped through and therefore there was no risk of strangulation.

'Straightforward…' she heard him mutter under his mask.

He inserted a laparoscope to check if there was herniation on the other side of the inguinal ring, but that was clear too. Next he tied off the sac with a suture, and removed the obsolete sac.

'Looks good,' she said.

He nodded. 'All that's left to do now is close up the incision.'

The relief in the room was palpable, as it always was after surgery on a baby. The fact that it had gone so well was reassuring, and she knew that Diego would be able to tell his friend that his son's surgery had gone perfectly.

She wanted to congratulate him. Before, whenever they'd been in surgery together and it had been a success, they would scrub out and she would give him a hug and a quick kiss. A kiss might be a step too far right now, but could she hug him? The desire to feel him in her arms again was dizzying…

But as they left Theatre a scrub nurse put her head around the door of the room and said, 'Are you guys looking after Zara Rodriguez?'

They both turned. 'Yes?'

'She's kind of upset. She's asking for you.'

'We'll be right there,' Grace said, before turning to Diego. 'What do you think is wrong?'

'I don't know. She seemed fine the last time I saw her.'

They dried their hands with paper towels, threw the towels into the clinical waste bin, and then headed down to Maternity.

Grace felt a deep sense of unease in her stomach. Zara had been doing well these last few days. Her infection was gone, and she was putting on some weight now that she was getting regular meals and hydrating properly. What could have happened to upset her?

As they raced down to the ward Gabbi stopped Grace as she passed. 'We had a nightingale baby. Zara heard about it.'

Grace took in a breath and let it out again slowly. A nightingale baby was the name the staff gave to a baby that had been stillborn.

She knocked gently on Zara's door, with Diego close behind her. 'Zara? It's Grace and Diego.'

The door opened and Zara stood there crying, wiping her eyes with tissue. 'I heard her… I heard her, Grace!'

'Hey… Shh…' Grace led her back to her bed, holding her hand. 'Tell me what happened.'

'Her baby—it…it died, and she was crying, and I've never heard anyone sound like that before, and…'

Grace swallowed hard. She didn't have to imagine what Zara had heard. She'd been there. She'd felt the raw, agonising pain that ripped through you when the baby they placed in your arms was lifeless. When you knew that baby would never open its eyes. When you knew that baby would never make a sound. When you held it, hoping beyond hope that some miracle would occur and it would begin breathing, only to realise with each passing second, each passing minute, that it would never, *ever* happen and that sweet, precious child would remain still.

The pain was like a volcano. A tsunami. An eruption. A wave of such grief and agony that there wasn't enough air, weren't enough words to describe what you feel when your very soul had cracked and shattered into tiny, fragile, broken pieces.

You'd stare at that baby in your arms, trying to absorb every detail of its face and its body through your own salty tears, through vision so blurred you were practically blind. You'd hold on to your child. Not willing to let go, but knowing that at some point you must.

That pain was the worst.

Watching them take your child away and leave you with empty arms.

Grace herself had been through it. To know that there was a woman on this floor who was going through that hit right at her heart and ripped open old scars.

And for Zara to have heard that, knowing that her own baby was facing immediate surgery after birth…

'Hey, it's going to be okay,' she managed, the words sticking in her throat as it squeezed so tight she almost felt as if she couldn't breathe.

On this floor, in the Nightingale Suite, was a mother whose heart had been irreparably damaged for the rest of her life, and her instincts were to go to that woman

and comfort her. Only she couldn't right now, because
Zara needed her more in this moment. Grace knew that
the other mother would have a dedicated bereavement
midwife. Probably Ana. They'd all received training,
but Ana specialised, as did Renata. That mother was
being taken care of.

'It's just… I heard her crying… I was walking the
corridor, trying to exercise a bit because I was having
these cramps from sitting down so much. And now
they're really beginning to hurt me and I'm afraid,
Grace…afraid something is wrong.'

'Where are you having these cramps?' Diego asked
gently.

'Down here.' Zara rubbed her abdomen just below
her bump.

Grace looked at Diego, feeling the tears in her eyes,
pleading with him to speak because she could not. She
was still stuck in the past. Held there by remembered
grief.

He understood. 'Let's put you on a trace. See if
you're having contractions.'

'You think I might be in labour?' Zara asked,
shocked.

'It's possible.'

She shook her head, adamant. 'No! I can't be! I'm
not ready! What if he dies, Grace? I won't be able to
handle it if he dies!'

Grace was so caught up in her own emotions at that
moment that she still couldn't talk. Knew that if she did
then she would cry herself.

Diego stepped forward. 'We're going to do our best

not to let that happen. Okay?' He turned to Grace. 'Why don't you go and fetch a trace machine?'

She nodded, grateful for the chance to escape the room, feeling her tears fall as the doors closed behind her and letting a deep, shuddering sob escape her as she stilled in the corridor.

Behind her, the door to Zara's room opened and closed again gently, and suddenly Diego's arms were around her and pulling her close.

It was something he'd hoped never to see again. That raw pain in his wife's eyes. Her reliving an experience neither of them would ever wish to go through again. It was as if they were right back there in the past, in their own birthing room.

He'd seen her try to be brave. Seen her try to stay strong for Zara, who herself was terrified and naturally so, but it had been too much, too soon, and his gaze had fallen on Grace as Zara had spoken, watching the crushing emotions silence her.

He'd known she needed to breathe. Needed a moment to gather herself. Known that Grace would be angry at not being able to control her emotions in front of her patient. A patient who needed her to be strong. She hadn't wanted to fail Zara. So he'd suggested that Grace go and fetch a trace machine. That way she'd be able to escape the intensity of that room for a moment and gather herself.

But then, when she'd left, something inside him told him to follow her, and when he'd slipped into the corridor he'd found her, tears streaming down her face, and he'd just known he had to comfort her.

'Hey… I've got you. You're okay. It's okay.' He held her tight, stroking her hair, fighting back the painful lump of emotion welling in his throat.

Why did he feel as if he'd been thrown back in time? Why did this feel like the moment after they'd taken their baby boy away and Grace had looked so broken with no one in her arms to hold?

He carried the blame for that in his heart to this day.

Renata had told them to take as much time as they needed to be with their son. They had held him, cried over him, taken pictures, his handprint and footprint. Dressed him in an outfit that had been way too big for his tiny body and given him a little soft blue knitted hat. Then they'd spent ages just holding him and staring at him, telling him all about who they were and how much they loved him and how his family was going to miss him. Hoping still that a miracle would occur and he would start moving. Breathing. Would open his eyes. They'd stared at him with such intensity. It had seemed a crime to look elsewhere…he'd been that precious.

He'd never expected that. To stand in a delivery room looking down at his stillborn child. Who did? And he'd looked so perfect! As if nothing was wrong. So how could it have been so terribly wrong?

Hours had passed in that room and yet they'd only seemed like moments. Much too fleeting. Much too fast. And then he'd caught Renata's gaze through the small window on the door and she'd told him that they needed to come in. Needed to take their son away.

He'd known Grace wouldn't give him up and he'd known he'd have to separate them, even though it was the last thing that either of them wanted. He didn't want to lose Luca. This was his boy! His son! And he had failed him. Failed them both. Unable to protect either of them.

'Grace...it's time.'

She had ignored him. Pretending not to hear as she'd gazed down at their angelic little boy.

'Grace.'

'No,' she'd replied, not looking at him. 'No, it can't be.'

'They need to take him.'

It hadn't been easy for him either. It hadn't been the way he'd imagined his journey towards having a large family of his own would go. He hadn't wanted to let him go either. But he'd known they couldn't keep Luca for ever, and that there were procedures the hospital needed to follow, and at some point they'd have to let him go.

Grace had shaken her head, tears dripping down onto Luca's shawl. 'No...'

'Grace...'

He'd hoped his tone would tell her that he understood. He'd hoped that his voice would show her that this was impossible for him too, and that he was only trying to be sensible. He'd reached for his son. His wife had tried to hold on to him. She'd cried out, twisting away from him, trying to keep their son for a few precious moments more, sobbing, her tears dripping down onto his blanket.

And then she'd released him.

He'd scooped his son up, for the last time ever in his life, and looked into his tiny face, memorising those features one last time. Memorising the feel and weight of him in his arms. He'd kissed his son's forehead, trying to ignore the coolness of his body, whispered *'I love you...'* and then he'd taken Luca to the doorway, where Renata waited.

The midwife had taken Luca with reverence. Laid a hand on Diego's arm as a thank-you. *'We'll take good care of him. Now you two take good care of each other.'*

There had been tears in Renata's eyes, too.

He had nodded and turned back to Grace, but she had already pulled away from him, her cries into a pillow heart-rending. Each one slicing through his heart.

He had felt a piece of his soul disappear that day.

Now, as he stood in the corridor, Grace held tightly in his arms, he remembered his son's face.

'I'm sorry. I'm so sorry...' he whispered into his wife's hair, and waited for her sobbing to subside.

Her shift was nearly over. Technically, in ten minutes or so, Grace could go home. But Zara was in labour and she didn't want to leave her. The poor girl was scared, and Grace and Diego had promised to be by her side to get her through this.

'You're ten centimetres now. With the next contraction you can start pushing.'

Zara's labour had progressed well—and quickly, considering she was a first-time mum. Her contractions had come rapidly and had been strong enough to soften, shorten and dilate her cervix over only a few hours. She'd used gas and air, but had asked for an epidural when she'd got to about six centimetres, so that she could rest before pushing began.

'I'm scared.'

Grace gave her a smile. 'I know. But I'm here to look after you, and when your little boy gets here Diego will take care of him.'

'What if I can't do it?'

'Give birth?'

Zara nodded.

'You *can* do it. Whether he gets here naturally, or you have him another way, you *will* give birth to this baby.'

'And then he'll have to have surgery. That's no way to start a life.'

'But it will *save* his life. That's what matters.'

'You're so certain. So sure. You believe in medicine, don't you?'

'Don't you?'

Zara shook her head. 'Not always. My mum, she... she had breast cancer. She did everything right. Operations, medicines, chemo, radiation. Nothing helped her. No matter what the doctors did, she still died. That's why I never saw... I worry that...that the same thing will happen to my baby.'

'You just have to believe. What's the alternative?'

Zara nodded. 'I know. That's why it's so scary.'

'Trust me, your baby is in safe hands. And when he gets here you'll be putting him in the hands of the best neonatal surgeon I know.'

'You sound like you really believe in him.'

Grace nodded, feeling something warm and wonderful growing in her heart. 'I do.'

Zara smiled, nervous. 'Are you saying that because you really believe it, or because he's your husband?'

'The first one.' She smiled back. 'He's a good man, Zara. The best. He knows what this means. He knows how scared people are, putting their brand-new babies into a surgeon's hands. He doesn't take that lightly. He's careful, and talented, and if I were in your place I would want Diego to take care of my child.'

'Do you have kids?'

How to answer? Tell Zara that they'd had three and lost every single one? When she was trying to convince her patient that Diego was the best person to look after her baby?

'No, not yet.'

Grace had her hand on Zara's bump and felt it hardening. She was grateful for the diversion.

'Okay, here's a contraction. I want you to take a big breath, curl up and bear down—like you're having a big bowel movement.'

Zara sucked in a breath and began to push.

Grace tried not to think of her three babies. What it might have been like to be a mother of three. She was acutely aware of their due dates and marked each one with a little candle and a whispered, *'I will love you for ever.'* She'd thought she was the only one to suffer their loss so openly. Diego had been distant. Buried under work. Barely at home. She'd not felt that she could reach out to him for his support.

Until today.

Today, Diego had held her as she cried.

Today, Diego had shown her that he was there for her and that her pain was a burden he also carried.

She'd never suffered alone. She'd just thought she had.

But what did this mean for them, as their relationship stood now?

Wrapped in her husband's arms, her head against his chest, listening to the steady and sure beat of his heart, she had felt so comfortable. As if she was home again. Safe. Relaxed. Cared for. *Loved.*

Was there still a future for them? Was there still hope?

'And again. Deep breath—and push!'

Zara was pushing as well as she could, but sometimes it was difficult to push with an epidural still in full effect. A woman couldn't always tell if she was pushing in the right way.

'Well done. Okay, take a rest. Do you need some water?'

Zara nodded, and Grace held a cup up to her mouth.

Behind them, the door opened and Diego came in. 'How's she doing?'

'She's started pushing.'

'Excellent.' He went to the other side of Zara's bed and picked up a small flannel, used it to wipe Zara's face.

Grace smiled at the gesture. He was so kind. So thoughtful. Had she misjudged him? Had she been too abrupt? She didn't want to throw away her marriage. She didn't really want to leave Barcelona and return to

England. This was her home now. These people, this country—she loved them all. And she still loved Diego. How could she not? He held such a big part of her heart.

Okay, so maybe they'd had a difficult year or two. The stress of losing three babies would test any marriage. It was what you did afterwards that counted. And perhaps neither of them had acted reasonably? He'd distanced himself from it all. Who was to say that was the wrong way to deal with grief?

I distanced myself from him. Maybe that was wrong, too?

All she knew in that moment was that she had to try. Had to try and get things back on a steady footing between the two of them. Had to let him know, somehow, that she was willing to give things a go if he still wanted her.

Did he still want her? That was the big question.

'Okay, here comes another contraction now. Big push!'

Zara groaned and bore down hard.

'I can see hair!' Grace smiled, looking up and meeting Diego's gaze.

He smiled back at her, and she could see that he wasn't just smiling at her because of the magical event happening in the room—he was smiling at a woman he loved still.

She felt sure of it.

'And again! Come on, you can do it!'

Zara pushed again and again and again, and finally, after claiming she had nothing left, she gave one last push and the head was out.

'Reach down, Zara. Feel your baby.'

She did, and a hesitant smile crept across her face. 'It's him!'

'Yes, it is. One last push and he's going to be here.'

Diego was ready with the incubator. Ready to take the baby and whisk him away.

Zara gave one last, strenuous push, and with a large gush of hind waters Baby Rodriguez was born, straight onto his mother's tummy, with a loud cry.

'Oh, my God!' Zara cried. 'He's here! Is he okay?'

'You hear that crying? He's okay!' Grace attached two clamps and cut the cord in between them. She used a towel to rub him down and get him dry. She was feeling optimistic. He was a good size. At least seven pounds. And although his exomphalos was sizeable, it was still neatly contained in its sac.

'Has he got a name?' she asked.

Zara shook her head. 'I didn't want to choose one. In case he…'

Grace understood. 'He's here now. You should think of a name for him. He's real. He has a birthday. Now he needs a name.' She knew how important that was. Even for the babies you lost.

'Give him a hug and a kiss, Zara. Because I need to take him,' said Diego.

'So soon?' Zara looked scared.

'He needs to be able to feed.'

Zara nodded, then she kissed the top of his head and whispered something to him that neither Grace nor Diego caught.

'Okay. I'm ready.'

Diego came forward and scooped him up gently. 'I'll take extra-special care with this young man, okay?'

Zara nodded, smiling through her tears. 'Make sure that you do.'

'I'll treat him like he's my own.'

Grace met his gaze then, feeling her heart caught in her throat, wishing she could say something. Wishing she could ask him what he was feeling. But he was gone, Zara was sobbing, and right now her patient needed her more than Grace needed to know what was happening between herself and her husband.

So she turned back to her, smiling as she checked on Zara's bleeding. 'He's in the best hands. So let's get you strong enough to look after him when he comes out of surgery.'

'How long will it take?'

'A few hours.'

Zara let out a heavy sigh and wiped her eyes.

Grace examined her and discovered she had a second-degree tear. 'You're going to need a stitch or two once you've delivered the placenta.'

'Okay.'

It was as if Zara was steeling herself. Or detaching herself. Grace couldn't tell.

Her placenta was delivered easily, and in one reassuring piece.

'Your epidural is still working, so I don't need to give you a local. You shouldn't feel this.'

The tear had ripped through the skin and muscle of Zara's perineum and extended slightly inwards. She would need at least five stitches, by Grace's judgement.

'Let me know if you do feel anything.'

Grace stitched carefully. Normally, new mothers didn't notice this part. They were too busy cuddling their babies or celebrating with their partners and taking photos. But Zara had no one with her, and her son was with Diego now, being prepped for surgery, and she just stared up at the ceiling, her face devoid of emotion.

'When your epidural wears off you shouldn't feel the stitches, really. Only a small amount of discomfort. And they'll dissolve on their own, so no need to come in to have them removed.'

'Mm-hmm.'

'We usually recommend that you don't have intercourse for four to six weeks. Until you're completely healed.' She was hoping that Zara would engage with her. Answer her. But she was getting nothing. Was this how Diego had felt, trying to talk to her after their losses?

'If you do feel anything you should apply a cold pack wrapped in a towel, but if the pain gets bad, or you think there might be an infection, then come back in and see us, okay?'

Zara nodded, her gaze still fixed on the ceiling.

Grace didn't like the way Zara was distancing herself. It hit too close to home. Had she done this? To Diego?

Yes, I did. But how hard did he try to reach me?

She remembered him sitting at the end of her hospital bed, trying to talk to her. How he'd kept saying her name, and how she'd not acknowledged him or spoken to him because she'd been feeling so awful, so terrible, that she couldn't carry a baby to term. How useless she'd felt. How guilty for trapping her husband with her, a woman incapable of giving him the family he deserved. How angry she'd been that he'd forced Luca from her arms and taken him away, leaving her with empty hands and a broken heart.

She'd not felt worthy of his love and affection and so she'd withdrawn. Ignored all attempts to engage with her. She'd been like Zara.

Grace cleared away her equipment, washed her hands, and then sat down beside Zara on her bed. She reached for her patient's hand and squeezed it. 'I'll wait with you. You're not alone in this—you hear me? You're not alone.'

A solitary tear trickled down Zara's face.

CHAPTER SEVEN

THE SURGERY WAS more complicated than Diego had expected.

There was a lot of swelling around the baby's exomphalos, and he wasn't able to reduce it as much as he wanted. He had to leave the sac in a silo. He fixed the throat issue, so that Zara's baby would be able to feed, but the baby's blood pressure kept crashing, and at one point his heart actually stopped. It was touch and go, and Diego's nerves were on edge. He knew this baby needed to rest and recover before it could have any more surgery, and he was glad Grace wasn't there to watch.

'Let's get him up to the NICU. I want half-hourly obs.'

'Yes, Doctor.'

He took off his gown and gloves and scrubbed out before heading out into the corridor and down to the maternity floor to speak to Zara and Grace. Exhaustion swamped him. He hadn't slept much during the day, his mind filled with what was happening between him and his wife and where they were headed. It was all he could think about these days. Now he needed a break. Things had been so intense for so long.

At Zara's room, he knocked on the door and went in.

Grace was sitting by Zara's bed, looking half asleep, but she woke up when she saw him. 'How did it go?' she asked.

'He's all right. He's in the NICU, Zara, so you can go up and visit him when Grace says you're ready.'

'And he's fixed? It's all done?' Zara asked in a low voice that betrayed no emotion. It was as if she was cautious about hearing his answer.

'I've fixed the fistula in his throat and joined the two ends, but there was some swelling in the abdomen and I was unable to reduce the exomphalos. I've placed it in a silo, and hope to reduce it when the swelling goes down.'

'What does that mean? That his organs are still on the outside of his body?'

'Yes. But only for the next day or so. We can go in again and reduce them further...maybe sew him up completely.'

'You mean he'll need further surgery?'

'Yes.'

'You told me you'd fix him.'

'I know, but these situations are all individual. As I said, there was too much swelling to—'

Zara held up her hand, silencing him. 'When can I go and see him?'

Grace glanced at her. 'I can get you a wheelchair and take you.'

'Now?'

She nodded. 'Now.'

Grace followed Diego out of the room, closing it softly behind her. 'Tricky case, huh?'

He felt frustrated. He'd almost promised this young woman that he'd work miracles and fix her baby. Why had he done that? Was it because Grace was involved?

'Yeah. But it happens…you know that.'

'I do. I'll talk to her—don't worry.'

'Thanks.'

'Are you okay?'

He looked at her. Looked into the beautiful blue eyes that were looking at him with such concern right now. He knew that she understood what he was feeling and he was grateful for it. Grateful to her for asking.

'I'm okay. You?'

She smiled back. 'I'm okay too.'

The machines created a reassuring rhythm and a musicality that was almost soothing. At least it was to Grace. For Zara, seeing her baby lying in an incubator, covered in wires and tubes and sensors, his intestines visible in the silo pouch, it must be terrifying. To her it would look unreal, as if some kind of awful nightmare was happening to her baby, right before her very eyes.

She burst into tears on seeing him, only stopping when Grace suggested she wash her hands and use the access panels to reach through into the incubator and touch him. Hold his hand and speak to him.

'Let him know that you're here,' she told her.

Grace's shift had been over long ago. Daylight was streaming in through the windows. But she knew she couldn't go yet. Zara needed her. And so she sat with the new mother and her baby for quite a while, before suggesting that Zara go back to her room to try and sleep.

'He'll be looked after…don't worry. If there's any problem someone will come and get you.'

'Will you be watching him?'

'It's really Diego's department rather than mine.'

Grace wheeled Zara back to her room and got her settled, then left her to get some rest. Then she headed back into the corridor and let out a big sigh. She was exhausted.

'Grace? You're still here?'

Diego's voice came from her left and she turned to see her husband striding towards her in casual clothes, a backpack slung over his shoulder. He looked good.

'I'm about to leave now. Zara's trying to get some rest.'

'You look shattered. Have you eaten?'

'No. I'll probably grab something on the way home. I don't think I've got the energy to cook.'

'Let me take you out for breakfast.'

She felt her heart accelerate. She couldn't remember the last time she'd eaten breakfast with Diego. But was it the right thing to do? Would she just be torturing herself with memories of how things used to be? However, she was so exhausted she decided to go with it. Besides, they'd been getting on so much better just lately.

'That'll be nice. Thanks. Give me two minutes to get changed?'

'I'll wait outside.'

Grace smiled. 'I won't be long.'

* * *

She felt as if she was back on her very first date with Diego. Only this time, instead of walking through the dark streets of London on their way to a show, they were walking through the brightly lit streets of Barcelona, with the hot morning sun beaming down upon their shoulders.

'How's Isabella?' she asked tentatively.

'She's well, as far as I know.'

'You haven't spoken to her lately?'

He shrugged. 'I've been kind of busy.'

She nodded. 'Zara told me you've been visiting her during the day. Have you been getting much sleep?'

Another shrug. 'You know me...'

Yes. She did. When he was worrying about things he worked. Long, hard hours. More than he should, putting himself last.

'You need to take care of yourself.'

'I know.' He smiled.

'How can you give your best to your patients if you're exhausted?'

'Is this wifely concern?'

She laughed. 'If it's still allowed.'

'It is.'

She nodded, smiling to herself, glad that he still considered her his wife. 'I'm serious, though. You can't burn the candle at both ends. You can't do nights and work during the day, too. Mistakes might happen.'

'I know. And now that Zara's baby is born I'll stop checking in on her during the day—how about that?'

'That sounds good. And no checking in on anyone else either. You must rest.'

'Yes, ma'am.'

She nudged him playfully with her elbow. 'I'm serious!'

He laughed. 'I know. I'm just kidding with you.'

They walked a little further, comfortable in the silence, not feeling compelled to fill it. It was nice to be with Diego again this way. She'd missed it. Missed *him*. Incredibly so.

'Still hungry?'

'Starving. I don't think I grabbed a bite all night.'

'Fancy heading over to La Casa?'

La Casa. Their place. Their special breakfast spot. She looked him in the eye. 'I'd love that. Yes.'

'Okay. Let's go.'

Normally she would reach for his hand as they walked, but she wasn't sure what the etiquette was for that now. So instead she fiddled with the strap of the bag that crossed her chest, occasionally risking a glance at Diego, admiring his profile, wondering how she'd ever got so lucky as to have this man fall in love with her and marry her.

Was he thinking about touching her the way she was thinking about touching him? When had she last let her fingers trail across his chest? When had she last touched him intimately? She knew every inch of him, and that was probably why she was finding it so hard only having her bag strap to fiddle with!

She wanted to reach out. Take hold of his hand. Feel his skin pressed against hers. Lay her head against his shoulder and stroke his arm. Feel his muscles. The solidity of his body. His quiet strength. To inhale him. Feel the brush of his stubble against her face. And so much more.

Her body was coming alive. She was next to him, away from the hospital, no longer hidden behind the barriers of work and her uniform. Their dedication to their patients had been taken away for now and they were in the open again. The possibilities were endless.

When they reached La Casa, Diego pushed open the door, holding it for her to go through first, and as soon as they stepped over the threshold, with the little bell above the door announcing their arrival, she heard the familiar voice of Felipe, the owner.

'Grace! Diego! My favourite couple! Where have you been? It's been so long!' Felipe clapped Diego on the back as he gave him a hug and then he reached for Grace's hand and raised it to his lips, kissing the back of it.

'Hello, Felipe.'

'Would you like your favourite table?'

'Yes, please.'

'This way.' He beamed, as if he was genuinely thrilled to see them, and Grace looked at Diego and they smiled at each other. They had always come to La Casa for breakfast if they'd both been on a night shift. Always ordered the same thing. It was a ritual they'd created in their marriage.

'Their' table was out at the back, in La Casa's rear garden. They liked it there because after a busy night-shift neither of them had any need to be surrounded by people. They liked the quiet and the privacy and the beautiful flower-filled terrace Felipe had created out there.

There were pots and baskets of geraniums and jasmine, ivy, bougainvillea and lilies. A large stone fairy in mid-flight reached out a hand, her fingertips caught in the water from a water feature that cascaded down various levels of slate and stone. Above, there were lanterns of many colours. It was the perfect spot. One they cherished.

Diego held out a chair for her and she sat down. Felipe laid her serviette in her lap with a grand flourish, almost as if they were in a Michelin-starred restaurant, before he poured water into their glasses.

'Would you like the menu, or should I just prepare your favourites?'

Grace looked at Diego.

'The usual, please, Felipe.' Diego smiled.

'Perfect. I'll have José bring out the coffee.'

'Thanks.'

'We haven't been here in ages. I bet he wondered what had happened to us.'

'I think we all probably wondered that,' Diego said, looking at her with a regretful smile.

She nodded. What could she say? At the time neither of them had known what was happening. Neither of them had known the implications for their marriage. The damage they were doing. They'd each just been trying to get through the day the best way they knew how.

When she'd had the miscarriages, when she'd lost the baby, the world had paused for her and Diego, but it had carried on for everyone else. The only way she could describe it was like a scene in a film where one person stood still and all around the world whizzed by so fast it was a blur. But they weren't still now. Were they?

'How do you see us now?' she asked, nervous about his answer.

He let out a breath, smiled. 'I think I like the fact that we can talk now. I've missed you, Grace.'

The last time he'd told her he missed her she'd berated him. Told him he had no right to say that to her. But this time she appreciated it more than she could say. She felt her heart swell with gratitude and happiness.

'I've missed you, too.' Her voice broke slightly on the last word and she felt her cheeks colour with heat.

The walls between them were coming down and that was good! Because if they could keep going in this direction then maybe something from this relationship could be saved? Whether that something was an actual future or not she couldn't know, but she liked what she was hearing. What she was feeling towards him.

People made mistakes. She might have felt that had Diego withdrawn from her and let her down once upon a time—but what had she done to him?

I'm not perfect. I've made mistakes, too. The solution is to learn from those mistakes, and maybe that's what we're doing right now.

'Here you go…' Felipe arrived at their table with a tray and a big smile upon his face. '*Torrada amb tomàquet* and *punxo de truita*. Enjoy!'

'Thank you, Felipe. This looks amazing—as always.'

She felt her mouth water at the sight, and at the aromas currently filling her nostrils. The sourdough toast was perfectly crisped, the rich red of the tomatoes was speckled with black pepper, and the omelette was rich with crisp potatoes. Hot steam was rising, urging them to eat at once.

Felipe disappeared like a magician and they both grabbed their cutlery, keen to tuck in and eat, to refuel after a long night shift of looking after Zara, delivering her baby and performing surgery.

The food was just as they remembered. If not better. It provoked memories of happier times, before their world had collapsed into ruin. Being here at La Casa, sitting opposite one another, eating the food they'd always eaten, looking into one another's eyes...

'Thank you for asking me to come here, Diego.'

'Who else would I bring to La Casa?'

She smiled. 'You know what I mean.'

'I do. Thank you for saying yes.'

'I wouldn't have missed this.'

They ate companionably, occasionally meeting each other's gaze and giving a warm, loving smile. Eventually their conversation turned to chit-chat about their friends at work, the cases they'd worked on, and towards the end of their meal Grace spoke of how Aunt Felicity had been when she had gone back to England.

Felipe took away their empty plates and returned with *churros* covered in cinnamon and icing sugar as their dessert. Grace wasn't sure she'd be able to eat anything else, but she couldn't resist at least one. And when they paid they hugged Felipe and promised they'd be back again soon, then headed out onto the streets of Barcelona.

It was busier. Filling up with tourists and locals. They walked through the market, casually stopping to look at stalls that caught their interest, and on through the streets to the beautiful Basilica de la Sagrada Familia—a towering masterpiece of gothic construction, resplendent with ornate stonework and filigreed spires and steeples.

Grace sighed. 'It's so beautiful… I can't remember ever having looked at it so carefully, and yet I must have passed it dozens of times since I've been here.'

'I think we're all guilty of not seeing the beauty of something that's right before us day after day,' said Diego. 'We take it for granted.'

She nodded. 'I think you're right.'

She knew she'd begun to take Diego for granted—expecting him to be there, expecting him to support her no matter what, so that when he'd been unable to she'd got angry with him, not allowing him the respite of understanding that he was hurting too.

They passed around to the Passion Façade. This side of the basilica was plain and simple, carved with harsh lines that she'd once been told represented the bones of a skeleton, to strike fear into the onlooker. She thought about the beauty of this place, how even something so wonderful had a dark side to it. Pain. Grief.

Maybe everything did?

'Do you want to go inside?' Diego asked.

'Yes.'

He reached out and took her hand in his, surprising

her. But she looked down at their entwined hands and smiled, and allowed him to lead her inside.

It was immediately cooler, and once her eyes had adjusted from the bright sunshine outside she looked up and gasped. The vaulted ceiling was the most incredible thing she had ever seen! Tall white columns rose up like flawless birches, and the ceiling looked like a collection of carved white flowers, each with a dark heart. Either side of them, along the walls, were windows of stained glass. All the colours shone down upon those inside, inspiring awe and moments of reflection. It truly was a building in which to just stop and breathe and take a moment to appreciate the wonder of life.

By the altar was an area where people could light a candle. Grace took a taper and lit four of them.

Diego looked at her. 'Four?'

'One for each of our babies and one for us.'

He smiled at her and raised her hand to kiss the back of it, the way Felipe had. But unlike Felipe's kiss this one meant something. Despite the beauty of her surroundings, the awe that it inspired, all Grace could think of was that kiss. The feel of his lips upon her skin and the way he'd looked into her eyes as he'd kissed her.

Something was happening here. Something was changing between them and she was ready for it! She was so happy that they were moving forward, past the pain of the last couple of years, past the hurt and the grief. Here they were reconnecting, rediscovering all that they'd felt for one another!

This was something they could get past. This was something they would conquer! She felt it deep in her bones and in her heart and her soul. She felt her heart quicken, her pulse thrum, as the sweet anticipation of Diego's kiss woke every nerve-ending in her body.

She wanted him. Wanted, in that moment, to forget all their pain, forget all their mistakes and just take Diego home and enjoy his body the way she always had.

But they were in the basilica, and their apartment was a few miles away. A good walk unless they caught a taxi. Right now she'd just have to accept what was happening and allow the anticipation of later to wait.

They spent a good thirty minutes in the basilica and then headed back outside into the morning heat, towards the Plaça de la Sagrada Familia—a beautiful tree-lined square filled with walkways and benches. It was packed with people. A lot of them were tourists, trying to get some good photographs of the basilica.

Grace and Diego walked past them all slowly, as if neither of them wanted their time together to end.

Diego had so much he wanted to say, but all the speeches and words he kept practising in his mind over and over again seemed inadequate for what he wanted to express. He was very much a man of action, and though he wanted so much to be able to say to Grace that he was treasuring this moment, he didn't want her to think that it was going somewhere it could never go. No matter how much they bonded again, and no matter how much they pretended that the past didn't exist, it did. And dining together, holding hands, lighting candles and spending time together, did not wipe out a past filled with pain and grief.

And yet…

He felt the lure of it. The desire, the temptation to ignore the past. This moment that they were sharing right now was just so wonderful, so hypnotic. Like a mirage promising a better life. A new way to be together.

It's easy, it seemed to say. *Just do this.*

He so much wanted to live in this moment. To just be present and forget the past, ignore the possible future. To revel in this gift he was being given of time with Grace and being kind and loving to one another again. When he'd taken her hand he'd done so without thinking about what he was doing. It had been natural. He'd forgotten they were split apart. He'd forgotten the arguments and the hurt. He'd just taken her hand in his and acted as if it was the most natural thing in the world for him to do. As it had been once upon a time.

'I should walk you home. I've kept you up far too long,' he said.

Grace nodded and they walked companionably side by side, in no great hurry.

He didn't want to think about getting back to the apartment they'd once shared. He didn't want to think about that moment when she'd disappear inside and leave him outside. That part was going to be hard. Because he wanted to continue to live in this fantasy land where he and Grace were partners again.

As they passed a flower seller he bought a small bunch of flowers and gave them to her. She held them to her nose and inhaled their scent, smiling, and then she went up on tiptoe and kissed his cheek.

He almost froze when she did so. Knowing she was

going to kiss him. Feeling the press of her soft lips against his face. Closing his eyes to treasure every nanosecond of it.

But then she was gone again, back to walking alongside him, and the kiss was over. And yet it was all he could think about. Her lips. Her mouth. Her tongue. Dear God, when was the last time they'd kissed? Passionately? Just thinking about it, he could remember how she'd tasted, how she would feel in his arms, and his body sprang to life, making it awkward for him to walk as they continued across the city towards their home.

He struggled for something to say. Struggled to think of a safe topic to talk about so as not to ruin the moment. In the end, he decided on silence. Her hand was still in his and that would have to be enough for him— though occasionally he was aware of her lifting the flowers to her nose, and one time she rested her head against his shoulder.

He wanted to rest his head on top of hers. Or maybe even reach up and stroke her hair, but if he did...

I'd want so much more! And I cannot in good conscience take any more from this woman who has already suffered too much because of me!

His mouth felt dry. His heart pounded in his chest painfully. Every step was a torture, when all he wanted to do was stop, turn and face her, and kiss her like there was no tomorrow.

They reached the street where he'd used to live with her and he felt his steps slow. He was not yet willing to give up this precious time. He wanted to eke it out for as long as he could. Because once he said goodbye, once he let her go and she went inside alone, the spell would be broken and they would go back to being colleagues again. Would they ever recapture the magic of this moment?

He gazed up at the window, saw the flower pots on the balcony, remembered how sometimes they would sit outside in the morning and share breakfast before work. The wrought-iron table and chairs were still there, with the bright red cushions still on the seats. He remembered how one morning they'd been sitting out there and Grace had used her foot under the table to stroke his leg, whilst staring intently at him…how he'd not been able to concentrate before she'd finally reached over, taken his hand in hers and led him into the bedroom.

They'd been so good together!

How had it all fallen apart?

'Well, this is me,' Grace said as they came to a stop outside the apartment door. It was still painted green and the paint was still peeling. He'd meant to redo it but never got around to it. Another failure of his.

'Yes. Thanks again for joining me for breakfast. It was good to spend time with you again.'

She nodded. 'It's been nice.'

She smiled back at him almost shyly, as if this truly were some first date and he'd walked her back to her door. And now there would be that awkward moment where you never quite knew if a kiss would be welcomed. And if you did go in for one should it be a kiss on the cheek? Or something more daring?

'So, I guess I'll see you tonight? At work? You'll check in on Zara's baby?'

'I'll bring her up to visit him, yes.'

'That's great.'

God, he wanted to kiss her so badly! He felt that if he could kiss her just once then it would get it out of his system… But he wasn't sure he'd have the strength to stop at a simple kiss. He'd want it to be so much more and then what would happen? But if he walked away without kissing her…he'd feel awful! He'd feel he was disappointing her again.

Because right now she was looking up at him as if she was waiting for a kiss.

And how could he refuse her that?

Diego swallowed hard, then leaned in for a goodbye kiss on the cheek. He figured that would be the safest bet. They would both get what they wanted, he wouldn't be rude, just walking away, and a peck on the cheek would be simpler than anything else.

But as he leaned in and pressed his lips against her cheek he found himself lingering, inhaling the scent of her—soap, and a faint perfume that he couldn't identify. Something floral, heavenly. He felt her turn her face to his lips, as if she was savouring the feel of his mouth upon her skin, and he pulled back slightly and met her gaze.

Those blue eyes of hers…so soft, so alluring…were darkened with arousal as she gazed at him and something happened in him. Something he couldn't describe…something he didn't want to think about too much. He just knew he had to kiss her properly.

He brought his lips close to hers, looked one last time into her eyes, aware that she was breathing heavily, and felt a jolt of lust hit him low and hard.

And then he kissed her.

Grace had thought he wasn't going to kiss her goodbye. She'd sensed his hesitation and even understood it. If he kissed her on the mouth it would signal a direction for their relationship that neither of them could possibly be sure of. They'd broken up. He'd moved out. She'd thought it was over. And now they'd had such a great nightshift together, a wonderful breakfast, an amazing walk around Barcelona... They were talking, enjoying each other's company again, laughing, living in the moment and remembering what had been so good between them.

If he kissed her and meant it, then... Well, she wasn't sure what that would signify. All she did know was that she wanted him to do it. So when he'd leaned in and pressed his lips against her cheek she'd pressed her face into them, enjoying that brief moment of feeling his stubble against her face, the rasp of his whiskers against her cheek, and she'd closed her eyes at the rapturous pleasure of knowing that her Diego, her *darling* Diego, was kissing her once again.

Maybe it would be the last time? Maybe this was it? A goodbye kiss? And if it was she wanted it to last and last, for ever and ever, because it felt so good to have him this close once again.

And then he'd hesitated, and she'd opened her eyes to look into dark chocolate pools, and she'd just known that this was no longer going to be a peck on the cheek. This was about to become something more. And she'd welcomed it, wanted it. Wanted *him*!

When his lips pressed against hers, softly at first, and his hands cradled her face, she felt herself sink against him, surrendering to whatever happened. His tongue began to explore her mouth and she met it with her own, entwining them, tasting him, letting their kiss become deeper and deeper and more passionate.

She let out a soft groan, her breathing heavy as they stood there in the middle of the street kissing, her hands grasping at his body, touching him, wanting more, wanting to rip off his shirt and feel his bare flesh, but restraining herself.

It was as if they couldn't get enough of each other and the tension of the last few weeks was exploding out of them as they rediscovered each other after so long apart.

And then, with his hands in her hair, he broke apart from her, breathing heavily, his eyes dark as he gazed at her, breathing heavily.

'Come upstairs with me, Diego,' she said, her intention clear.

They could build on this. They could move forward. If they could get over this, they could get over anything. She knew they had it in them.

She felt him let go of her hair and he took a step back, suddenly looking around him, as if remembering they were in public. She could see that he was aroused, and it pleased her, but what didn't please her was the look on his face.

'I'm sorry. I shouldn't have... I wasn't thinking.'

'Neither was I.' She smiled. 'Come home with me.'

He took another step back, shaking his head, checking his watch. 'I can't. I...er...need to go back to the hospital.'

'Diego—'

He held up both his hands, palms outward, as if placating her. 'I'm so sorry.'

And he turned and walked away from her.

Grace watched him go, her heart breaking.

How could she have misread the situation so badly? She'd thought he wanted the same thing. She thought that he wanted her back.

Only he didn't.

Perhaps that *had* been a goodbye kiss after all?

Diego forced himself to walk away, fighting the tremendous urge he felt to simply turn around, rush straight back into her arms and take her upstairs and ravish her the way his body wanted.

Only he couldn't.

And she would never know the strength it took him to keep creating distance between them. He couldn't wait to get to the end of the street so that he could stop and breathe and gather his will and his composure.

Kissing Grace had been like...heaven.

Kissing Grace had been everything he'd wanted.

The way she made him feel...the way she made him yearn for her...it was killing him! But he had to walk away. Had to be logical and sensible and ignore everything that his heart and body was screaming at him and

instead listen to his head, remember just how complicated they would make things if they became intimate
with each other again.

Because although it might have been wonderfully
magical to enjoy her kiss and remind himself of everything about her that he loved, it would, in the end, have
done neither of them any good at all.

Nothing had changed. Nothing had been resolved.
They would have just become stuck again. Stuck in a
relationship with major problems that they still needed
to talk about.

When he'd written that note about moving out, he'd
said *For now*. He'd thought a break apart would do them
both good. But then somehow Grace had come back
from Cornwall and told him that they needed to tell everyone it was over between them. He'd assumed she'd
made her choice. He couldn't give her the family she
desired so she'd ended it. He couldn't comfort her because she would never allow it. He couldn't talk to her
because…well, because he hadn't been ready. He hadn't
known what to say. But their time apart had given him
the space he'd needed to formulate his thoughts.

They needed to talk to one another before they did
anything else, and if he'd gone up those stairs with her
the only language they'd have been expressing would
have been bodily. Sexually. Intimately. Emotionally.

And even though his body wanted that, he wasn't
interested in just scratching an itch. Grace deserved
better than that—and so did he.

Going upstairs to the apartment together might have
seemed like a step forward for them, only it wouldn't

have been. It would have been a sticking plaster on a gaping wound that was still gushing blood profusely. They'd not fixed things between them. Yes, he could have been greedy and sated himself with her body, but that would have been wrong. Especially when she'd soon have realised they were still in the same situation and the arguments would have begun again.

He couldn't face that. He wouldn't use her.

Walking away from her before she left for Cornwall had almost killed him.

Walking away now...?

He could barely breathe.

But it was the only sane thing to do.

And maybe one day she would understand.

CHAPTER EIGHT

THE NEXT NIGHT Grace sat at the midwives' desk, twirling her pen and staring off into space instead of writing up notes as she was meant to be doing.

She just couldn't concentrate! She'd even considered taking a night off and not coming in, but the night shifts were already understaffed, and Renata had begged her to work them. She couldn't let others down. Not her friends and colleagues, nor her patients.

But she was alert to any new people coming onto the ward. Alert for Diego.

What would they say to each other after this morning?

That kiss. That kiss had been everything. *Everything!* Grace had kissed her husband as passionately as he had kissed her, and had stupidly believed—naively or not—that it meant a turning point for them. That they were moving forward and there didn't have to be a separation or the breakdown of their marriage. That there was still enough between them to work it out.

It had taken a lot of courage to ask him up to the apartment. To blatantly ask him to stay with the implication that it would lead to sex. Diego was a very sexual being—as was she. Sex was something that had always been brilliant between them.

And he'd turned it down.

Turned *her* down.

Mortifying. Horrifying. It was… It was…

Grace groaned and dropped her head to the desk, crossing her arms over the back of it.

'What's wrong?' Gabbi asked as she swiftly walked up to her, holding an armful of notes and plonking them down on the desk.

Grace sat up. 'What makes you think something is wrong?'

'Women only make noises like that when their spouse or their boss is making their life hell. So which is it?'

Grace smiled. 'Diego.'

'Ah… Want to talk about it?'

She wasn't sure. *Did* she want to discuss her personal life with Gabbi? She almost decided against it, but who else could she talk to? Gabbi was about her age, and married, so she might understand.

'You know Diego and I have had a few issues?'

'He's been sleeping in staff accommodation for a while, so…yeah.'

'Well, we've grown close again over Zara's case… as you know we've been working together.'

'Uh-huh.' Gabbi swept her hair up into a knot, sticking it in position with her pen.

'After last night's shift he took me out for breakfast. It was lovely. We talked, we chatted, we went for a walk over to the basilica. We lit candles for our babies.' She smiled sadly. 'And then he walked me home.'

'I feel that it's about to get complicated at this point.'

Grace grimaced. 'We kissed, and it was like…' she looked around to make sure no one else could hear '…a damned good kiss. Hot. Sexy. The kind of kiss that leads to more, if you know what I mean?'

'I'm a midwife. I understand how kisses lead to more. So what happened?'

'He said no, and he walked away. Said he had to get back to the hospital. I felt…' She shrugged, recalling exactly how she felt that morning. 'I felt abandoned again. Like I wasn't good enough and that maybe I'd misread the signals, or something. But surely a man doesn't kiss you like that and then just walk away?'

Gabbi sighed, clearly thinking.

'I mean…have I got it all wrong? I thought we were going to be okay. I thought we could save what we'd lost and we were rebuilding our relationship… But he couldn't get away from me fast enough, Gabs.' She could feel the tears. The lump in her throat. The old hurt. The old pain resurfacing, announcing itself with a roar. 'Are we truly over?'

Gabbi reached out a comforting hand. 'Only you and Diego know that. But is it possible that he got scared?'

'Of what? Me?'

'Of what might have happened if he had followed you into the apartment.'

Grace shook her head. 'He's not scared of sex or intimacy, Gabs.'

'Perhaps you need to speak to him?'

'I don't know what to say.'

'I'm sure you'll think of something. Now, don't you have to take Zara up to see her baby?'

'Yes. But what if I get up there and speak to him and he wants to call off the whole thing? End the marriage. Walk away.'

'I'm sorry, honey, I don't know. You two have been through some terrible times. That does damage to a relationship. Did you ever have counselling?'

Grace shook her head. 'No. Not really.'

'You need to talk to him. Look, the floor's not busy right now. Why don't you take Zara up for a visit to the NICU before she goes to sleep, and see if you can speak with him whilst Zara is with her baby?'

Grace nodded. 'Yeah. Thanks, Gabs.'

She got up and headed down to Zara's room, knocking gently before going in.

'How are you feeling?' she asked her.

'Sore.'

'That's to be expected. Have you been getting up? Moving around?'

'A little.'

'Think you could manage a walk up to the NICU?'

Zara nodded, albeit reluctantly. 'Sure.'

'I'll pass you your dressing gown.'

She waited for Zara to be presentable, and then slowly escorted her down the long corridor towards the lift that would take them up a floor to the NICU.

The closer they got, the more the butterflies in Grace's stomach built. She kept picturing herself in those moments after Diego's scorching kiss, smiling up at him, asking him to come inside, and then see-ing the look on his face and the way he'd backed away from her—as if he'd just discovered she had the plague, or something!

But she couldn't hide for ever. Problems didn't get solved by hiding from them or avoiding them. That just made them worse.

Their marriage was proof of that.

He saw Grace and Zara come out of the lift and, know-ing that they would be heading to see Zara's baby, he decided to stay in his office.

He wasn't hiding. He was simply undecided. Un-decided what to say. How to behave. Grace had in-vited him in, and although every fibre of his being had wanted to accept and go with her, revisit her body, he had walked away instead.

She must have felt so rejected! And he had no idea if she was angry now or just disappointed, resigned to ending their marriage?

He didn't want that. At all. But he'd known he needed to leave that morning, no matter how much he still loved her and wanted her. He had simply known that it was not the right thing for them to do.

He knew she would be confused by his walking away, but he hoped she'd see the sense in it. Though that kiss they'd shared was etched onto his brain, into his very being, because of how wonderful it had been, he'd known deep inside that to protect this woman he would have to go.

She probably wouldn't understand that, and he

couldn't tell her his reasoning right now—neither did he want to bring up the traumatic memories of her miscarriages. This wasn't the time and place. There was no way he wanted to see that hurt in her eyes again. To know that he'd caused it.

No. What he needed to do was wait for the right moment. Keep his distance. Stay away from—

'Hey, there.'

He looked up from his desk and frowned. Grace was standing in the doorway to his office, twiddling her fingers as if she didn't know what to do with her hands.

He felt heat inflame his face as he recalled his rejection of her. But if they were going to stay friends through this he knew he had to respect her, keep his distance until he could make his message clear—they could not revive their relationship sexually, no matter how much they wanted it. That part was over. Otherwise they'd allow themselves to get carried away. Would believe in the mirage until all the pain got raked up again.

'Hi.' He got up to put a patient file away in the filing cabinet, then went back behind his desk and sat down. 'Can I help you with something?' He tried to keep his tone neutral.

'Zara's with her baby boy. I brought her up to see him before she tries to get some rest.'

He nodded and tapped at his keyboard, bringing up his list of surgeries for the next week and pretending to scan them.

'I just wanted to see how you were doing after… well, you know…'

After the kiss. That was what she meant. Well, he

was nearly exploding right now! Did she have any idea how difficult it was to have her this close again, after that kiss this morning? His body was responding to her the way it always did, and the willpower it was taking to control himself and not just march over there and take her in his arms was terrifying.

'I'm fine. Look, I don't mean to be rude, but I'm quite busy and I don't really have time to chat with you. Maybe later?'

He made eye contact with her, keeping his face neutral, so that she knew he wasn't trying to be mean, just that he was busy. *Very* busy. And that he didn't need his very hot English rose of a wife lingering in his doorway, biting her bottom lip and curling her hair behind her ear. It was driving him crazy!

'Of course. Sorry. I'll…er…let you be. I'll be in with Zara if you need me for anything.'

'Fine.' He forced a smile that didn't reach his eyes, his signal to her that she could go.

This was killing him! Being so distant. They'd made up so much ground between them since her return from Cornwall and now he was destroying it all over again! Hurting her again!

Why didn't I just ask to see her later? Arrange a date? No. Not a date. A coffee.

'Right. Okay. Bye, then.'

She was gone before he could clarify.

He watched her retreat and sagged in his chair, unaware of how much tension he'd been holding in his body. What the hell was he doing? Playing with her emotions like this? Moving out, then being friends. Taking her out for a meal. Kissing her, then walking away. Being rude.

It was not how he saw himself. Diego had always prided himself on being a decent guy, always trying to do the right thing for other people. Thinking of others' feelings before his own.

But perhaps he was viewing this all wrong? Just because she'd suggested sex, it didn't necessarily mean she wanted anything else. She hadn't asked anything of him. Perhaps he needed to push his own wants to one side and just maintain his distance from his wife as much as he could.

Either way, once Zara's baby was fixed properly and discharged from the hospital they could both just get on with their lives.

Separately.

Grace walked away from Diego's office feeling her heart crumble into little pieces. He could not have made it clearer. The kiss had been a mistake and so had she, and he had no intention of making things right between them.

She had to accept that it was over.

Grace wiped at her eyes and took a few deep breaths before she entered the room where Zara sat beside her baby.

'Hey, how's he doing?'

'He looks awful. I can see his intestines. It's just so *wrong*!'

'He won't be like that for ever. Once the swelling goes down Diego will be able to put them back.'

And once Zara's baby had his medical condition corrected she and Diego would have no reason to work so closely on a case together.

'This is my fault. I knew I was pregnant and I never took any of those vitamin things, or had myself checked out! I caused this!'

'No. No, you didn't. This condition happens to babies with mothers who follow all the rules! You can take your vitamins, you can rest and not overdo it, you can eat the right foods, avoid alcohol and soft cheese and whatever else they tell you to avoid, and it can still go wrong.' She thought of all the rules *she'd* followed. Especially the second time. And the third time she'd got pregnant she'd been almost afraid to move. 'You can't blame yourself.'

Zara looked at her, and then down at her baby. 'I haven't held him yet.'

'Do you want to? I'm sure if I asked a nurse we'd be able to find a way.'

She shook her head. 'No. I don't want to hurt him any more than I already have.'

Grace laid a comforting hand on Zara's. 'Just give him your love, Zara. That's all he needs.'

She'd thought giving all her love to Diego would be enough. But love hadn't fixed the fact that she'd stopped him from having the large family of his dreams. Love hadn't fixed the fact that their marriage was most definitely doomed.

That kiss had been a lapse in judgement, and Diego was trying to make that clear without saying so outright.

I need to face facts.

* * *

'Have you heard?' Gabbi asked as Grace came onto her shift the next night.

'Heard what?'

'Zara's baby... Diego has said he's ready to go back in for the final surgery to reduce his exomphalos.'

Grace pressed her backpack into her locker, closing it. 'That's fabulous news. When did you hear that?'

'Day shift told me. I think he's waiting for you, so you can both go in and tell Zara the news together.'

Grace nodded. It was good of him to wait. He could have told Zara alone. 'Right. Okay. Is he on this floor?'

'I think he's in with Renata.'

'I guess I ought to go and find him, then.'

Letting out an anxious sigh, she straightened her uniform and headed down the corridor towards Renata's office. As she passed, the door to Zara's room was open, and for the first time she was dressed in normal clothes instead of a hospital gown.

Grace said hello and gave her a wave. 'We'll be in to talk to you in a moment. Looks like Diego can finish your son's surgery. Don't go anywhere.'

And then she was past Zara's room and at Renata's office. The door was open and Grace's boss was inside, having a chat with Diego.

'Grace! We were just discussing you.'

'All good things, I hope.' She glanced at Diego, but he didn't meet her gaze, and she felt the hurt hit her right in the solar plexus.

'I was just informing Renata that I'm going to take Zara's baby up to Theatre.'

She nodded. 'I heard.'

'You've been involved in the case from the beginning. It would be remiss of me not to invite you to see the surgery through.' His voice was neutral and he barely looked at her, clearly uncomfortable with being in the same room as her.

It made her feel a little angry. 'Thank you. I'd like that.'

And maybe they could talk? In Theatre he couldn't back away from her, could he? But would he appreciate her discussing their failing relationship in front of the scrub nurses, the neonatal team that he had to work with, and the anaesthetist?

Probably not.

It would be embarrassing to start off with, and completely unkind. But she wanted to tell him so much about how rejected he was making her feel, and she just couldn't see when they'd get a chance to talk again.

As they walked down the corridor side by side she felt…small. As if somehow she'd lost who she truly was, as if part of her was missing, and she knew that missing part was wrapped up in Diego still. How to tell him that he'd dashed her dreams of reuniting? That his cool tone had broken her heart? That if they couldn't do this and be friends then she most definitely would be leaving—because she couldn't stand to stay here and be spoken to as if she had never been anything more than a colleague?

But then they were at Zara's room and it was empty, the covers half thrown off the bed, the room in disarray.

Grace frowned. 'She was here just a second ago.' She

looked at the door to the en-suite bathroom, which was closed. 'Maybe she's in the bathroom?' she knocked on the door. 'Zara? It's Grace and Diego.'

But there was no answer.

Diego looked down at the door to the Vacant/Engaged sign. 'It's not locked.'

Had she collapsed inside the bathroom?

Grace knocked again. 'We're coming in!' she said, and yanked open the door—only to find that the bathroom was empty, too. Puzzled, she turned to look at Diego. 'Where is she?'

He shook his head. 'I don't know.'

'I saw her just seconds ago. I told her we were coming in to talk to her about her baby's surgery.'

'Could she have gone up to the NICU?'

That seemed the most likely answer. She must have felt she needed to see him before he went into Theatre and hadn't wanted to wait for Diego and Grace. Felt that every second she could spend with him would be precious, just in case.

They didn't bother waiting for a lift. They both raced up the stairs, Diego's longer strides taking the stairs two at a time, before they burst out onto the NICU floor. Diego slid his card through the security reader and they headed for the room where Zara's baby lay.

She wasn't there either.

'Have you seen Zara Rodriguez?' he asked one of his nurses, who shook her head before going to look at the visitors' log.

'The last time she came up to see him was at lunchtime today. She didn't stay long. Only five minutes.'

'How did she seem?' asked Grace, feeling a terrible sense of doom approaching.

'Weird. A nurse has written a request for a follow-up check for postnatal depression.'

Grace looked at Diego. 'She could still be in the hospital. She might be just...'

'Might be what?'

'I don't know. But we need to look for her inside before we assume anything bad.'

'I'll alert Security.'

She watched him stride over to the desk and pick up the phone, giving a description of Zara and asking for anyone who spotted her to notify Diego immediately. When he got off the phone, he came back to her.

'So where do you think she might have gone?'

'Let's go back to her room one last time, then let's check the café—or even outside in the gardens.'

'Okay. How did she seem when you told her we were coming to talk about her son's surgery?'

'I don't know. It was said in passing as I came to find you. She looked...' Grace thought back to that tiny glimpse of Zara. Wearing street clothes. Trainers on. When Grace had said they were going to talk about the surgery she'd looked... 'Scared. She looked terrified.'

'I think she's done a runner.'

'She wouldn't leave her baby, Diego!'

'Wouldn't she?'

She opened her mouth to speak, to answer, to reprimand him for his outrageous suggestion, but a tiny voice inside told her that he could be right. Some mothers did abandon their children. They did it because they couldn't cope. Or they did it because they thought the child would have a better chance in life with someone else. Or they did it because that had been the plan all along. They couldn't afford to keep a child, so they gave birth and then they left.

But Zara hadn't left the second her baby had been born. She had stayed. She had visited him. Grace was convinced she cared about her son. Loved him the way that Grace had loved and wanted her own babies. Only now it was crunch time and she'd got scared.

They began searching the maternity wing but found nothing. They searched the NICU again, but there was no sign of her. Then Diego's mobile phone rang.

'Hello?'

Grace watched him listen, then turn to her as he put his phone back in his pocket.

'She was spotted in the security feed leaving the hospital and heading towards St Aelina's Park.'

Grace stared back at him. 'The folly... Isabella found her at the folly when she was first brought in.'

'Let's go.'

They went down the floors in a lift and then ran out into the cool evening air. Lights were coming on across the city, and though it was still busy it was nothing like it was in the daytime.

'Where is the folly?' Diego asked.

'I don't know. I've never really explored the park.'

There were signposts directing them to certain paths, but it seemed to her that they were going in circles for ages—until she finally spotted a sign saying Secret Folly in both Spanish and Catalan.

'This way.'

It had been a long time since Grace had done any running, and by the time they arrived at the folly she was completely out of breath. But as they rounded the south-east path that brought them to the stone building they both saw a dejected-looking Zara, sitting on its steps, looking out over the lake. They slowed to a walk.

'Zara?' Grace called.

Zara turned to look at them and they could see the tears in her eyes. When she saw them she looked embarrassed and turned away, wiping the tear stains from her face. 'You must think that I am a terrible mother.'

'No. Of course not. You're just scared.'

'It's just that…he's so little, and he's already been through so much, and I don't want to be responsible for putting him through more surgery so soon. What if he dies? What if I lose him? He's all I've got.'

They sat either side of her, Grace taking her hand in hers. 'It's natural to be scared. But you can't leave him as he is. He needs that surgery, and he needs his mother to be there waiting for him when he comes out the other side.'

'Grace is right,' Diego said, his tone soft. 'He needs his mother to be strong for him. That's all any child needs from a parent. For them to believe in them, to love them and to protect them. You can do all of those things.'

Zara shook her head. 'I've already run from him. I tried not to visit him too often because it hurt to look at him like that, and now… Now I've run away from him. I abandoned him. I could never be a good mother.'

'My guess is you've never been shown what a good mother can be,' said Diego. 'Maybe that's why you chose to live on the streets. Who knows? But what I do know is that you are a mother who wants the best for her son. You want him to live, don't you?'

'Of course I do!'

'You didn't not visit him because you didn't care,' Diego went on. 'In fact you cared so much you couldn't bear to see him suffering. That hurt you. Left scars in your heart that will never go. I know what it is to feel that way, Zara. I understand. Sometimes you love someone so strongly, with an all-or-nothing love, that when you see them suffering it tears out your heart, so you think the only answer is to run. To get away. To hide from it. But you're wrong. It's the worst thing you can do. And you're not alone. You don't have to do this alone. Grace and I will help you find somewhere to live. We can set you up with support groups and maybe even some financial aid, so that you can give your son the kind of life you want him to have. A normal one. Just like anyone else's.'

Grace felt her eyes well up at Diego's words. What had he said? That he knew what it was like to see someone suffering? That it left scars in your heart? That when you saw someone you loved suffering you thought the only thing to do was to run from it?

He was talking about *them*.

'You don't know this yet, Zara,' he said, 'but you are brave and strong. And although a love like this makes you want to run from it, because of its overwhelming nature, you will embrace it—because it is yours and it belongs to you and no one else. That little boy back in the hospital has no one but you. He needs you and you need him.'

Grace wiped away a tear at his words. The fact that he could speak so eloquently and show that he was capable of understanding such intense emotions when she'd once thought him so barren of them... Well, that left scars on *her* heart. For thinking badly of him. For thinking that he was unfeeling and shallow.

Diego felt things. He might never express those feelings outright, but they were there and that gave her hope.

'That feeling you're experiencing right now is something so unique, so rare, and it's also the one reason that makes you stay. It's *love*, Zara. And you *love* your baby.'

Zara threw her arms around Diego, surprising him. Grace watched them both. Proud of Diego. Proud of Zara. She'd learned something about both of them today.

She wanted to tell Diego she understood now. Understood why he'd run from her. Why he'd turned his back. But this wasn't the right time or place, so she tried to break the tension another way. 'Anyone know the short route back to the hospital?' she asked with a smile.

Zara nodded, letting go of Diego with a thank-you. 'I do.'

'I'll be with you in a minute,' Grace said to Diego as he went to prep for surgery.

She watched him walk away, feeling all different kinds of emotions, seeing the world with new eyes.

Diego hadn't left her because he didn't care. He'd left her because he couldn't bear to see her in so much pain.

Why hadn't he just told her that? Why put her through the torment of making her feel that she wasn't good enough? That she was failing in her duties as a wife to provide him with children?

Why couldn't they have just talked about it?

She got Zara settled in her room again. 'I'll be in Theatre with Diego. When we can, we'll send a nurse out with updates, to keep you informed on how it's going. Okay?'

Zara nodded.

'We're going to take good care of him.'

'I know.'

'Just don't run. Stay. Can you do that?'

'Yes.'

'Okay.'

Grace was about to go when Zara spoke again.

'Are you and Diego okay?'

'I'm sorry?' Grace pretended she hadn't heard. She didn't normally discuss her private life with patients.

'You're married, right? Only, there's a tension between you two. I've noticed it. I only mention it because...well, Diego is going in there to operate on my son, and I need to know that he's in the right frame of mind to do so. I appreciate all that you've both done for me. How you've put yourselves out for me. But that's my baby boy in there, and I need to know he's in the right hands.'

Grace let out a sigh. 'We've had a few issues, I'll admit. But we're okay. And when Diego is in that theatre our personal lives don't follow him in. He'll focus on the patient on the table—they always come first. I don't want you to worry.'

'I will, though. Until I know he's all right.'

'I know.'

'And it will all be over? After this surgery no more? I'll be able to hold him and he can be a normal baby?'

Grace smiled. 'He can be a normal baby and you can be a normal mum.'

She headed off towards the theatre, feeling proud of how far Zara had come—from the surly teenager she'd first met in the ER to the caring mother she saw now, who'd been at her wits' end with worry.

Zara's case had shone a light on her relationship with Diego in ways she could never have expected. She felt she understood her husband a little more now. But although she wanted to talk to him about it she'd promised Zara she would not bring anything personal into Theatre. She would wait until afterwards and ask to speak to him then. Clear the air.

In the scrub room, she reached for a scrub pack, cleaning her nails with the pick and brush, then washing her hands with water and the special antimicrobial soap, up to her elbows. Through the viewing window she saw Diego, already in Theatre, being helped into his gown and gloves, and their tiny patient, already anaesthetised, lying on the table.

Zara's fears about losing her child were understandable. Grace knew that more than most. And so did Diego…

Heading into Theatre, mask already in place, Grace smiled at Diego. 'Ready?'

He nodded. 'And raring to go.'

'Okay. Let's do this. Let's give Zara a healthy baby.'

She stood back, opposite him, beneath the theatre lights.

'Scalpel.'

The scrub nurse placed the blade into his hand.

As the surgery began, Grace watched her husband with new eyes. Once again falling in love with the man behind the mask, who saved babies' lives every single day. That he had the skills and the talent to do so was remarkable, and it was something about him that she adored. He moved adeptly, cleanly, each practised move sure and steady, as if he'd done this a million times.

She watched as he reduced the exomphalos and began to put the intestines inside the baby boy's abdomen.

I'm going to talk to him when this is over.

I'm going to tell him that I understand him now.

I'm going to tell him that there's still a chance for us if he wants me.

She wasn't fearful about putting herself out there and having him reject her. She'd done that before and she'd survived. This time it would be different.

You had to be brave when it came to love.

You had to be willing to step out of your comfort zone and put your heart on the line.

Because loving someone meant you had to be vulnerable. You had to be open.

And she loved this man and wasn't willing to let him go any more.

And when this surgery was over she would reveal her heart to him, knowing that he would reach for it and take her back.

Of course he would.

He wouldn't have said those words before if he didn't want to.

He'd shown her, through Zara, that he'd suffered too. That he'd run away from her because he'd been protecting *himself.*

I did the same thing when I ran away to Cornwall.

They'd both made mistakes.

The important thing was to admit them…

CHAPTER NINE

THE SURGERY WAS going smoothly, but Diego was struggling internally. Outwardly, he was like a swan. Calm, graceful. But underneath his heart was pounding and his mind was racing.

All those things he'd said in the park to Zara, to get her to come back to the hospital…he'd said them in front of Grace. Exposing parts of himself he'd never meant to show her because they would hurt her, too. Remind her of their past. Their terrible, painful, grief-wrecked past. Would reveal to her that when he saw someone suffering he wanted to run…

Embarrassing. He'd shown himself to be weak—she must think him a terrible fool. She had to be wondering what she'd ever seen in him. How she could have been with someone who didn't have the strength to stay when life got tough.

It was pitiful.

But the words had simply poured forth. He'd seen Zara suffering and had understood her fear of the unknown, her fear of the surgery, her fear of not being good enough.

He knew that last one too well.

All he'd wanted to do was let her know that she wasn't alone. That she wasn't the only person ever to feel that way and that she was strong—that she did have it inside her to carry on, because he'd seen it in her. She was someone who had the ability to stay alive on the streets and not use alcohol or drugs to numb the pain of being unwanted. That took huge reserves and he knew she had more inside. He'd just wanted to remind her of that…that was all.

But then he'd exposed parts of himself he'd always thought he would keep hidden. He'd run from Grace not just because he hadn't been able to bear to see her suffer, but because seeing her suffer had made him feel…helpless.

Helpless was not a feeling that Diego often associated with himself. He had lost his parents early. Isabella had helped protect them all, but he'd been the eldest boy and he'd often felt he needed to be the man of the house. He'd taken on responsibility at an early age. He was used to being strong, to being the one who coped, who remained stoic and in control, because that was what everyone needed to see. Someone who didn't panic. Someone who didn't fall apart at the slightest hiccup.

He'd become a neonatal surgeon because it needed the utmost confidence. Not everyone could find the nerve to operate on a newborn baby, using tiny instruments on tiny organs and tiny arteries and nerves. He'd wanted to show he could compete with the best because he'd always felt like the best.

Until his wife had lost a baby. And then another. And then another.

He'd spent a lifetime proving he could save babies, but he'd never been able to save his own. That changed a man like him. Saving babies was his reason for being. Every baby saved was a life saved. A family saved.

Losing his three children had lost him his wife and his family.

Watching his wife fall apart, watching his marriage fall apart, had not been something he could handle. Observing what it did to him when he saw his wife bent double, sobbing with pain and grief, had not been something he could deal with at all—because what was he supposed to do?

Hugs and cuddles had been useless. They hadn't made things right. They hadn't brought their babies back. And his words had seemed empty.

So he'd stopped using them.

It had been easier to return to work and prove that he *wasn't* helpless—because at work he could be a god. He could save lives and restore limbs and remove tumours and give people the healthy babies that they deserved. He could help everyone else.

Except Grace and himself.

When this surgery was done…when they got Zara settled into a place where she could live securely…then his time with Grace would be over. He would be able to get that distance again. Maybe even apply for a transfer to somewhere else? He'd always fancied seeing the world. Seeing how they did things in different countries.

Cairo would be good. Maybe Saigon? Or Cambodia. Somewhere far, far away from Barcelona.

It would give Grace the space she needed too. Neither of them could breathe with the other so close. Living and working in each other's pockets only served to confuse them even more, and caused them to make mistakes—like on that morning when he'd kissed her outside their old apartment.

The thought of that kiss made him briefly look up at his wife, standing opposite him across the operating table. That kiss had been…something else. She was so beautiful. So perfect. But he'd failed her and she didn't deserve that. He loved her enough to let her go and find happiness with someone who could give her the babies she wanted. He'd been wrong to try to hold onto her.

I'll do that for her. Because I've got to be the strong one.

With the exomphalos reduced and all the internal organs inside the boy's abdomen, where they should have been all along, Diego began to sew up the small abdominal hole. He let Grace snip the final suture.

'Done.' He looked at her from behind his mask and nodded. It was done. He couldn't allow himself to think *what if?* any more.

'Let's keep him in the NICU for a few more days' monitoring, but I don't see any reason why his mum can't give him that first cuddle.' He went to step away from the table, pulling at his gloves and gown.

'Diego? Do you have a moment?'

He closed his eyes in pain at hearing Grace's voice. She wanted something. Clearly she did. But he had nothing left to give her now. He couldn't. He had to forbid himself from thinking he could give her anything again.

'No, I'm sorry.' He began to walk away.

'Diego!'

He turned. 'Grace. No. No more. We've done enough.'

And he walked away, hoping that she would finally get the message, even though his heart was breaking and tears burned the backs of his eyes.

Grace stood there, cheeks flaming in shame, surprise, and more than anything else anger.

That was it? He was *done?* He thought that he had the power to decide when they were over all by himself?

How could they be over? He'd said all those things…

She'd thought it was his way of telling her he was sorry and that they would be moving on. A new beginning for both of them. *Together.*

She watched him go, walking away from her without looking back. The set of his shoulders certainly made him look as if he was fed up with all the nonsense and that he was done. Just *done.*

How many times would he break her heart?

How many times would she *allow* him to break her heart?

This wasn't good enough. She deserved more. She deserved her moment in the sun and to say exactly what she wanted to say to him.

But first Zara. Grace needed to go to her and tell her how the surgery had gone, then take her up to see her baby. Let them have that first cuddle. That was more important than any grudge she had with Diego. He could wait. He wasn't going anywhere.

She removed her own gloves and gown, scrubbed down, and then went in search of Zara. Grace found her in her room, sitting in a high-backed chair, looking anxious.

When she saw Grace she got to her feet. 'Is it done? How is he?'

Grace smiled. 'It's all done and he's absolutely fine. Do you want to go and see him?'

Zara let out a pent-up breath and then rushed into Grace's arms, crying and sobbing, thanking her for getting her through it. For getting her son through it.

'It wasn't me. It was Diego.'

'Where is he? I want to thank him.'

What could she say? She didn't know. 'I think he got called to another case,' she lied. 'But it all went perfectly.'

She walked Zara up to the NICU, her stomach churning at the thought of seeing her husband again, but he was nowhere to be seen.

When Zara was sitting with her son in her arms for the first time, Grace grabbed hold of a passing nurse. 'Where's Dr Rivas?'

'I think he's left already. Said he needed some time away.'

Grace smiled and thanked her, the smile dropping from her face the second the nurse turned from her.

He needed 'time away'?

She knew where he would be. The place he always went when he wanted time to think away from the hospital. The beach. She checked her watch. Soon the sun would rise. He'd gone for that. He'd always said he found watching the sun rise soothing.

'How does it feel?' she asked Zara, looking at her holding her son for the first time ever.

'Amazing! He's so perfect! So small!'

'When you hold your baby in your arms for the first time it changes you, doesn't it?'

As always, Grace felt a little spike of envy. The only baby of hers that she'd held in her arms was Luca. Stillborn. So, so tiny. So, so still. She had no idea what it would be like to hold a baby that was not only hers, but alive and breathing. A baby that would look up at her face and yawn, or sneeze, or give a little crooked windy smile.

Her whole body ached at the thought.

Her story couldn't be over. *Their* story couldn't be over. Not yet. Neither of them had *tried.* They'd both just given up when the going got tough and that wasn't them.

At that moment Renata tapped on the window of the unit to get Grace's attention.

Sucking in a deep breath, she excused herself for a minute and popped outside to see her superior. 'What's up?'

'I've just had a call from a women's shelter that has a space for Zara and her baby. Just a one-bedroom place in El Poblenou, but it's hers if she wants it.'

'Really? That's amazing. I'm sure she'll say yes. Would you accept it for her?'

'Of course.' Renata looked in at Zara. 'It all went well, then?'

Grace smiled and nodded. 'Yes.'

'And for you?'

Now she frowned. 'How do you mean?'

'You and Diego? I know you've been having problems, and I didn't want to pry, but... I'm short-staffed, and I really don't want to lose my best midwife if you decide to return home.'

Grace was stunned. She hadn't realised that everyone knew. But should it be a surprise? Gossip mills in hospitals picked up on any kind of rumour, and she and Diego could easily have been overheard in this place.

'I haven't decided anything yet.'

'But you'll let me know? As soon as you can? I'd hate to lose you, Grace.'

Grace gave her a sudden hug. A thank-you, for showing that she cared. That she didn't see Grace as just another employee, but as a valued member of the team whom she didn't want to lose.

'Of course I will.'

Renata wiped away a small tear and squared her shoulders before walking away.

Grace watched her go, then went back into the unit and told Zara about the housing opportunity.

'Wow! I can't thank you enough. You and Diego have done so much for us.'

'It's no problem.'

'No, don't downplay it. I was a street kid. Mouthy, surly. I didn't trust anybody. But you showed me that people care. You both went out of your way to look after me and my son. You saved the only family I have. You gave me a future. I just hope that you and Diego have one too.'

For the second time in moments Grace was stunned. 'Thanks.'

'I don't know what your problems are with each other, but to me you guys are amazing. And I'm sure whatever your problems are you can solve them if you just talk to one another and look for the good. It's so easy to focus on the bad all the time that we can forget the good times.'

Grace stared at Zara, wondering how such a young street kid had got so wise. But she was right. She'd spent so long focusing on all the bad things in her and Diego's relationship she'd forgotten the good times—and there'd been plenty of those.

Lazy mornings in bed, when neither of them had had to work. Cooking together in the kitchen, testing long strings of pasta by feeding them to one another, laughing. Snatching moments together at work in between cases, when just seeing him had given her the extra burst of energy she'd needed to get through a shift. Shopping together…browsing old markets and bookstores. Going out on a boat that time for their first wedding anniversary, intending to sunbathe and have a champagne picnic only to discover that Diego got seasick. Watching movies. Sharing ice cream in that small café in Sarrià.

Marrying him—even if it had been a small ceremony with just a couple of witnesses. Standing there next to him, holding a small bunch of flowers that they'd bought from a florist's beforehand, looking into his dark brown eyes and promising him for ever.

For ever.

She'd meant it when she'd made her vows, as brief as they'd been. She'd stood there, holding those flowers, promising herself to him for the rest of her life and she'd meant it. She couldn't let him walk away like this. She needed to remind him of the promises they had made.

And, okay, maybe they'd made those promises to each other when they'd thought life would be easy for them, and that there wouldn't be any problems with having babies, but surely she still had value to him? She couldn't have just been a womb to him—a means to get the family he wanted. He must have fallen in love with her, and not just her ability to have a family...or not.

She turned back to Zara. 'If you're all settled here, I've got some things I need to do. You'll be okay?'

Zara nodded. 'I'm going to be fine now. We both are.'

'I'll come and check on you later, okay?'

Zara nodded, but her attention was already back on her son, just as it should be.

Grace quietly slipped from the room.

His marriage was well and truly over. He'd never thought he'd be the one to sound the death knell, but someone had needed to be strong enough to do so. He'd never expected this ache inside. This hollowness. This emptiness that he felt in his chest—as if someone had ripped out his heart and all that was left was the empty cage where it had once been kept.

He tried to tell himself that he had tried to save their

marriage, but knew he wasn't fully telling himself the truth. Diego tore off his tie and flung it into the nearest bin, opened up his shirt and headed onto the sand. He needed to feel it, so he kicked off his shoes, pulled off his socks, rolled up his trousers and walked across the cool sand towards the water.

The sun had not yet risen, but it would soon, and when it did it would rise on a new day. A new beginning. A day that promised many seconds, minutes and hours for him to fill in his new life as a single man.

It was not a joyous thought. He'd loved being married. Adored being dedicated to one woman. To Grace. She'd been everything he'd ever wanted in a woman… and now he'd walked away from her for the final time.

It felt…wrong. It felt painful. But it was a sensation he was used to because that was what he did, time and time again, when things got tough. He walked away. He shut down and threw himself into work, where his life *could* be successful. He used work as a balm. A soothing agent to make him feel better.

I should have turned to Grace to make myself feel better. Only I couldn't because she was hurting too.

He kept telling himself that he'd been trying to protect her, but in all honesty he knew he'd actually been trying to protect himself, too. Why not claim he was being the strong one if it made him feel even a tiny bit better? Why not lie to himself?

Because lying to myself hasn't exactly worked out, has it?

Lying to himself had caused him to end up on this beach alone.

He stared out across the dark water, feeling it lap at his ankles, the coldness enveloping his lower legs, his toes sinking into the wet sand beneath.

Lying to myself caused me to lie to her.

She ran through the streets, knowing he would be at the beach, waiting for the sun to rise. It was his thing when he was troubled. He said it always helped clear his head of muddled thinking when he was stressed about work or a project or a patient. He'd begun going after each baby was lost. She had to assume he was there now, because… Well, because there were still some things that needed to be said.

Grace did not want to let her marriage go unless she'd told him exactly how she felt. If he still decided it was over after all that then she would have to accept it—because you couldn't *make* someone love you. She would walk away if she had to, but right now she felt that there was still a chance.

She'd seen a sliver of the real Diego when he'd talked Zara into coming back to the hospital, and then there'd been that kiss, too, showing that somewhere inside he still had feelings for her. So, this wasn't over. It couldn't be over until Diego was in full possession of the facts.

The street lamps were still on and there were hardly any people out and about at this early hour. She heard her feet slapping against the pavement as she ran towards the promenade, her gaze scanning the dark horizon, looking for him in the darkness.

She stopped, panting heavily, not knowing why it felt so urgent that she had to tell him how she felt right now. Maybe because so much time had been lost between them already and she didn't want to miss any more unless she absolutely had to. She had to try everything. And then, if it didn't work out, she would at least know that she had given her all.

There. Out by the water's edge. A solitary figure stood. It looked like him. The stance. She'd know him anywhere.

Letting out one long breath, she began to walk across the sand, at one point pulling off her shoes and walking barefoot, carrying her shoes in her hand.

She could hear the gentle lapping of the water. Her stomach twisted into knots as she approached, trying to think of what she should say first. What was important? What did he actually need to hear? It seemed impossible to settle on one actual thing and her pace slowed as she neared him, suddenly uncertain and unsure. If this went wrong…if he rejected her one more time… could she bear it?

Grace stood alongside her husband, about a metre apart from him, staring out to the dark sea. To the horizon, already beginning to turn a lighter blue, with hints of orange and red as the sun started to rise.

'I thought I'd find you here.'

She sensed him turn to look at her and she knew that it was important, in that moment, that she didn't meet his gaze. She continued to look out at the array of colours beginning to slowly materialise in the sky.

He let out a sigh and she panicked. Was he about to tell her that she should never have followed him here?

'How's Zara?'

Relief. 'She's very happy. She was holding her baby when I left. And Renata came. Told me she'd found a home Zara can have when she gets discharged.'

'That's good. A home is important.'

She nodded, risking a glance at him now. His tie was gone, his shirt unbuttoned…his trousers were rolled up and he was barefoot. She saw no sign of his shoes and briefly wondered what he had done with them.

'You always wanted a beach wedding.' He turned to face her. Waited for her to meet his gaze. 'I wish I'd given that to you. I wish…' He sighed, looked down. 'I wish I'd done a lot of things differently.'

Grace felt her breath catch. 'Me too.'

'I wish I'd never thrown myself into work. I wish I'd never stopped talking to you. I wish that things had been different.'

There was a massive lump in her throat suddenly, making it difficult to talk. 'Me too.'

'I used work as an escape, didn't I? But you need to know, Grace, that I didn't use it to escape *you*. I used it to escape having to confront the emotions that I was feeling staying at home. Your pain, your grief, just made me feel *powerless*! And that wasn't something that sat easy with me.'

She listened intently, feeling all the old emotions swimming to the surface.

'I wanted to hold you. I wanted to tell you that everything would be all right. But how could I? When evidence wasn't there to show us that we could have the family that we both dreamed of? You didn't seem to want me after life kept telling us no. My words, my actions, felt empty, so I simply stopped—because of how it made me feel. I was so busy fighting off feeling impotent that I forgot you were still suffering. No.' He shook his head. 'I still knew… I just felt I couldn't do anything about it—and that was wrong. I'm sorry. I'm *so* sorry!'

He turned away from her, looked out at the first glimpse of sun as it emerged over the horizon.

'I don't blame you for leaving me. I don't blame you for walking away. Because we weren't happy any more. And I was the one who had made you sad. I was the one who had caused you pain. I couldn't protect you, or our babies. I accept now that I have to let you go, so that you can find the happiness you deserve with someone else.'

'No!' The word came out of her with such strength, such force, it surprised her. 'I'm not leaving you, Diego. You didn't cause me this pain. I couldn't carry our babies to term—that was just sheer bad luck. It wasn't your fault. And, yes, you pulled away from me, but I pulled away from you, too. Don't you see? *I* felt guilty. *I* was the one who couldn't carry your babies. *I* was the one who couldn't meet your eye because of the guilt that I felt. *I* was the one who caused you pain. I pulled away from you when you tried to help. I shut down even as I watched our marriage fall apart, I did nothing to save it. I let you down, Diego.'

She took a step towards him. And then another. And another.

He looked at her uncertainly, and so she did what she knew she would have to do to show him that her love for him was still there if he wanted it. She slipped her arms around him and looked up into his eyes.

'Yes, we stopped being happy with each other—because I think neither of us knew what to do to make the other feel better. We've both had time away now, and I think it's helped us to see…well, it's helped *me* to see… that I miss you terribly and just how much I still love you. We're equally to blame for not communicating with each other. I should have told you how I was feeling when I lost our babies. I should have listened to you to find out how you felt. But when you're in the depths of grief you sometimes forget about others. I became so used to hiding my feelings that I forgot how to show them. But spending all these nights together, working on Zara's case… I feel… I feel it's given us a second chance. If we want to take it. *Do* you, Diego? Do you want to take a second chance on me? Because I'm here for you. I want to try. I love you so much.'

Diego smiled down at her, wiping her tears from her eyes. 'I love you, too. Can we do it, do you think? Are we strong enough? What if it happens again?'

Grace smiled. 'We make a vow. Right now. That we'll make time every day to talk to one another. To tell each other how we're feeling even if it's just about work.'

'And what about…the babies?'

'We talk about them, too. We loved all three of them. And they were gone much too soon. But we *should* talk about them. They were real. They were loved. We had hopes and dreams for each of them and no matter how hard it is we'll talk. I promise you.'

'I'm so sorry I hurt you, Grace. I never want to do that ever again.'

She smiled. 'Ditto.'

'I love you, and I'm never going to let you drift away from me ever again.'

'I love you, too.'

And he bent his head to kiss her as the full glory of the sun rose above the horizon, lighting the sky in a fanfare of orange, red and yellow.

A new beginning for a love that had never died.

EPILOGUE

THE LAST FEW weeks had been a whirlwind of preparation and planning, but somehow they had managed to pull it off.

The beach looked perfect. The perfect backdrop to their event. A white pergola had been erected in front of the water, its trellis interwoven with white flowers. Roses, dahlias, peonies, carnations and tulips. Snapdragons hung from the centre arch, along with gypsophila to make it look ethereal.

Wooden boarding had created a walkway down the centre of the rows of chairs that were now filled with guests for the renewal of their vows.

Grace could see Diego standing at the end of the aisle, waiting for her, along with his best man and the minister.

Had she felt this nervous at her actual wedding?

She could see their friends from the hospital were there too. Santiago, Carlos, Javier, Caitlin... Her colleagues Renata, Gabbi, Ana, Mira—even Olivia, back from her mother's in Andalusia. And on the front row, for the first time, Diego's family. The people she'd always hoped to meet. There was Isabella—whom she already knew, of course—but there was also Eduardo and Luis, looking like younger versions of Diego, and his other sisters Paola and Frida.

This was the big family ceremony she'd always dreamed of and her happiness knew no bounds. Even Zara was there, with her baby boy Jacobo.

Grace stood listening for the violinists to begin playing their music, waiting for her walk down the aisle. It was a shame there was no one to escort her, but—

'Want to take my arm?'

Grace turned and gasped. 'Aunt Felicity!' She threw her arms around her and hugged her. 'How come you're here?'

'Diego told me you were renewing your vows and he paid for my flight out here.' Her aunt gave her a big smile and looked her up and down. 'You look the perfect bride. You're beautiful.'

Grace smiled and slipped her arm through hers.

'Are you ready?' asked her aunt.

'I am.'

Aunt Felicity gave a nod to the violinists and they began their music.

At the end of the aisle Diego turned to look at her, and she saw a broad smile cross his face, his eyes lighting up at the sight of her.

Her heart leapt at seeing him. She had never felt so happy, and she knew that this happiness was more important than any she had ever felt before. Because this happiness—she and Diego had earned it. They had walked through fire with each other. And although life had tried to ruin what they had, they'd somehow survived and fought hard to keep what had drawn them together.

Their love.

As she stood there in front of all their friends and family, holding his hands, saying her vows, she knew this was the happiest day of her life. And that no matter what—even if their future didn't include children—she and Diego were lucky to have such intense love in their lives, but most importantly they were lucky to have each other.

He was the love of her life.

And she was his.

And that was all that mattered.

* * * * *

FROM
WEDDING GUEST
TO BRIDE?

TINA BECKETT

MILLS & BOON

To those around the world
who are involved in equine assisted therapy.

PROLOGUE

THE GROUND WAS so much harder than Elena Solis remembered. She lay there, weird sounds emerging from her throat as she tried to draw a breath and failed. A bolt of panic surged through her. But despite all that, despite the continued gasp for air, despite her fear, she searched the area for her horse.

The music from the speakers at the boarding barn was still blaring, even though she and Stratosphere were no longer moving to the same beat.

It wasn't the first time she'd taken a hard fall. She'd pulled plenty of stupid stunts in her eighteen years, so she doubted it would be the last. Only this time, it wasn't a stunt. She'd been practicing for a show, the way she'd done hundreds of times before.

Her eyes arced over the space again, finding Sandra standing nearby.

"Don't worry. I have Strato. Are you okay? You hit pretty hard." Elena's closest friend had dismounted from her own horse and now held Strato's reins as well.

The poor boy had tripped as she'd rounded a corner during their freestyle routine, not an unheard-of occurrence. Thankfully he hadn't fallen on top of her. As always, she would just hop up and carry on. You had to get right back on after a fall, right? Wasn't that how the saying went? Except right now everything hurt. Her shoulder, her left knee.

But the worst was her back.

"Just give me a minute." She dragged in a shallow breath, then another, the tight band around her chest slowly easing, even as her pain levels crept higher.

She filled her lungs with air, eyes closing in relief that she could finally breathe normally again. Okay, now to get up. As she tried to roll onto her side, sudden shards of pain slashed at her back, and she felt a horrible burning sensation in her spine. Then nothing. Nothing at all. She immediately fell back and lay still, trying to think.

Okay, that had never happened before. The pain in her knee had vanished, though. That was a good thing. Right?

She wiggled her hands, her arms. Her toes.

Everything worked. Wait. Had her toes wiggled? She couldn't tell. She tried again.

Dios!

"Sandra?" Her voice shook in a way it hadn't a moment ago.

Her friend took a step closer, the horses moving with her. Strato's head came down, and he nuzzled her shoulder, giving a soft nicker.

"Do you need a hand?" her friend asked.

"I—I don't know yet."

"What's wrong?" A hint of alarm had entered Sandra's voice.

"Can you look at my left foot?"

Her friend's attention moved downward. "What about it? Does it hurt?"

"Is it moving? Look at it. My left foot. *Is it moving?*"

"No, should it be?" Her friend's eyes met hers. "Elle? Talk to me. Are you in pain?"

Terror rose up and clogged Elena's throat, threatening to steal her breath all over again. Her riding helmet pressed against the back of her skull. At least she'd worn that. "No, it doesn't hurt. And it should be moving. I'm telling it to move." *Please move! Please!* "Are you sure? Look again."

"Okay." Sandra's gaze flitted back toward her foot. "It's not doing anything. *Dios*, Elle, I think I need to call for help."

Elena swallowed, remaining very still, knowing she'd made a terrible mistake in trying to get up before she'd assessed the damage. How many times had her father warned her not to move someone who might have a back injury? "I think so, too. Because, for some reason… I—I can't feel my legs."

"Oh, Elle…" Her friend pulled out her cell phone and dialed.

Through a tunnel she heard Sandra telling someone where they were and what had happened and begging them to send help. Now.

All Elena could do, though, was lie there and pray. Pray harder than she'd ever done in her entire life.

CHAPTER ONE

Santiago Garcia had never seen his friend Caitlin look more radiant or more beautiful as she glided down the aisle to meet the man she called *el amor de mi vida*. The love of her life. Santi had once had one of those, too. But not anymore. And he'd never felt less festive about an event like this than he did right now. It was the first wedding he'd agreed to attend since Carmen's death had ripped his life apart six years ago. And right now, as he sat in a plush pew in the ornate estate chapel, he was sorry he'd come. But he'd traveled all the way to Andalusia from Barcelona, and to skip the wedding at the last second would have raised eyebrows. And Caitlin didn't deserve to have one second of her happiness affected by his behavior.

A slight movement to his left caught his attention. The woman seated next to him rearranged her skirt over her legs for the third time since she'd wheeled herself into her spot moments earlier.

She looked almost as unhappy to be here as he felt.

Without turning his head, he studied her out of the corner of his eye as a way of avoiding the joy that radiated from the front of the chapel. With raven-black hair that wound its way down her back, the woman sat proud and erect, her slender shoulders bared by a green slinky dress. The color was perfect against her smooth skin. She was stunning. And evidently alone. Just like him. Not that it made the slightest bit of difference.

Santi wasn't here to meet women. He was here to wish his friend well. Once that was done, he was free to return to Barcelona. Back to his life.

He forced his attention back to the front, more anxious than ever to get out of here.

Caitlin and her soon-to-be husband were holding hands and the officiant was instructing Javier to place a ring on Cait's finger. Their eyes met, and Javier leaned over to whisper something in Caitlin's ear. Something that made her lips curve.

Santi's muscles tightened in remembrance of doing that exact thing with Carmen. Whispering about how much he loved her. How he couldn't wait to walk down that aisle as husband and wife. Some strange impulse made him glance across, searching the fingers his neighbor had clasped in her lap. No ring. Not on any of her fingers.

Why had he just done that? It didn't matter if she was married or available. He'd taken off his ring a couple of years ago but had felt a vague twinge of guilt when he had, his empty finger whispering an accusation that wasn't true. Because *nothing* could make him forget his wife.

The woman next to him glanced his way without warning, making him jerk his gaze back to the front, where it belonged. But not before he saw the slight frown that furrowed her brow. He agreed with her. He'd had no business staring at her.

The rings were exchanged and vows repeated back to each other, and as the strident chords of the organ began to play, Javier bent over to kiss Caitlin on the lips, lingering there long enough for the guests to chuckle, a few whistles echoing off the formal walls, where stern saints seemed to chastise the interruption. Then the couple parted and turned to face the back of the chapel. Javier raised their clasped hands, kissing his bride's knuckles before they began their march down the aisle. Caitlin smiled at him as she went by. Or had it been at the mystery woman to his left? She was seated on the bride's side, so they had to know each other.

From where?

It didn't matter. Maybe she was a childhood friend, or someone from school.

As soon as Caitlin and Javier and their wedding party exited through the massive doors, the woman beside him whirled her chair around and disappeared into the crowd that now streamed toward the back. Anxious to get away from him?

Hell, why wouldn't she be? He'd stared at her for most of the ceremony, although most of that was out of avoidance.

Avoidance? Was that all it had been? The woman was beautiful. She probably had men staring at her all the time. Maybe that's why she'd seemed so irritated when she'd caught him in the act.

Well, he didn't need to worry about it. Once he got

through the reception dinner, he was free to leave for his hotel. Or maybe he'd try to catch a flight straight back to Barcelona and his apartment, which was not far from Santa Aelina Hospital. The university hospital had been new when he'd been approached to come and be a part of it, and he'd jumped at the chance. He didn't regret the move. Even though he'd lost Carmen a year after moving to Barcelona.

He took his time making his way to the reception, which was held in one of the ballrooms of the huge estate. Sliding through the doors, he winced at the strands of white lights that were artfully draped throughout the space, giving it a sense of intimacy that made him balk at moving farther into the room. But the people coming up behind forced him to move away from the entry, deeper into the belly of the beast. The love and romance fairly pulsed through the space. And it was evidently contagious with people everywhere holding hands and murmuring to each other. The occasional outburst of laughter made him even more uncomfortable.

His eyes scanned the area, and it took a second before he realized what he was unconsciously searching for. The woman who'd sat beside him in the chapel. To apologize?

Maybe she'd think his staring was because she was in a wheelchair. But she'd be wrong. And trying to explain that seemed worse somehow. So he was going to let it go.

Besides, he didn't see her anywhere.

He went over to the bar, waiting in line for a drink. Anything was better than standing against the wall and watching the rest of the world enjoy themselves, while he tried to plug a hole that was spewing memories of Carmen like a broken water main. This was why he didn't do weddings. He'd toyed several times with returning to Argentina, but he didn't want to get his parents' hopes up that he would take over the family business. While he loved horses and polo—having grown up with them—that wasn't where his heart was.

Santi loved medicine. Loved being a pediatrician. Even more so now that his dreams of having a family of his own had been snatched away by the cruel hand of fate.

He ordered a Scotch on the rocks, taking a sip before stepping away from the bar. He savored the bite, the chill of the ice burrowing beneath the warmth of the liquor. It was a sensation he knew all too well. After Carmen's death, he had taken far too many slugs of room-temperature whisky over a period of months. He'd cut back before it had gotten completely out of hand, and he'd found the addition of ice made him slow down and think, rather than mindlessly toss back shot after shot.

A flash of green caught his eye before disappearing again. He squinted in that direction while taking another sip of his drink.

It probably wasn't even his mystery woman.

His?

No. She wasn't. And he had no intention of trying to change that.

Caitlin and Javier appeared in front of him. They must be making the rounds rather than standing in a reception line. He couldn't blame them.

"Thanks for coming, Santi. I wasn't sure you would."

He knew Caitlin and some of the rest of the staff at Santa Aelina's had been worried about him after Carmen's death. He'd refused to talk to anyone and had brooded in his office whenever he didn't have patients. He refused to go to any events not related to the hospital and had equally rebuffed Caitlin's mentions of going to the hospital's counseling center.

"I told you I would."

She smiled. "I know. And you always keep your promises, don't you." She leaned forward and kissed his cheek. "Well, I'm glad you're here. It means a lot to me."

Javier held his hand out, and Santi gripped it.

"Congratulations to you both. I'm happy for you."

The lie slipped out so easily that it sounded true. It wasn't that he *wasn't* happy for them. He just found it hard to bleed an emotion that no longer flowed through his veins. Nowadays, he found his fulfillment and purpose in his work. It filled his days with meaning, and right now, he couldn't ask for any more than that. Didn't really deserve any more than that.

His friend eyed him. "Sorry to talk shop right now, but there's a case I might ask you to look at when you get home, since we'll be gone on our honeymoon for a while. Teenage patient complaining of leg and foot pain."

"Tomás?" Javier glanced at Caitlin.

She nodded at her husband before looking back at Santi. "He was born with hypoplastic left heart syndrome."

Santi frowned. HLHS was a congenital malformation of the heart where only half of it was capable of pumping blood. It was normally a death sentence. "And he's a teenager?"

"He had the Fontan procedure as a child and has done remarkably well with it."

He didn't understand where he came in. Fontan circulation was a complicated rerouting of the heart vessels that helped bypass unusable portions of the organ. It was a delicate balance, since cardiac output never became what was considered "normal."

"You're both cardiologists, and I'm a pediatrician, so I'm not sure how I can help."

Javier inserted, "We've basically ruled out the pain being caused by the circulatory system itself. We've talked about bringing you in, there's just been no time—"

"You helped me with a case a few weeks ago, remember, Santi? And there's a new doctor coming on board—a diagnostician. I think I mentioned her to you before. She's already said she'll examine him." She squeezed his arm. "Anyway, look at his chart and see what you think. His name is Tomás Lopez."

"Okay, I will." He hadn't needed to contact the diagnostician last time as he'd solved the issue himself. He welcomed complex cases. They used brain cells that might otherwise be occupied with things he couldn't change. And what was the worst that could happen? The new diagnostician telling him to mind his own business? If she did, she did. He no longer worried much about stepping on toes.

Caitlin hugged him. "Thanks. Keep me updated."

Her husband shot her a look that made her grin.

"Okay, I know I promised no work on our honeymoon. But I'd like to know what they find."

Javier tipped her chin and planted a kiss on it. "I'm kidding. I want to know, too."

With that, the happy couple turned to speak with the person on his right.

Blowing out a breath, he took another drink and found that too much ice had melted during their conversation, taking the bite out of the Scotch. Setting the remainder of his drink on a tray designated for discarded glasses, he forced his mind to work through what little information Caitlin and Javier had given him.

The sound of a spoon rhythmically tapping against a wineglass broke through the chatter, and more people joined in until it became a solid clanging wall of sound. Folks moved to sit at the large round tables where food would soon be served.

Santi knew what was coming. Before Javier kissed Caitlin to appease the crowd, or the first person had a chance to propose a toast to the happy couple, he slipped out of the room.

Shoving his hands into the pockets of his dress pants, he wandered down the hallway, the quiet click of his shoes on the tile a marked contrast to the noise of all those people in the ballroom. At last he could hear himself think, although that could be a double-edged sword.

An open door to his right caught his attention and he peeked inside and saw a huge area of shelves lined with books. A library. Perfect. He could find a quiet corner and sit for a while. He didn't dare leave quite yet, when his absence might be noted.

Ducking inside, he made his way over to look at a tile mural tucked between two of the bookshelves. He studied it, giving a snort at what the scene depicted. A couple dressed in ornate period clothing sat astride a galloping horse. Not only were they sitting, they were, in fact, sidesaddle. Both of them. The couple kissed, the draped reins flapping uselessly against the steed's neck as it raced across the countryside. Evidently romance trumped reality everywhere, not just in the chapel.

"Seriously?" he muttered.

"I thought the same."

The soft words came from somewhere behind him. He closed his eyes as he realized he wasn't alone. He certainly hadn't meant for anyone to hear him scorning the local decor. Especially since the painter was probably someone famous.

Well, at least it sounded like the person agreed with him. So maybe someone besides a horse person could spot how ludicrous the scene was.

Well, even a wedding contained ridiculous promises of forever, didn't it? No one knew what the future held. And no one knew that more than he did. So why had those wedding vows not changed to any large degree over the last couple of centuries? Plagues, pestilence, wars…cancer. Any one of them had the power to grind those promises into dust.

Realizing he was still standing there in the same position he'd been moments earlier, and probably seeming very rude to whomever had spoken to him, he slowly turned around, trying to explain as he did.

"Sorry, it's just that I was raised on a—"

His words faltered for a second before dying away completely.

The flash of green he'd spotted in the ballroom... It was repeated here. What the hell were the odds of that?

The faint sounds of laughter carried in from the ballroom, and he tensed before he realized his focus was fixed on the mystery woman.

He was staring at her just like he'd done in the chapel less than an hour earlier. He blinked and forced his eyes to move away before looking at her again.

"It's you."

As soon as the words were out of his mouth, he felt a swell of irritation wash over him. He'd sounded shocked. And pleased.

And the last thing he wanted was to sound like a breathless teenager.

Her quick smile wiped away his irritation as her brows went up in question.

"Yes. It's me. Although I'm not sure what you mean by that. Should I be flattered or insulted?"

Elle was good at hiding her feelings. So she hoped the sense of shock had been veiled beneath an air of lazy amusement. When the man had wandered into the library, she hadn't realized who he was at first. But the sound of disbelief when he'd gone over to the picture had made her smile. The impulse to glide away on silent wheels had come and gone as curiosity made her sit there and see what he would do or say next.

She'd come here to get away from the crush of people in the ballroom. Crowds gave her a strange sense of claustrophobia as they towered over her. At times, she felt invisible, which she knew wasn't what anyone intended, and there wasn't much they could do about it, other than sit down.

So observing this one man as he studied the mural was much more interesting than going back into the reception. She probably knew a few of the people there, although she hadn't really seen anyone besides the bride and groom.

But when he'd turned around and she recognized him as the man who'd sat next to her in the chapel, shock had shot through her. It was evidently the same for him, judging by his words.

His mouth twitched. "Sorry. I thought I was alone. It seems you've seen my bad side twice now."

"Twice?" She had no idea what he was talking about.

"Never mind. I just needed to get away for a minute and then I saw…" He motioned back toward the mural. "Did the painter never once throw a leg over a horse?"

She blinked, eyes going wide. "I haven't heard that expression in a while. You ride?"

"I haven't recently, but I used to quite a lot."

"So did I." She expected to see disbelief go through his eyes, but there was nothing.

Nothing…except something she wasn't quite sure of.

He came over and took a seat in one of the gilt chairs in front of her and smiled. "Okay, so tell me. Have you ever ridden bareback while kissing someone—as your horse charged across a field? And actually stayed seated?"

She flinched as she remembered her fall all those years ago, but quickly covered by saying, "Nope, I've never done that. Never even wanted to do that. You?"

He laughed, glancing back. "You mean you don't recognize me in that painting?"

Her answering laugh took her by surprise. He was talking to her as if she could do anything. People often tiptoed around her, being careful with what they said, afraid they would hurt her feelings. They didn't realize that very act hurt. Even the few dates she'd gone on had been full of men rushing to do things for her that she could do for herself. After a particularly disastrous encounter, she finally decided she didn't need a life partner. They were just too much work, and she was pretty sure they thought the same thing about her. Her college professor being one of them.

"Well, I thought you looked vaguely familiar."

There was suddenly a sense of relief about him that she wondered about. He'd seemed so ill at ease seated beside her in the chapel, and she'd thought maybe it had to do with her chair, but there was none of that now. It had been embarrassing, because what she'd noticed first and foremost about him was that he was a man. A very, very attractive man.

And hearing him talk… *Dios*, his voice only increased that awareness. His voice had a low gravelly quality that caught at her insides and made them quiver. All the way to the middle of her left thigh, which was the lowest part of her body that had retained sensation. Her injury hadn't completely severed her spinal cord. And the parts that could still feel had the ability to detect the most minute sensations. The lightest brush against her skin. So the pleasure of his voice...

Oh, man, it was nice. More than nice.

She cleared her throat. "Anyway, you can kind of see why the painter concentrated on the couple rather than the horse in that mural. After all, Caitlin and Javier only had eyes for each other during the ceremony."

"Yes. I guess that's true."

The words were said in that same gruff intonation as before, but it was as if a shutter had suddenly slammed down in his eyes. The uneasiness had returned as he leaned back in his chair, arms going across his chest.

Okay, so this was a subject that was touchy with him for some reason. It didn't take a diagnostician to read his body language. She could have done it with no medical degree at all.

He wasn't angry. More like he was putting up a roadblock that read "Closed to through traffic."

She could understand that. There were still areas of her life that she didn't talk about with just anyone. But she mourned the loss of the playful conversation they'd had just minutes earlier. All because of a careless comment.

But how could she have known?

She reached for the books she'd found when she'd first come into the library, hoping to recreate the ease between them. "Do you know much about the history of the Maravilla estate? It's kind of fascinating actually."

She stumbled through a couple of more sentences about the house and grounds before taking a breath. And in that time there was a silence that made her teeth clench.

This was why she didn't talk about stuff like this. Her fixation on the smallest details didn't sit well with most people. She waited for his eyes to glaze over and for him to make an excuse to leave.

Only she didn't want him to leave. Not just yet. And she wasn't sure why.

Surprise washed through her when neither of those things happened. Instead, his arms uncrossed, and he leaned forward. "I don't actually know anything about it."

"Oh, really?" Her eyes met his, and she swallowed, fumbling with the book she'd grabbed. She flipped to the first page that had a picture. It was the one from the mural on the wall. "Oh! Well…"

The man chuckled. A warm sound that made a rush of pleasure run through her. This man could be very dangerous. "You planned that didn't you?"

"I didn't. Honest." But her words came out breathy with a strange huskiness that wasn't familiar.

She recognized the attraction for what it was and knew it was risky to continue down this path. But somehow, she didn't want to exit the conversation. Wanted to see what would happen if she stayed here and let things take their course.

His gaze locked on her face, shifting subtly to her mouth and pausing there. It knocked the breath from her lungs.

"Didn't you?"

A buzzing started up in her head as he continued to look at her. Her tongue flicked out to moisten her lips, and she watched him capture the movement before forcing herself to answer him.

"Why would I do that? You don't even like that mural."

"The mural? Hmm… No. I'm not impressed by that."

Said as if he was impressed by something else, instead.

Her? Surely not. But what if…?

How long had it been since she'd engaged in back-and-forth banter like this? It could almost be considered flirting, couldn't it?

And was she? Flirting?

Yes. She thought she was. She was never going to see the man after tonight, so what was the harm?

Against her volition, her back curved, as if something in him was pulling her toward him. Some magnetic force. Her hands went to her knees, pushing slightly to keep herself balanced in her chair.

The chair was the only place she was balanced. Her mind, her heart, her body… They were all rocking on some sort of precipice. One tiny push and…

"So what impresses you?" She couldn't believe she'd just asked that. And yet she didn't want to retract the question.

"All kinds of things. This country. This place." There was a slight pause before he continued. "And you."

She realized they were now inches away. The buzzing in her head spread to her body, until her entire being vibrated with a strange kind of urgency.

She recognized it a second before warm fingertips touched her cheek, sliding down it until he reached the corner of her mouth and cupped her chin. Tilting it up. Her pulse skyrocketed, and everything in her willed him to do it. Wanted him to do it.

"Yes," he murmured. "Most definitely you."

And then he leaned forward and did exactly what she'd been waiting for. He pressed his lips to hers.

CHAPTER TWO

SOMEWHERE IN THE back of his mind, he heard something clatter to the floor.

The book.

Except that's not what he wanted to think about right now. Not with this woman's sweet mouth pressed against his. And instead of moving away, she was inching closer.

Her hands curved around his shoulders. Maybe it was to help support herself, but the sudden touch rocketed through him like a missile, sending all kinds of crazy thoughts pumping through him. It was insane and heady and he never wanted it to end.

Her warm fingers toyed with the hair at his nape and a rush of need pumped through his body, making him want things he hadn't wanted in what seemed like forever. Things like intimacy. Sharing.

Caring.

Things he hadn't wanted since…

Carmen.

He sat back in a hurry before he realized he was dragging her with him. Reaching out to steady her and help her regain her balance, he ground his teeth together. Hell, what had he been playing at?

Diablos! Kissing her made as much sense as the scene in that damned mural!

He didn't even know this person, yet he'd been locked in an embrace that he almost hadn't been able to break. If not for...

"*Santo Dios.* I'm sorry."

Up went her chin. "Don't be. It was just a kiss. It meant nothing."

She smiled, but there was a brittle edge to it. She'd gone from soft and warm and so passionate it had made his blood heat, to a state that was chillier than those cubes of ice in his drink a half hour earlier. Only there was nothing watered down about this. And her words were sharp and biting and filled with an anger he didn't understand.

He shouldn't have kissed her. And now she wanted him to leave. That much he understood. So he climbed to his feet, staring down at her for a few seconds trying to find a different way to apologize, one that would make for a softer exit. But he found nothing. No words that would work in a situation like this. Not that he'd ever been in one.

It meant nothing.

Hell, he wished that were true. And maybe for her it was. But for him...?

What they'd shared a moment ago was the first time he'd felt out of control since his wife's death. Other than two quick encounters with other women, he'd pretty much been celibate. And he preferred it that way.

And this? Well, this was the first real kiss he'd had since that time. The first kiss with no end goal in sight. He'd kissed her simply because he'd wanted to. And that fact just made the guilt rise higher. He knew he wasn't betraying Carmen, but it sure as hell felt like he was.

The woman's head was bent, and she stared at the splayed hands in her lap. He didn't want to leave her like this, wanted to at least ask her what her name was. But he didn't think she'd welcome anything he might say right now. So with one last look, he turned and walked away.

Away from her. And most of all, away from that damned mural on the wall.

"Elle?"

She'd zoned out again. For the third time, since her friend and mentor, Letizia Morgado, started showing her around Santa Aelina Hospital. And it all centered on that surreal experience at the Maravilla estate. It had almost been like a scene out of *Cinderella*. Only the man had been no prince. And Elena was no downtrodden stepsister. But that kiss… As short as it had been, its memory still had the power to send shivers of need through her.

And she didn't like it.

"Sorry."

"Are you okay with this? Staying in one place? Caitlin said you were but…" Her friend's worried glance said volumes.

Elle had preferred to travel from hospital to hospital, justifying it with the idea that she could learn more and be better at what she did by having a wide range of experiences. But maybe the truth was that she'd had a hard time trusting people since her accident. The world had turned into a dark and scary place for a few years after her fall, and some of her friends had silently slid away, including her high school boyfriend, who'd sent excuses for why he stopped coming to visit her in the hospital.

Sandra was one of the few who hadn't deserted her. And Strato now resided with her at her home on the island of Mallorca. Elle had retired him after her accident, not able to bear the thought of selling him and not knowing what might happen to him down the line. She was happy knowing he was loved and cared for, even if she hadn't been out to visit him in the last three years.

"I'm sure. Caitlin has a case she wants me to look at. Besides, you've done a wonderful job with accessibility at the hospital. We haven't been one place where I had trouble getting around."

Letizia smiled. "Thanks. It was a hard battle, just like it is everywhere. It's not that people don't want accessibility. It's just something they don't always think about. This hospital really wanted to work on that." Her friend spun to face her. Their wheelchairs were as unique as their personalities. Letizia's green spiked hair and the bold stickers plastered all over her transportation were in stark contrast to Elena's sleek chair that was built for maneuverability and comfort. Elle also had a racing chair at home that she'd used for various walk, roll or run marathons.

"A new case. I heard about that. Must be interesting if Caitlin is asking for another set of eyes."

"I know. I'll look at the patient's chart as soon as I get to wherever you guys are putting me. Fifth floor, right? In the research and teaching departments?"

"Actually, if you're okay with it, we have an office on this floor you can use while working this particular case. You may be shuffled around the hospital a bit when there's a complicated case to make it easier for you, but you're right, your 'home' department will be up on the fifth."

She smiled. "Well, see there? I'll still be moving from place to place. It'll just all be in the same building." Actually that made her feel better. If she bounced from one department to another, she wouldn't get that claustrophobic sense of panic that she'd had her last year of high school when everything had changed. She still got that whenever she was in one place for too long. It was irrational, and she'd done her best to combat it, but it was still there. That fear had chased her away from any relationships she'd had since her accident. You never knew when life could change completely. But if she just could stay ahead of it…if she could just outrun it—or out roll it, in her case—she would be fine. She hoped.

Letizia headed toward the end of the hallway, pushing a button to open a door on the right. "Okay, then. This will be your office, for now."

Elle moved past her, eyes widening as she took in the large space. "Are you sure this is the right place?"

In the back of the office, there was a huge window that looked out over Aelina Park, the green space the hospital had put in as the facility was being built. With a tree-planting program and dirt paths made for walking or jogging, the park spanned the space between the hospital and the staff quarters just beyond. She couldn't wait to take her other chair out on that path and get back to her workouts. There was also a little man-made creek that ran along part of the trail that was stocked with fish and could be enjoyed by birds and small wildlife. It was beautiful. And peaceful. Something that really resonated with Elle, who desperately needed that peace.

"This is it. Caitlin requested it especially for you. It'll make it easier for you and Dr. Garcia to work on the case."

Dr. Garcia must be the pediatrician her friend had told her about. She just hoped the person didn't get his feathers ruffled, the way some doctors did if she didn't kowtow to their every thought.

Maybe that's why she had this space. For meetings about their patient. There was a table with four chairs and a plush sofa that looked like it might pull into a bed.

Okay, she could get a little too used to this. "Well, thanks. I'll take good care of it. While I'm here, anyway."

"Are you planning to leave again? I hope not."

Elle hesitated. "No. I just meant while I'm using the office." Had her words contained a hidden meaning? Was she thinking of her stay at Santa Aelina's as being temporary?

No. She needed to overcome some of her hang-ups, and this was the perfect time and place. She rolled over to the desk and reached behind her for the backpack that contained her laptop and some items for her workspace. Setting it on the light wood surface, she glanced again at the park.

Letizia must have seen her look. "Did you get into your apartment yet?"

"Yes. I think it will work out perfectly. Do most of the staff live there?"

"Some of us do. But not everyone. Those who live farther out normally either take the bus or ride bikes—another way Santa Aelina's is different."

"I noticed the bike racks near the main entrance."

"Yep. That reminds me." She went behind the desk, motioning Elle to follow her. "The outlets that are blue have electricity supplied by solar panels on the roof on the west side of the building. We try to plug phone chargers and computers into those to cut our power consumption."

"I'm impressed. Thanks for letting me know."

"You're welcome. And I'd better head back to work myself. Let me know if you're free for lunch anytime soon."

"I will. For now, I just want to grab the notes on this case and get up to speed before Dr. Garcia wants to meet."

"All right, *querida*, I'll let you get to it, then."

Elle smiled at the endearment. She might not have a ton of friends—by choice—but she loved the ones she did have. "See you."

Letizia closed the door behind her, leaving her to get set up in the office. Opening the backpack, she pulled out her pencil cup, laptop and a picture of her family, hesitating over the snapshot of her with Strato, pre-accident. She'd thrown it into her pack at the last minute. But it might bring up a lot of questions she wouldn't necessarily want to answer. So maybe she would hold on to it until she started using her space on the fifth floor.

Zipping her backpack up again, she managed to drag the chair out and away from the desk so she could park her wheelchair there. She shifted the weight off her left hip and seat bone. She was fortunate to still have feeling in part of that leg, but the price had been a form of neuralgia that ranged from a dull ache to a sharp pins-and-needles sensation at times.

She plugged her charger and laptop into the plug Letizia had indicated and popped open the top of her computer. Pulling her access code out of her purse, she linked into the hospital's system and found her patient. His name was Tomás Lopez.

"Okay." The file was long. She scrolled trying to find the end of it but gave up. Instead she sorted the case file by dates and came to the most recent entries that included a long list of symptoms. "Okay, here we go."

She'd been staring at the screen for about five minutes when a knock sounded at her door. "Come in." Not wanting to lose her place, it took her a minute to look up.

Shock swung through her like an ax, severing whatever concentration she'd had minutes earlier.

It was The Kiss! Er…the man. The one from the wedding. Oh, God! Why hadn't Caitlin warned her?

Because her other friend had no idea what had transpired in that library. And even if she had, she'd probably have been urging her to explore the possibilities.

There were no possibilities.

Maybe this wasn't even Dr. Garcia. *Dios*, she hoped not.

The man finished coming into the office, the dismay on his face obvious. He was just as shocked as she was. He frowned, a heavy furrowing of brows that made her cringe.

"I'm sorry," he finally said. "I'm looking for Dr. Solis."

She couldn't stop a laugh. Of course he was. Because that's just the way her luck ran. Or maybe she should say the opposite of luck.

"That would be me."

"Diablos."

The swear word was almost too low for her to hear but hear it she did. She also saw the muscle that worked in his cheek for a minute. In a voice that was a little gruffer, he continued. "Why didn't you say something at the wedding about working at the hospital?"

A familiar tingle went through her abdomen. One she was quick to suppress.

"I'm sorry? Was I *supposed* to say something?"

"Did Caitlin tell you who I was?"

"Nope. I had no idea. If I had…" If she had, she would have what? Not let him kiss her? And missed the best kiss ever? Somehow she didn't want to wish that away, so she submerged it instead.

"Yeah. Me, too." The words were said with a sense of quiet…regret.

So she might not regret what had happened in that room, but he did. It was obvious in the stiff way he held himself. In his reaction when he realized exactly who she was.

It made a thread of anger go through her. It was okay to lock lips with her as long as he never had to run across her path again?

To be fair, wasn't that what she had thought as well? That it was something she could look back on with... what? Fondness? Maybe. As if they'd been at a masquerade party, had flirted with each other, but never removed their masks and revealed their identities. It was titillating in some weird way.

Whatever it was, she didn't want to erase it.

But what was happening right now was not titillating. Or exciting. And it definitely wasn't comfortable.

Her lips twisted as she tried to think of something to say, before grabbing at the first thing that slid through her mind. "We can't take back what happened. So let's just put it behind us and move forward." She reached out her hand. "Elena Solis. But you can call me Elle. Most people do."

He grasped her hand. "Santiago Garcia. Santi."

Santi. One letter away from being a saint. Only this man was no *santo*. Saints didn't kiss like that.

"I take it you and I will be working together. At least for this one case."

"That's what Caitlin said. She and Javier have exhausted all cardiac issues as being the cause of Tomás's symptoms."

"Which are? I just started looking at his file, can you fill me in?"

"Sure. He's been having leg and foot pain for the

last three months or so. It's been steadily getting worse. They thought at first it might be due to a lack of perfusion caused by the Fontan procedure, but—"

"Wait. Back up. I haven't heard most of this. What tests were run? How did they rule out circulatory issues?"

Dr. Garcia didn't have to look at notes, he just went through Tomás's diagnosis at birth straight through to where things stood now. She was surprised by the details he remembered. That had always been something she prided herself on, her memory. It looked like the pediatrician's was every bit as good if not better than hers.

Not that any of that mattered right now.

"And there were no issues with his feet or legs until now."

"No. They thought maybe he was getting ready to go through a growth spurt or puberty, which I'm sure you know is sometimes delayed in Fontan circulation patients. He's also near the bottom of the growth chart for his age."

"Liver? Kidneys?"

"Nothing outside of what would be expected in a case like his. Enzymes are no more elevated than they have been in the past. His circulatory system is as stable as it can be, although it will never be normal without a heart transplant. He'll go on the transplant list if something changes."

"Okay, thanks. So other causes? Growth plate pain?"

"Caitlin said they thought of that and had one of Santa Aelina's orthopedists look at the X-rays. Nothing showed up. And the pain is only in a section running from his thighs all the way down to and including his feet."

She shifted again at the memory of her own transient pain. "Neuralgia?"

"It's on my list of differentials. But I want to run through all the possibilities before just slapping a label on it."

She smiled. "I totally agree with that." She'd had enough labels slapped on her to last a lifetime. And medical opinions were sometimes a dime a dozen. Her parents had taken her to a long list of specialists, some of whom said she'd never regain any sensation and others who claimed they'd be able to make her walk again. But she also knew how it felt to be poked and prodded until you were ready to scream. There was a balance there between the oath to do no harm and the pain they had to cause to help with the healing process. "Can we go see him?"

"Yes, that's why I came over. I was getting ready to go meet him and wondered if you were at a place where you could join me. Caitlin said he's not been the most cooperative of patients." He paused. "He's in the system."

"System?" As in a juvenile offender?

"No. More like his latest in a long line of *padres de acogida* who've turned him back over to the group home he was living in."

Foster parents. Her heart ached. "And his biological parents?"

"Single mother who couldn't handle the special

needs baby who'd been born to her. Not and continue to work and care for her other children."

"I see." So this child had no one, other than the government…and his doctors. "I definitely want to go see him."

She hoped Santi hadn't seen the flash of compassion that went through her when he'd told her about Tomás's situation. As much as she tried to maintain a professional distance, it wasn't always easy. That went for this doctor evidently, too, because she'd caught the way his eyes quickly went over her when he'd sat down to talk to her. Suddenly she was wishing she'd worn something snazzier than her gauzy navy blouse and cream pants.

Was she trying to impress him? No. Absolutely not.

Their wordplay from the library at Maravilla came back to her in an instant, threatening to hijack her thoughts.

She quickly brought them back under control. "Shall we go?"

"Sure." He waited for her to get her phone and backpack, slinging the latter over the handle of her chair before she exited and hurried away from Santi…from her weird awareness of him.

"He's around the corner, the last doorway on the right."

"Okay, thanks."

He moved to walk beside her. "Any thoughts on where to start?"

"I want to see him, first, before I even start to speculate. Things like, is there any weakness accompanying the pain? Is the area of pain expanding? Contracting?"

He nodded. "Yes, it's hard to just read a case file and come up with a plan, although that seems to be how the game is played at times."

"I don't think of it as a game, but I remember being frustrated by that in med school. How were we supposed to come up with a differential diagnosis from a set of words put to paper?"

He smiled. "So I wasn't the only one who thought that."

Elena hadn't even wondered about it until she'd met her first patient and realized how different it was to hear someone describe in their own words what was going on with their body. She could remember when she was injured and doctors made pronouncements that hadn't resonated with her. At the time, she'd been too young and scared to challenge anyone. But now that she was a doctor herself, she found she wanted her patients' input, although there had certainly been times when a colleague from another hospital had sent her a case file and asked her opinion. So it wasn't that she couldn't work that way. She just preferred not to.

She also preferred not to work with someone she'd once kissed. She'd gone out and slept with one of her professors from medical school—after she'd graduated, of course—which was an unmitigated disaster. One that had never been repeated. And one-night stands were not for her.

So she wouldn't have slept with Dr. Garcia, given the chance that night at the wedding? She had a feeling she might have, breaking one of her self-imposed rules.

There. The door to their patient's room. Time to stop thinking about things she couldn't change.

Santi knocked and a second later entered the room holding the door for her.

"Hi, Tomás. I'm Dr. Garcia and this is Dr. Solis. We're here to check on you and see if we can figure out a way to help you."

The boy on the bed, who was probably fourteen or fifteen, lifted his shoulder in a shrug as if he couldn't care less who they were. But surely that was all for show. His notes had described his pain as a seven or eight at its worst and a five on good days.

Elena maneuvered so she was closer to the bed, but far enough away to allow him to have some personal space. "I've been reading your chart. Can you tell me when you first started to have pain?"

His chin jerked up. "I thought you said you read it. So you should already know."

She smiled, not put off by his abrupt manner. "I did, but I'd like to hear it in your own words."

Tomás shrugged again. "Don't know. My legs hurt. That's all I can tell you."

Okay, so he wasn't going to make this easy on them. That was okay. Because she didn't need "easy" to do her job. "Let's start with an easier question, then. What is your pain level right now?"

He jabbed his thumb at a picture on the wall as if he'd done it thousands of times. "Frowny face guy."

The pain level chart had both a set of numerical indicators and faces depicting different expressions.

His description made her smile. "So, *fuerte*. How long have you been in this much pain?"

"Since you guys arrived. Maybe you should just leave me alone."

She laughed. "I assume you're talking about Dr. Garcia's arrival and not mine." She shot the other doctor a grin.

"I was about to say the very same thing." Santi sat on the chair next to her. "We will need to examine you, though, Tomás. Seriously. The sooner we figure this thing out, the sooner you'll get out of here."

His chin went up and he fixed them with a glare. "You mean leave the hospital?"

The pediatrician nodded. "Yep. I know you must be looking forward to that."

The boy's expression underwent a subtle shift that made something in her stomach churn. His cloak of anger seemed to lift for just a brief second before his eyes went hard all over again.

"Well, then, you don't know anything. Because I don't want to leave."

CHAPTER THREE

I DON'T WANT to leave.

He'd said it with as much surliness as Santi had ever heard, but what was he hiding underneath that? How much emotional pain would it take to make staying at a hospital preferable to wherever he would go after he was discharged?

He'd watched Elena's face contort at the words before getting herself back under control. Who could blame her? This boy's case was one of the most heartbreaking things he'd heard since becoming a pediatrician.

Who knew how many people had let this boy down. Including his latest foster parents. He pushed back the sympathy that threatened to interfere with his objectivity.

"The only way things are going to get better is if you let us help you."

"Who says they'll even get better? Maybe I'll just be stuck in a..." His glance snaked over to Elena, and he nodded at her. Santi was pretty sure he knew where the teen had been headed with his comment. But to let Tomás use his anger as a weapon to hurt someone else?

No way. But before he could intervene, Elena spoke up instead.

"If you are, then you'll deal with it. You'll have no choice but to deal with it." Her soft voice came through, not hurling angry words back at the teen, but just being firm and matter-of-fact. "But you're not there. So let's see if we can find an answer. Help us do that."

The compassion he'd seen a second ago in her face was there in her words. And suddenly, Santi wanted to find an answer just as badly. Not because he didn't want Tomás to wind up in a wheelchair, but because he wanted to keep whatever was happening from progressing any further than it already had. Wanted to be someone this boy could trust.

He glanced at Elena. Her hair was pulled up in a long sleek ponytail today and her toenails were painted a light pink, something he hadn't noticed at the wedding due to her long dress. Her fingertips boasted no color, but those long, slender digits had propelled her down the hallway as if she'd done it her whole life. And maybe she had. Not something he was going to ask.

But if anyone knew what was at stake here, she did.

"So I'll ask again. Is it okay if we examine you?" Santi watched the boy's face.

Tomás shrugged. "Whatever. You gotta do what you gotta do, *tío*."

The kid was calling him *dude*? Really? Frustration sprouted all over again. He didn't like wasting his time. He was looking at this case as a favor to Caitlin. She'd said the boy was prickly. But that was putting it mildly.

If he wasn't going to share anything outside of what was on the case notes, then this was a useless endeavor.

Santi leaned forward. "Listen…*tío*…" He purposely used the same term Tomás had used. "It's no hardship on me if you don't want to tell me what I need to know. I'll just call Dr. McKenzie and tell her that you evidently don't want to get better." He wasn't going to do any such thing. Caitlin deserved her happiness and he wouldn't do anything to upset her.

"Yeah, well *she* left me, too."

The words were a punch to Santi's gut. He could see how it might appear that way to this kid. He'd been left time and time again. "No. She got married. And she's very concerned about you. So is Dr. Torres. That's why we're here."

"And if you can't figure it out, either?"

Elena pushed a lock of hair off her face. "You're not giving us much to work with, though, are you?"

The teen crossed thin arms over his chest. "Fine. I was reaching across the dinner table one night to get another piece of meat and my *padre* yelled at me for being rude. I suddenly felt something hurt in both of my legs and screamed, clutching them." He stared at Santi and then Elena. "You know what he did? He claimed I was making it all up. He even told Dr. McKenzie that. Said I was doing it to get attention. So I agreed with him and went to my room. And the next day when they hurt again, I didn't say a word. I wasn't going to give him the satisfaction."

"What were you doing when they hurt the second time?" Santi asked.

Tomás looked at him as if trying to judge whether he really wanted to know or if he thought the illness was feigned as well. Santi knew better. A kid like this didn't use weakness to get attention. They made themselves as large and scary as possible. Just like he was doing here in this room.

"I was sitting on the bed and bent over to get my shoes off the floor."

Tomás's eyes came up and he pointed at his legs. "Just so you know, he was wrong. I wasn't making it up then, and I'm not making it up now."

"I believe you. So do some other people. That's why you're here now. Do your legs hurt all the time now?"

"Pretty much."

Santi stood. "I'd like to examine you now. Would that be okay?"

"I can't stop you."

"Yes, you can. All you have to do is say the word, and we'll leave."

Elena shot him a glance but didn't contradict him. Santi knew he was taking a risk, but he had to believe the boy didn't want to just sit in this room and let things play out. He and the diagnostician needed to keep on tackling this problem, one point at a time.

Another shrug. "Whatever. Go ahead."

"So yes?"

Tomás head gave a jerky nod, which he took as permission. Going to the side of the bed, he reached in his pocket for his stethoscope, looping it around his neck.

"Don't bother. My heart doesn't sound like other hearts."

"That's fine. I wasn't going to listen for that. I'm

going to use it to listen to your belly and your lungs. But first I'm going to turn your head and bend your neck. Tell me if anything hurts."

He felt Elena's eyes on him and Tomás as he manipulated the boy's neck, turning it this way and that. "Does any of that hurt or make your legs hurt?"

The kid gave a harsh laugh. "My legs already hurt."

"Does it make them hurt worse?"

"No."

The one-word answer was evidently all he was going to get. He moved in front of him and stood just out of reach. "See if you can take my hands."

Tomás rolled his eyes, but did as he was asked, stretching his arms toward him, even as Santi took another step back. "Keep reaching."

"I can't."

"Humor me and try."

As he bent forward slightly, Tomás's face contorted. "Yeah, that hurts."

"Where?"

"My legs. And my stupid head."

Santi went very still as he mulled this piece of information. "Okay, you can relax, Tomás. Have you been having headaches?"

"I'm in the system. My whole life is a headache."

Santi held his tongue and waited the boy out.

He was rewarded with a rough exhalation. "Fine. Yes, sometimes my head hurts."

Elena wheeled herself a couple of inches closer. "Did the headaches start at the same time that your legs get worse?"

Tomás's mouth twisted. "I think so. So what does that mean?"

Not saying anything, Santi finished his examination. "I'm not sure yet. But your lungs sound good and so does your belly. What I'm going to do next is send you for a CT scan. Do you know what that is?"

"Yes. I have a bad heart, remember? Lots of scans and tests."

"I'm sure you've had more than your share. But this time I want to look inside your head." He glanced at Elena, and she gave a slight nod as if to say she was thinking along the same lines.

He hoped they were both wrong. That there was nothing growing inside this kid's head. Although manipulating his neck hadn't brought forth anything, leaning forward to grasp Santi's hands sure had. And it was a similar movement to stretching across a table and to bending down to get his shoes. If there was a brain tumor growing in there, the changes in blood pressure by bending or hard stretching could theoretically cause pain, depending on where in the brain a growth was.

It was something to rule out. And better to start with the most grave possibility and work their way backward.

He pulled his cell phone out and put in the order.

"How long do I have to stay in there this time? Because I'll need to get my earbuds or something."

"I'll make sure you get some. And I don't know what tests you've had, but it might take longer. We may need to give you a little shot of dye if we can't see anything without it. You're not claustrophobic, are you?"

"It's going to happen even if I am, right?"

"Yes. It needs to. But I can give you something for anxiety if you need it."

"I don't need anything."

Yes, he did. Tomás just wasn't willing to admit it. Yet. But Santi hoped with time that they could build his trust. He'd talked about Caitlin leaving him just like everyone else, so it meant that he'd trusted the cardiologist. Most of this had to be rooted in fear. And honestly, Santi couldn't blame him. For any of it.

"Okay, then. They should be here in a few minutes to take you down. We'll be close by, though."

"You're going to watch?"

"We are. I want to make sure everything goes smoothly."

Was Tomás afraid of being alone? Of being left?

Hell, if anyone could relate to that, Santi could. Carmen's death had ticked both of those boxes. But if he could do anything here and now, he was going to make sure this boy didn't feel abandoned, like he'd obviously felt in the past.

He knew he should ask Elena, though, before including her in his plans. "Is that okay with you?"

"Yes." Her eyes met his and she gave a slight smile. "I don't know where anything is yet, so you'll need to direct me how to get there."

"You can follow me. Imaging is on the next floor up."

Elena backed her chair a few inches. "We'll see you soon, Tomás."

He answered with yet another shrug, but Santi could swear there was a hint of relief in the way his shoulders relaxed, in the way the tension in his jaw eased.

Just then a nurse came in and began to get things ready for the teen to be wheeled down.

That was their cue to leave. Santi could only hope the CT gave them the answers they wanted.

Elena pushed a button near the door, and it opened with a whisper of sound. She went through it. Turning slightly to look over her shoulder, she said, "You'll have to remind me where the elevators are."

He went ahead of her, walking with his normal speed in the direction they'd come earlier. "Let me know if I'm going too fast."

"You're not." There was a hint of irony to her words that wasn't lost on him.

He decided this was someone who didn't want or need him to ask about every little thing. If she needed him to change pace, she would tell him. He liked that. She'd been pretty direct at the wedding, too. It was one of the things that he'd found so attractive about her. Maybe that's why he'd ended up kissing her, when it was the last thing he should have done.

But man had it been good. That made it even worse.

They got to the elevator, and he pushed the up button. The car pinged as it arrived, the doors sliding apart. He put his arm across the mechanism, holding it open while she made her way inside. He got in, and she pushed the button for the next floor. They were the only passengers, and standing beside her, the ventilation system stirred the air, and he caught a slight whiff of clean lemon. From her shampoo? It tempted him to lean down and investigate a little more. If he pulled the tie from her hair, would those locks tumble down around her shoulders like they had that night, releasing more of that fragrance?

He gave an inward groan. *Stop it. Not the time. Or the place.*

Not that there was a right time or place. She was off-limits. Not just because of Carmen, but because of work as well. But why was that, really? What was it about business and pleasure that didn't mix?

Because things could get very messy very fast. And because he didn't do relationships or forever. Not anymore. Besides, he no longer believed that forever existed outside of romantic fiction. Or gorgeous wedding settings.

That had to be what it was. Why he'd been drawn to her. Why he was still drawn to her.

The elevator arrived at its destination before he had a chance to dissect that last statement. And just as well.

The imaging department was busy, as usual, and Tomás was sitting on his gurney, shoulders slumped, waiting his turn. The teen didn't look any happier now than he had in that room. While Elena went over to let him know they were there, Santi went to the desk to find out where they were in the queue.

The nurse checked her paperwork. "It shouldn't be long. He goes in as soon as the current patient comes out."

"Thanks."

He joined Elena and Tomás. "Looks like it will be just a few more minutes."

Tomás didn't look up, just continued staring at the floor. "It doesn't matter how long it is."

Santi gave an audible sigh that there was no change in the boy's attitude. He was surprised there wasn't a representative from the group home here as an advocate, but it could be they had more than one child here or had asked to be called if there was a problem. But despite the attitude, a pang went through him that the kid was having to handle this completely on his own. If Santi had had trouble handling things after Carmen's death, how much harder would it be for a kid like this?

"So what do you want to do when you get older?"

Tomás shrugged and for a second he didn't think the teen was going to answer. But finally he said, "I want to have a dog."

The ache in his chest grew. Most kids grew up dreaming of buying a home and having nice things. Tomás wanted a dog. A companion. Something that would never leave him or hand him back when the going got tough.

Maybe this is where he could make a connection.

Santi smiled. "I have a dog. She's a Labrador retriever named Sasha. I could bring her in to meet you, if you'd like."

A pair of dark brown eyes swung up. "Hospitals don't let dogs come inside."

Okay, so it wasn't actually a yes. But it wasn't a no.

Sasha had been his and Carmen's. He'd brought her home as a puppy from a nearby shelter while his wife had been going through treatment. Carmen had loved that dog, whom she never got to see grow up into an adult. Sasha was now going on seven. And with every year that went by, he was aware that one of his last links to his wife would be severed when Sasha died.

Although she wasn't a certified therapy dog, Santi had taken Sasha through training so that she could be brought in to see Carmen. It had worked like a charm. It had also sparked his interest in hippotherapy—where horses were paired with differently abled people as a form of therapy. His background with the polo ponies on his dad's ranch in Argentina helped him realize how important the partnership between an equine and a person could be.

"They'll let Sasha in. She has special training. How about tomorrow? She can spend the day with me in my office. I have a couch in there. Maybe we could even arrange for you to hang out in there as well, rather than in your hospital room, to keep Sasha company." He eyed the teen. "As long as you don't overdo it."

"I don't have anywhere else to be. So I might as well be there."

Had he just seen a crack in Tomás's demeanor? Time would tell.

"I think Sasha would appreciate that. Thank you." He understood the need not to appear weak. Especially in a boy of his age who'd bounced from place to place. He didn't want to form attachments.

Santi could relate to that all too well.

He glanced at Elena and found that she was staring at him. What? She didn't like dogs?

She turned and wheeled away without a word, making him frown.

"Tomás, would you excuse me for a minute?"

He went over to where she was. "You disapprove of me bringing Sasha to visit him?"

When she glanced up at him, her eyes were bright. A little too bright.

"On the contrary. I approve. I really approve. I just…" She shook her head as if she couldn't find the right words. "I think that is just what Tomás needs right now. He's scared out of his wits, despite his bravado."

"I know. And we need him to cooperate if we're going to help him. Maybe Sasha can provide him with some company, if nothing else. I'll check and make sure that's okay with the people responsible for him, and that the nurses know where to find him. Since my office is on the same floor as his hospital room, I don't think it'll be a problem."

She smiled. "You'd better be careful, or you'll have everyone in the pediatric wing clamoring for their turn with you and Sasha."

Including her?

There was something about her smile that punched him right in the chest. That made him want to take a step or two closer to catch another hint of that elusive fragrance he'd noticed on the elevator. He forced himself to stay where he was.

"Sasha has come to the hospital several times with me, especially if I know I'm going to be working late and don't want to ask my housekeeper to stay over."

"And the hospital is okay with that?"

"She's well behaved. And the kids seem to love her. Especially in her Christmas elf costume."

"Your dog has costumes."

There was shock and an element of bland amusement in her voice that he liked. As if his words had been truly unexpected. "Several, actually."

She blinked. "You're very…surprising, you know that?"

"Am I?" He let one side of his mouth slide up in a half smile, not wanting her to see how much her words warmed him.

No one spoke for several seconds.

Elena glanced back. "Well, I think they're ready for him. Can you tell me where the observation room is?"

"Yep, I'll take you there."

Elena had needed to get away. Something about the idea of a strong man like Santi putting a costume on his dog and bringing her in to mingle with his young patients had made her heart clench. And his offer to let Tomás stay in his office with the dog had brought tears to her eyes. She needed to be careful. There was something about him that made her want to trust him. To move closer to him like she had at Caitlin's wedding. But she'd been burned going down that road once before.

Her professor had shown an interest in her while she was in his class, and like any student, she'd developed a crush on him. He never asked her out while she was at the school, but a few weeks after she graduated, Renato called her and asked her to dinner. She'd been thrilled. His noticing hadn't just been part of her imagination. He actually had liked her. And she had liked him. A lot. Enough to be a nervous wreck as she'd spoken to him on the phone.

Dinner had been at a swanky, intimate restaurant. The atmosphere as they ate had quickly changed, little touches over the table leading to her going back to his apartment with him. And when he'd kissed her, the sparks had ignited.

Just like they had with Santi.

Renato had carried her to bed and had been an attentive lover, taking a lot of time with her. But then at the height of passion, he'd rolled onto his back and tried to haul her on top of him to straddle his hips. "Sit on me, *querida*."

Horror had zipped through her.

"I—I can't," she'd stammered, the blood rushing from her head. How could he not know that?

He'd sat up dragging a hand through his hair and apologizing profusely, but the mood had been completely shattered. While her paralysis wasn't complete and she could bear weight on her left leg—bracing herself with her arms—long enough to transfer from one place to the other, it didn't mean that she could do everything other people could. It hadn't been his fault. Not really.

But it had evidently bothered him enough that he'd never contacted her again. She'd been devastated. But even if he'd called, she didn't think she would have gone out with him again. And she wasn't sure why.

It had left her wary of being caught in a situation like that again. After Renato, she'd never let a date go further than dinner and a chaste kiss, not that there'd been many over the years. She was pretty sure she now gave off warning vibes that could be read for miles.

But Santi… Well, the man was a temptation. A big one. They worked together, though, which would amplify any awkwardness if she got carried away and then suddenly found she…couldn't.

And aside from that one kiss in the library, he'd shown no signs of wanting to kiss her again. For that she was grateful. It made things so much easier.

The observation room was surprisingly large with several open areas near the chairs where she could park with ease. She had a feeling Letizia had a hand in designing this room. She could move freely and change locations depending on what angle she wanted to see. Letizia said Aelina was the model she wanted other hospitals in Spain to use when they were thinking about accessibility.

And she was also surprised that there even *was* such a large observation room in the imaging department. Those were normally reserved for surgical areas of the hospital, although the booth where the techs sat usually had a couple of extra chairs where doctors could watch the scans roll out.

She'd expected Santi to go in there, actually. But he made no move to leave.

"They're getting ready to put him through." Santi settled in a chair next to her. "The tech will let us know if they see anything. And I'll decide then about the need for a dye."

The glass wasn't one-way and when Tomás glanced at the window, Santi gave him a thumbs-up sign to let him know they were there. Not that the boy returned it or even acknowledged the sign.

"Are you thinking tumor?" She hoped he wouldn't concentrate all his efforts on this one possibility. She preferred to keep things wide open and narrow them down a little at a time.

"No, it's just a starting place. Ruling this out lets us move on to the next possibility. Any thoughts?"

"I have several. A dystrophy, MS—"

"MS? I know it's possible, but I haven't come across a case of multiple sclerosis in a child yet."

"It's rare, but I don't want to rule anything out. Like I said, some of the dystrophies. Spinal cord lesions. The laundry list of possibilities is pretty long." She paused. "Caitlin said they looked at everything they could think of that was related to his heart, but there's still the possibility of neuropathy caused by perfusion issues."

Neuropathy could strike any part of the body that involved nerves. Elena experienced it herself with her injury. Although the attacks weren't as bad as they were after her fall, there were still times when she got zings of pain near what she called her dead zone. The band that separated the numb areas of her body and the areas where she retained feeling. Most especially in her left hip and thigh. Hers wasn't caused by perfusion problems, however, but by her spinal cord injury.

"Perfusion certainly makes it a little harder to identify the cause, since his circulatory system isn't ideal. But from the looks of it, Tomás has done better than some of the other hypoplastic left heart syndrome patients. The survival rates are better than they used to be, but chronic lack of oxygen eventually takes its toll."

"Yes, it does. Caitlin said he could go on the transplant list if and when that started to become an issue."

The flat bed area of the CT machine started to move into the doughnut-shaped hole, stopping when Tomás's head was inside the field. The tech's voice came through. "Try to hold your head and neck very still, Tomás, okay?"

No response.

Although the teen appeared to be doing as he was told, she could tell by the flexing and unflexing of his feet that the position wasn't comfortable for him.

"Santi…"

"I see him." The pediatrician paused. "He said sitting was the most comfortable for him. I've been trying to puzzle through why that is. Although he said when he was sitting on the bed and reaching down for his shoes he had an attack of pain. Which is why it made me think the problem was positional."

Santi pulled out his tablet and scrolled through whatever was on the screen. He glanced over at her. "They did a tilt table test on him and there were no major changes in his blood pressure."

"I'm going to try to sit down with his chart tonight and comb through everything and see if I can find any holes in his testing. Although Caitlin is very thorough."

"Maybe we can brainstorm that together in my office tomorrow. Sasha will be there to keep Tomás company, and he'll be close by in case either of us have any questions for him. Hopefully he'll start opening up more."

That made sense. There were times, though, when she liked to really sit down by herself and study the charts. But she could do that tonight. At least she thought she could. "Can I access patient files remotely? I'm staying in one of the staff housing units across the park and would like to get up to speed on everything."

"Yep, just ask HR for the code, if you're doing it from a different device than the one in your office."

"Okay, thanks. I'll check in with them." Before she could capture her next words, she blurted out, "Are you staying in the housing area as well?"

He glanced at her. "No. I live about twenty minutes from here."

The words were a little curt, and she couldn't blame him. It was really none of her business where he lived. *Cielos!* Did he think she was making a pass at him? She wasn't. And she wasn't even sure why she'd asked the question. It was just straight-up curiosity. One that she needed to toss aside before it got her into trouble.

Like with that kiss?

Yes. Exactly like that. Except she hadn't really tossed it completely aside, because she kept thinking about it.

If she were smart, she would weigh any future words with care. The last thing she needed was to make Santi uncomfortable or give him the wrong idea.

The same went for her. She had to make sure she got no funny ideas about the handsome pediatrician, not if she wanted to continue to enjoy her time at Santa Aelina.

CHAPTER FOUR

THE PARK WAS nicer than she expected. Her racing chair flew down the pathway, and she passed a jogger who was traveling at a nice leisurely pace. Elena did leisurely during her nights working at the hospital. The evening shifts were like that. Quiet with periods of frenetic activity.

When she got off work at six in the morning, she wanted a real workout. Felt the need for speed. Maybe it mimicked what she used to have when she raced Strato across the beach on days they weren't training for competitions. She sighed. Those days were over, although Sandra had offered to help her get on Strato, if she wanted to try to ride again. She did. But she'd been too angry at her condition over those first six months to even think about it. And she'd been afraid she wouldn't be able to mount, much less handle any kind of cues involving her legs.

Then she went to college and her days had grown busy.

And now?

She wasn't sure what held her back. Maybe the idea

that she could never have what she'd had before. She wasn't sure she could stand the sting of regret or the what-ifs that might follow.

She turned another sharper corner in the running path, the cool morning invigorating her and loosening her muscles. Suddenly she had to swerve hard to avoid another jogger coming at her from the opposite direction. "Sorry!" She threw the word over her shoulder before realizing the person had stopped and turned in her direction and was now jogging after her. Worse, she now recognized who it was.

Dios! It was Santi. What the hell was he doing out here? She thought he'd said he didn't live in the hospital housing unit.

That didn't mean he couldn't use the park. It was for anyone, whether they lived on-site or not.

The impulse to put on a burst of speed and try to outpace him came and went. What would doing that accomplish besides make it obvious she didn't want to interact with him? And it would make working with him even more awkward.

She wasn't embarrassed that he'd found her getting some exercise. No, her avoidance radar had to do more with that stupid kiss than her physical condition.

Every time she saw him, she still pictured the exact moment when he leaned closer…when she realized what was about to happen. The second her eyelids slid closed in dreamy bliss. And the first glorious touch had been—

"You're out and about early." The gravel of his voice stopped her wayward thoughts, and her fingers tightened around the wheels of her chair, arms almost forgetting to keep pumping. She forced herself to concentrate. The last thing she wanted to do was jerk to a stop and dump herself onto the ground.

It's not that she couldn't brace her left knee on the ground and use her arms to haul herself back into the chair. She could. But even before her accident, she would have been embarrassed to fall flat on her face in front of someone.

And she still worked her legs, putting a brace on the one that still had a modicum of feeling left and using it to support her weight. But she did that in a more controlled setting, which reminded her that she needed to find a gym with a trainer who specialized in spinal cord injuries. Working her muscles in the pool was her favorite way to train. That and propelling herself in her racing chair.

"Early? Well, I just got off work and ran home to change clothes and chairs. I could ask you the same question." Why did she sound so much breathier than he did?

"Could you slow down for a minute?"

The surprising request made her muscles go slack instantly, and only then did she realize her arms were shaking. Not so much from exertion but from nerves.

He slowed to a walk, glancing at her. "I do like your ride, by the way. Especially the reflective fabric."

Her racing chair was neon orange with those reflective flecks woven right in to help make her more visible. Sometimes runners whose line of sight was over her head and who were "in the zone" might not notice her until she had to jerk sideways to avoid them. This way, their peripheral vision caught sight of something other than green trees or asphalt.

"The better to see you with, my dear." The lines of the well-known fairy tale came out before she could stop them.

"Or maybe to be seen?"

She blinked, surprised he'd caught her drift so easily, without her having to explain. She nodded. "I'm easy to miss."

His mouth twisted slightly. "Oh, I know for a fact that's not true."

A shiver went through her. He wasn't talking about the same thing she was. And her tongue tripped over several flippant responses before the truth came out. "You'd be surprised how invisible you feel, sometimes." Going from almost five foot ten at eighteen to about half that height sitting down had been one of the biggest shocks she'd had to get used to. She'd always been visible. Sometimes painfully so. How silly it seemed now to be so embarrassed about being tall.

In an instant her life had changed in almost every way. From the way she ambulated, to the way she drove a vehicle…to the way she made love. She could still do it all. The mechanics just had to be tweaked.

She glanced down at her breeches. They were one of the last remnants of her riding days, but one that she held on to. She found that the grippiness the garment had afforded her in an English saddle worked to keep her stuck in her chair when she was racing across a surface or while shifting her weight to navigate tight turns. The same things she'd done while riding.

But those knee patches might look weird to Santi. If so, he didn't say anything.

Instead, he smiled. "Someday I'll race you."

He hadn't offered platitudes or tried to convince her that how she felt wasn't real or valid. A weird pinging sensation started in the region of her heart, and she had to force herself not to visibly react. She understood that people wanted to make her feel better, but they didn't realize that sometimes it just made her feel worse. Like no one understood. But Santi hadn't done that. In fact, he acted like he really did understand what she went through sometimes. How?

"You mean as in chair against chair?"

"I think you might have an unfair advantage there."

She laughed. No one had ever even hinted at that before. She decided to go with it. "I think I might have an unfair advantage whether you're on foot or on wheels."

His smile widened, showing a flash of white teeth. "Is that a challenge, Dr. Solis?"

Was it? Exactly how dangerous would it be to challenge a man like Santi? Probably very dangerous. But since when had she shied away from things that weren't so safe?

"It is indeed, Dr. Garcia."

"Be careful what you wish for. It might just come true."

Elena pushed a lock of hair out of her eyes, trying to ferret out the expression on his face. But it suddenly shuttered against her probing stare, his smile disappearing in an instant. The same way Renato's face and demeanor had changed during their lovemaking session.

Her chest tightened. She and Santi had never been involved. Had certainly never made love. Barely even knew each other. So why did she feel a boulder in the place where her stomach normally sat?

His cell phone pinged, and he pulled it out of one of the pockets of his navy jogging pants, glancing at the screen just as her phone went off, too. Another sense of foreboding settled over her.

She pulled her phone out of her belt bag and looked at it. It was from Grace Rivas, a midwife she'd consulted with briefly in the past and met in person on her first day at Aelina.

Emergency situation. Can you come back to Aelina?

Caitlin had told her how Grace and her husband, Diego, had patched up their rocky marriage.

She and Santi looked up from their devices at the same time. Their eyes met.

"I need to go."

Their words matched syllable for syllable, and his face softened. "They called you back, too?"

"Yes. Any idea what it is?"

"No, just that it's a teen and the other pediatrician is stuck in traffic." He nodded at her chair. "Are you okay to work in that?"

"Yep. Let's go."

They raced back to the hospital and when they got to the desk, Carlos, one of the ER nurses, stopped them. "They're up in maternity."

Santi frowned. "Are you sure that's the right patient?"

"Yes. Very."

"Thanks, we'll head up."

That was weird. Pediatrics was on the third floor while maternity was on the first. She could understand being called to a case there, but Santi? He wasn't a neonatologist.

They went up the elevator, with Elena trying not to be weirded out at going to work in breeches, of all things. At least the sweat had dried in the air-conditioning. She'd been dragging when she'd left the building, but her workout and the adrenaline of knowing there was an emergency had reenergized her.

And maybe that had a little to do with meeting Santi on the path?

Diablos, she hoped not.

The doors opened and Grace met them. "Thanks for getting here so fast. I'm about to have the patient wheeled down to the maternal intensive care area. She's now comatose."

As they went back to the room, Grace filled them in. "Sixteen-year-old who's twenty-four weeks pregnant. She's been emancipated and is technically married, but neither her parents nor the baby's father are in the picture anymore. A friend called paramedics when they found her passed out on the floor." She paused to take a breath as they reached the doorway. "We've taken bloods, but her sugar is normal, which is the first thing both Diego and I thought of—he's prepping for a different surgery, which is part of the reason I needed you guys back. It's a race to figure out what is going on."

That was why Santi was here. At sixteen, the patient was still considered a pediatric case in some areas despite the emancipation.

Elena's mind went through a labyrinth of possible causes. Gestational diabetes would have been high on her list as well. But with no elevated sugar…

"And the baby?" Santi had gloved up and was now standing over the patient already doing his own examination and Elena moved to the area beside him.

"A quick ultrasound reveals everything as it should be. No molar pregnancy. Nothing to suggest that the pregnancy itself is to blame. But the baby's vitals are showing some downward trends that we need to correct, if we hope to save either of them."

Molar pregnancies—when the beginnings of a fetus turn into a tumor that overtake everything and threaten the life of the mother—could be fatal in and of themselves. But this was a viable pregnancy.

She began to sort through some options. "Tell me if something I throw out isn't something you've looked at. Stroke—" she paused as she went through the list being generated in her head and watched Grace for a reaction to each "—brain tumor, cancer of any type—"

"We haven't gotten as far as MRIs and such. She's just come in. We've only had time to check the baby and her. She really needs to be down the hall in ICU. But I didn't want to move her until you saw her."

"Blood ox is low. COVID?"

"We did two rapid tests for that and the flu. Both came back negative."

Elena's head tilted as something caught her eye. "Santi, look at her neck."

His gaze shifted as he looked. "What am I... Wait. I think I see something." He palpated her throat and then fingered a strand of hair. "Hmm... Did you send for thyroid levels?"

"I did. I asked them to be expedited."

"Okay. Heart rate is low. So are respirations."

Elena pulled down the sheet and checked the girl's ankles. "Puffy here and so are her hands."

"I noticed that, too," Grace said. "Which is why I thought maybe diabetes. You're thinking she has hypothyroidism? That makes sense. She's not had prenatal exams from what I'm gathering. Unfortunately, I'm seeing more and more of this in younger patients who are trying to hide pregnancies. I had a case like that just a few weeks ago that was touch and go."

Grace's phone rang. "This may be it." She put the device to her ear. "Mmm-hmm... Oh, wow. I think that explains it. Thanks. Send over the numbers, okay?"

She hung up. "You were right. Extremely high THS. They're sending over the labs."

Elena breathed a sigh of relief. "What we know, we can treat."

"Absolutely," Santi agreed. "Checking dosages now. Let's go ahead and move her and add some levothyroxine to her drip. I also want to start hydrocortisone in case there's pituitary involvement besides just her low thyroid levels." He looked at her as if seeking her opinion.

"I agree. If we're right, we should start seeing some

improvement pretty quickly. I want her to stay on oxygen until her blood ox is above ninety percent."

Grace reached down and gave her hand a squeeze. "Thank you. To both of you."

"You're more than welcome." Elena smiled back. "I want to know how she and the baby do."

Santi got off the phone call he'd made as she and Grace had been talking. "I've called Dario Mileno, who's still a few minutes away. He agrees with treatment and will come down to see her when he arrives. He's seen one of these before. This is my first."

"Who's Dario Mileno?" Elena hadn't yet met everyone on staff. Working more on the night shift made it hard.

"He's our endocrinologist. He's one of the best. She'll be in good hands." Santi glanced at her. "Are you exhausted, or can you hang around for a few minutes in case Grace needs us back?"

Grace nodded. "I would really appreciate that. And good catch, you two."

"Elle did the catching. If she hadn't noticed her neck, we might still be looking."

The midwife's eyes widened, mimicking her own, which Elena tried to hide. Normally only her good friends called her that. The fact that Santi had…

Meant nothing. She'd called him by a shortened version of his name lots of times, so why was it different for him to do the same? It wasn't. But her heart had given a hard couple of thumps when he had. And that mellow voice curling around that one syllable…? Oh, man. It might turn her to goo, and that was not good.

She covered her reaction the best she could. "The TSH numbers would have cued you in. We all did our part."

"So we did." Santi moved so the two nurses who came in could gather equipment and move the bed to a room down the hall where at-risk pregnancy patients could be monitored. "Are you good, Grace?"

"I think we have it under control now. I'll text you in a few minutes once we get the drip started."

Another man crowded into the room, and he and Santi shook hands. "I just got in. Have you started treatment yet?"

"They're just moving her now," Santi said. He then turned to Elena. "Dario, this is Elena Solis. She's our new diagnostician."

His head tilted as he looked at her. "Didn't I work with you once? Over at Santa Pedro's a year or so ago?"

"Oh, yes, I do remember. The dengue case that came in from Brazil."

"That's the one."

For some reason it felt good to have Santi see that she actually did know what she was doing. Most of the time, anyway. It seemed her brain worked in a way that other people didn't always understand. But that was probably due to her trying to absorb every minute detail about the way her body had worked before and after the accident. It was almost as if she could float above the scene and "see" it. Could put things together that didn't always seem to go together.

Dario smiled at her. "Okay if I consult with you from time to time when you're around?"

"I will be around. I've decided to settle in at Aelina's for a while."

"Great! No more roaming from place to place?"

Her eyes darted to Santi and saw him frown. What was wrong? Was he sorry she was staying at Aelina's? He hadn't seemed that way a minute or so ago, but now…?

Her chin lifted as if daring the pediatrician to say something. "No, not for the foreseeable future."

"Very good. I'll see if I can drum you up some work." Dario gave her another smile, moving so they could wheel the patient out of the room. "But for now, I have patients to see. Check in with me when you get a chance. I'm on the fifth floor."

Her eyes widened. "That's where I'll be once I'm done in pediatrics."

"Well how lucky is that? Looks like we'll be seeing a lot of each other."

The endocrinologist followed the patient from the room.

Once he had disappeared from sight, Grace bumped shoulders with her and gave her a smile. She didn't say anything, but she knew what the other woman was thinking. And she agreed. Dario Mileno had been flirting with her. If Grace could see it then maybe… When she looked again at Santi, she saw that she was right. He'd noticed. And he didn't look happy about it.

Why? It wasn't like *he'd* shown a lot of interest in

her. Oh, he'd been friendly, but the way he'd recoiled from that kiss had stung.

Still stung, if she were honest with herself, and to have a man show some interest in her helped soothe that hurt just a bit.

She started to say goodbye to Grace and the other woman said, "When you have some time, I can show you around the area, if you want. You're staying in the housing on the other side of the park, right?"

"I am. And I would love for you to show me what's what. I'm the last house on the left when you step off the pathway. Come over sometime."

"Thanks. I will." She threw Santi a smile. "Stop looking so grumpy. You haven't looked so put out since Carm…" Her words died away, and she looked mortified. "That didn't come out right. I'm sorry."

"It's okay. And I'm not grumpy. It's just a been a long night. To prove it, I'll treat you both to breakfast. Cafeteria style."

Grace wrinkled her nose. "No thanks. Besides, I have babies to deliver. Take Elena. She needs to experience El Café Aelina at least once." With that, the midwife walked out the door.

She was quick to try to retract the other woman's offer. "You don't have to—"

"Yes, I do. Besides, Grace is right. You do need to experience it. At least once."

He escorted her out of the room and down the hallway, making Elena wonder what the hell to think. One minute there were storm clouds hanging over his head and the next…?

Well, she had no idea what was hanging over his head now. Except for trouble. Trouble that Elena would do well to avoid.

CHAPTER FIVE

ME CAE GORDO. Maybe Santi was being irrational, but Dario Mileno really did rub him the wrong way. Ever since they'd almost come to blows that day when Carmen was having tests run at the hospital. Before she was diagnosed.

Thinking about that would do no good. And Carmen had insisted the man wasn't flirting with her. But Santi remembered exactly how he'd felt when he laid eyes on her for the first time. He'd been completely *enamorado*. If there ever was a love at first sight, it had been that day she'd come to visit Argentina and had wound up on one of his father's polo ponies. Santi had been on another, actively hitting the ball around with some colleagues, when she trotted over and asked to join the game.

Her accent, the way she moved with this unconscious seductive air, had bowled him over and he'd been... *enamorado*. There was no other word for it. They'd exchanged numbers and when she flew back to Spain ten days later he'd called her. He was already a doctor at the time. And soon he was applying at hospitals in

Spain. He'd jumped at the first position in Barcelona. The rest was history.

And now it really was history.

As he walked beside Elle, he tried not to think about how Dario had brought all those memories back with his talk of collaborating with the new diagnostician. Maybe Carmen had been right. Maybe it was all in his imagination. But he didn't think so. The endocrinologist had dated a lot of female staff on the fifth floor, and it never seemed to end well.

A little girl stood in a doorway as they neared the end of the hallway and stared at Elle.

"Are you going home? Where's your baby?"

A voice called from inside the room. "Maria! Don't ask such questions!

But Elena didn't flinch. "It's okay. She's fine."

Her voice was soft as she continued. "I'm not going home. Not yet. And I don't have a baby."

The child's tiny brow puckered. "But my mom said she has to be wheeled out like that."

Santi's chest tightened. His mouth opened to stop the questioning when a hand touched his.

Elena glanced up at him. "I like answering questions." She turned back to Maria. "I'm not riding in this chair because I'm going home. I'm in it because I have to be. I can't walk, like you can."

Her words were so even. So full of confidence that it took him aback. It had never crossed his mind to ask her what happened. Maybe because of his work with hippotherapy.

"Why? You have legs."

That made Elena laugh. "I do, don't I? But mine don't work the way yours do. You see I was riding a beautiful black horse a long time ago. It was like I was riding the wind. I loved my horse very much. And then I fell." She smiled at the child. "Have you ever fallen down?"

The girl gave her a grave nod. "I hurt my knee when I fell once. I cried."

"Well, I got hurt like that. And I hurt my knee, too. But I also hurt my back, very badly. So badly that my legs can't hold me up anymore. So I ride in this chair."

"It looks like fun."

"It is. Sometimes."

Maria seemed to ponder that for a minute. "Do you have a picture of your horse?"

"I do, but I don't have it with me. His full name is Vientos de la Estratosfera, but I call him Strato for short."

"That's a funny name."

Santi kind of liked it. Winds of the Stratosphere. He could picture just the kind of horse he was. And Elle probably did feel like the wind when she rode him.

Her riding trousers suddenly made sense, and his chest tightened even farther. Were these like the breeches she'd worn when she'd been hurt? She'd mentioned that she rode when they were at the wedding, when they'd seen that crazy picture in the library. But he'd had no idea she'd injured her back while doing so.

"It is a funny name. But he's a funny horse."

Said as if the horse was still alive. And maybe he was. Maybe Elena kept tabs on him. He could see her doing that.

"Maria, that's enough, come back inside and help me with your baby brother."

"Okay." She turned back to Elena. "I have to go. I hope you have fun with your horse."

Elena smiled, but her lips had tightened. She waved at the child and started moving away from the door.

"I'm sorry, I didn't know."

She shrugged. "Well, now you do."

They didn't say anything further until they got to the ground floor, where the cafeteria was. They entered the eatery and Elena expertly went through the line making choices and asking for help when she couldn't reach something. Santi remembered the first time he was at the café line at the first hospital he'd worked at. Everything had looked so different from what he was used to in Argentina, but he'd liked it. And later, he'd learned he wasn't supposed to like hospital food. At least everyone else complained about it. Even Grace had.

They sat down at a table just as Elle got a text from someone. She looked at it. "Dario says treatment has started, and he'll let us know when there's some improvement. He says he's hopeful. About a lot of…" Her voice died away, and he could swear he saw a hint of color flush her cheeks.

Dammit. He was right. Even Elle… Elena knew. When had he started thinking of her as Elle? He wasn't sure.

"He's hopeful about a lot of things, huh? I think maybe Grace's sly hints are right."

"Of course they're not. I'm sure he was just talking about the patient's chances of recovery."

Whatever she said. But he didn't believe it. And he didn't think she did, either.

"Well, I'm glad he thinks his chances are good." Too late he realized he'd made a Freudian slip and made it sound like Dario thought *his* chances were good rather than their patient—who was a girl.

She giggled, killing his hopes that she'd misunderstood his words. "I'm pretty sure *he* has no chance at all."

"I'm not telling you anything that's not common knowledge when I say that Dario Mileno has a bit of a reputation."

"I know. I can spot them a mile away. Now."

Said as if there was a time when she couldn't. "Sorry. I had no right to say anything."

"No, I appreciate it. It's just that I can take care of myself."

"Of that I have no doubt." He was seeing more and more of that in her. She was a self-assured, confident woman. Maybe that's what had struck him about her. Carmen had been the same, but underneath there'd been this kind of vulnerability about her that brought out his protective instincts. That was probably what had led him to warn her about Dario. What Carmen hadn't been able to see—because she always saw the best in everybody—Elle had spotted in an instant. Because of what had happened to her? Because she relied on herself? Probably.

But more than that, she'd made it sound like she'd met Dario's type before. Maybe had even been pulled in by someone.

Demonio! He hoped not.

She popped a grape into her mouth, while he struggled for something to say. "So I knew you rode before, from what you said the first time we met. But I didn't realize you'd had a horse of your own. Where did you grow up?"

"In Mallorca, actually. I was a typical horse-crazy girl. My parents brought home a pony." She smiled. "I was ecstatic. Except Bom-Bom didn't match his name. He wasn't a good-good boy. He was actually quite *travieso* and liked to stand on my foot, or zig when I asked him to zag. Maybe my parents thought it would cure me. But it just made me more determined. Then, when I was a little older, they bought Strato. And that was it. He was...*is*...my heart horse. Always will be."

She had certainly made it sound like he was when she was describing the horse to Maria a few minutes ago.

"I had a favorite horse as well."

"Tell me about him." She leaned her chin on her palm and looked at him across the table.

"His name was Diablo."

"Wow. Did he live up to his name?"

One side of his mouth quirked. "He did in more ways than one. He could be a devil. But he was also a devil to catch, which came in handy on the polo field. I think my family was disappointed in my decision to become a doctor rather than helping run the business."

"I can imagine."

He shifted the subject back to her to avoid going into some of the heated discussions that had transpired when he told his dad what he wanted out of life. "Do you still ride?"

"No. A good friend is taking care of Strato. He deserves the best life can offer. I'll probably never ride again."

That surprised him. "Why?"

She looked at him as if in disbelief. "Strato wouldn't know what to do with me."

"He could be retrained. There are lots of ways."

"And sometimes there aren't." Her mouth tightened. "Do *you* still ride?"

"Yes. Not as often as I'd like, and it's been a while."

"Oh." She deflated as if she'd been expecting to question him on his decision, like he'd questioned hers.

"I actually met my wife while riding. Carmen loved horses. She introduced me to hippotherapy."

Was he still trying to steer her toward the idea that riding wasn't beyond her grasp?

"You're married?"

Oh, hell, she'd latched onto the wrong thing. And her question was anything but curious. There was an anger behind the words that he totally understood and was quick to correct.

"Carmen died six years ago."

Her cheeks burned with color like they'd done when Dario had texted her a few minutes ago. "I'm so sorry. I just thought…"

"You were angry that I would kiss you, if I was married. Believe me. I wouldn't have. I never cheated on her. It never even crossed my mind."

"I should have realized. I'm sorry again."

"It's okay. Unlike Dario, I have no reputation. None at all."

That got a smile out of her. "None? Surely everyone is known for something."

"Hmm. Then what about you? What are you known for?" He wanted to know what she thought people saw when they looked at her.

"I think I'm known for solving puzzles."

Ah, that made sense, especially with the work she did. It wasn't quite what he'd been looking for, but he wasn't going to backtrack and try to make her rephrase her answer. He'd asked…and she'd told him. *El fin.*

It also explained why he'd told her about Carmen, when he rarely talked about her, not even to the people at the hospital. Ones who had known her. Elena was good at coaxing information from patients. He'd seen that for himself with Tomás.

With a wry chuckle, he said, "And from the looks of it, you're very good at finding the pieces to whatever puzzle you might be trying to solve." Like trying to solve the puzzle of him? Not likely. Santi didn't know if there was anything left to solve.

"Thanks. I try. But I don't always succeed."

"I don't think any of us can claim to solve one hundred percent of the cases we're given. All we can do is try. And when it's not enough, when there's nothing left to be done… We have to accept that, too."

Like he'd done with his wife, when he'd wanted to try treatment after treatment, hoping for a magic bullet that would kill her cancer. She'd finally said enough and called hospice herself. By that time, the disease had overwhelmed her system, and he realized how stupid he'd been to throw away the time they could have spent building memories. It should have been Carmen's call all along.

When Elena started speaking again, he shook away the thoughts.

"So are you involved with hippotherapy?"

"I volunteer at a center called En Alas de Caballo."

She blinked, then slowly repeated the words. "'On horses' wings.' I like that. I always did feel like I was flying."

It was on the tip of his tongue to say she could still feel that way, but she'd made it pretty clear that riding wasn't something she saw herself doing. At least not right now. And he wasn't going to push where he wasn't welcome. But he could offer something else.

"I'd be happy to take you over to see it. I take a group of kids from the hospital over there once a month to see and interact with the horses. This Friday is the day, actually. There would be no strings attached. I'm not trying to convince you to ride or anything else. I've taken a lot of Aelina's staff over there. A few of them even volunteer."

She stared down at her plate for a moment or two before lifting her head to look at him. "I think I'd like that. No strings attached, though, right?"

"Not even a little one." A weight seemed to roll off him, and he wasn't sure why. Maybe because he was so passionate about the equine therapy center that he wanted to share that love with others. Or maybe he really did hope she'd eventually get back on a horse.

"How do you even find time to volunteer? From what I've seen, your night-shift work takes up most of your time."

It does, but Friday afternoons are sacrosanct. There are two other pediatricians who have offered to work a few hours in the evening so I can go, and they trade off. It gives me time to be at the center to lead Billy."

"Billy?"

"Billy was my horse here in Spain. I donated him to On Horses' Wings six years ago."

"Six years ago…" She seemed to mull something over, then she gave a visible swallow.

She'd figured it out. And maybe like Elle, he'd given up something he loved after losing something he'd loved even more. "He has a good home. A good purpose. And I see him every single week. Billy and Lirio, his rider."

"I like your horse's name. Sounds like a cowboy name."

"He's kind of a cowboy horse. More like the Criollos of Argentina. Rugged and famous for endurance. Billy's not sleek and elegant like the Andalusians you have here in Spain."

"You live in Spain too, remember? Or did you never fully leave Argentina?"

"I think part of my heart will always be in my homeland. But I've chosen to make my home here in Barcelona."

"Even if you can't own another Criollo?"

"There's always a way. I've learned that every time I step into the arena with Billy and Lirio."

She sighed when her phone pinged again. But this time when she looked at her screen she smiled. "The patient's respiration and heart rate are going up. They're hoping she'll wake up soon. Baby's stats are improving along with his or her mom's." Her gaze traveled a little farther, and she rolled her eyes.

Evidently the endocrinologist was still hinting at something. He ignored her look and concentrated on what the body of the text had said.

"That's good news."

"Yes, it is." She sighed and picked up her now-empty tray, setting it in her lap. "And with that, I think I need to head home so I can shower and go to bed. Before my shift starts back up again tonight. I really want to work on Tomás's case and see if he'll tell us any more. He was still kind of sullen again when I visited him today."

"Same here. Maybe we should try to do like we did a couple of days ago. Go in together and tag team him. Maybe this time we'll be harder to resist as a pair."

The second the words were out of his mouth, he wished he could retract them. Maybe the traits he detested so much in Dario were being transferred to him. Wasn't that what they said happened? That if you weren't careful you'd take on your enemy's characteristics?

Demonio! If so, he'd better damn well put a stop to it. Before she started rolling her eyes at him, too.

Instead she smiled and said something completely unexpected. And completely unsettling.

"Yes. Maybe we are."

Grace called her the next afternoon, just as she'd pulled on her clothes for work. Her heart started pounding. "Our hypothyroid patient?"

"Yes. I just came in a few minutes ago, and Patricia is awake. Thought you might like to hear."

"That is great news, Grace, thanks for letting me know!"

"I hope you don't mind me calling your cell phone."

She smiled. "Of course not. I don't know very many people at the hospital, so it's nice to get a phone call relaying happy news. I don't always hear the results when I've worked on cases."

"Well, this time you will. Her THS numbers are coming down, too. They're thinking maybe something autoimmune crashed her thyroid. But for now it looks like the levothyroxine and cortisone combination are going to do the trick."

"When is she going to be discharged?"

"Probably tomorrow or the day after."

"Fantastic. I hope she starts coming in for follow-ups. She needs to be seen regularly, especially expecting at such a young age."

"Yes, and having no support system to boot. Hey, do you want to go out for dinner before work tomorrow? Diego has surgery scheduled earlier that day, so I'll be on my own and could use some company."

Elena pulled in a breath, a sense of relief washing through her. "I would love that, thank you."

She'd wondered if she would like being stuck in one hospital, if she would have enough work or feel like an outsider, but so far she really liked Aelina. Despite some of her uneasy feelings about Santi. Most of those were of her own making, though. It wasn't like he'd made her feel unwelcome. In fact, they seemed to work well together, most of the time, which in itself made her feel odd.

Maybe we're harder to resist as a pair.

She didn't know about them as a pair, but one thing she did know. He was pretty hard to resist all on his own. After their conversation this morning over breakfast, she'd been unable to resist looking up Criollos. They might not look like Strato—who was as Andalusian as they came—but they were beautiful in their own right. She'd expected something scruffier from Santi's description. Instead she'd found they came in different colors, many with at least some kind of roaning—where a darker-hair coat was interspersed with white. They were known for their agility and quite popular as polo ponies. Which made complete sense, given what he'd told her about his family's polo business.

She arrived at the hospital and decided to peek into Letizia's office. "Just wanted to say hi."

"Well, hi, yourself. I've been meaning to sneak up to the third floor and see how you're doing. Aelina is treating you okay?"

She pulled the door farther open. "It is."

"And the case with Dr. Garcia?"

"We haven't found the answer quite yet, but we're still working on it. I'm heading up there in a few minutes."

"If I know you, you won't quit until you get to the bottom of it. That's what makes you so good at your job."

There were some things she might never get to the bottom of. Like the reason she'd gotten so defensive when Santi had asked her about riding. Because when he'd asked her to go to the equine therapy center, a trill of excitement had shot through her. Why? It wasn't like she was going to ride one of those horses. Maybe it was the thought of seeing a horse again.

Or maybe it was the hint of excitement over accompanying him somewhere outside the hospital.

Well, whatever it was, she'd better get a hold of that feeling and quick. Once she did, she needed to fling it so far away that she'd forget all about it. Ha! Like that was even a possibility.

Well, it needed to be not only a possibility, she also had to work to make it her reality. Before something happened that she might regret.

Something far worse than going to the center with him. Far worse than the simple kiss they'd shared. Something subtle kept hanging around trying to get her to look at it. So far, she'd succeeded in refusing.

But for how long? She might be good at solving puzzles, but she was pretty sure this was one she didn't dare tackle.

CHAPTER SIX

SANTI WAS LOOKING through papers when a knock sounded at his door. Sasha, who'd been lying under his desk at his feet, got up and looked toward the door, her tail wagging. She was wearing a pink tutu around her midsection. He hoped Tomás liked her. He glanced at the sports watch on his wrist. Just before six. It had to be Elena coming to ask about their visit with the teen. *"Entra."*

He motioned for the dog to sit just as the door swung open using the automatic system they all had on the wall. And, yes, it was Elle.

Sasha ducked her head under the desk to look, still sitting exactly where Santi had told her to.

"You're not afraid of dogs, right?"

"No. Why? Are you hiding one?"

He murmured to Sasha, who ran around the desk and sat beside Elle's chair.

"Oh, my goodness! I love her. Is it all right if I pet her?"

"Yes, absolutely. She'd be hurt if you didn't."

While she stroked the dog's head, Santi glanced at

her. Today she was dressed in a long beige skirt that had a kind of purposeful crinkling. Her top was a white button-down that had to be murder outside in the heat. But here in the air-conditioning, it was fitted and crisp and molded over some features he was doing his best not to glance at, especially as she leaned over to take Sasha's proffered paw. But it was tricky, as in virtually impossible. His eyes moved to her wrists and fingers, which were devoid of jewelry, and her feet, which had on pumps today rather than sandals.

"Have you taken her to see Tomás yet?"

He frowned. "No, I thought we were doing that together."

"Oh, we are. But I thought you might have peeked in on him before I got here. I was running a little late. And that ballet skirt is adorable on her."

"The kids seem to like it. And no, I haven't peeked in. I just got here a few minutes ago myself. Did you hear that Patricia Gomez is awake and set to be discharged soon?"

"Grace called me before I left the house and told me. That's great news. Any idea exactly what caused it? I heard it was autoimmune related."

With a sigh, Sasha plopped down at Elle's feet, making her smile.

"Yes. They're doing some more tests. So far they haven't narrowed it down, but I'm sure Dario will explore all of his options."

Right on cue, Elle's face colored slightly. Had the man texted her again? She said it had been Grace who called her. Besides, what business of his was it? Hell,

even if she wanted to date the man it was of no conse-
quence to him.

She didn't have to worry about any of that with
him. He had no interest in dating anyone. He'd had
exactly two one-night stands with women since Carmen's death. Totally about physical release. The women
hadn't wanted anything further, either, which had made
it perfect.

He hated to admit it, but Elle would have been his
third encounter in those six years, if that kiss had gone
any further than it had. But this weird sense of home-
coming had flooded his system the second their lips
collided. It had made him yank away from her. And
thank heavens he had or working with her would have
been…impossible. He was already highly aware of her
this afternoon, maybe because of their talk yesterday.
He had a feeling she didn't get asked about her riding
all that often and the fact that she'd opened up about it
had made something in his chest turn all soft.

Soft? It wasn't only his chest that was going soft. His
brain evidently was, too. He needed to pull himself together. And fast.

"Are you ready to go see him?"

She nodded. "Any other thoughts on what's causing
his leg pain?"

"Not yet. You?"

"I'm still going through some lists of differentials.
Blood clots in the femoral being one of them, but there
would have to be one on each side and only partially
obstructing the vessels. The chances of that happening are…"

"Infinitesimal."

"Exactly. One of the dystrophies, like we mentioned earlier?"

He thought about that for a minute. Becker's was a possibility, although it didn't normally present with pain. But if Tomás was trying to force his muscles past any perceived weakness, there could be some soreness involved afterward. "Yes, there are a couple that come to mind for this age range. Becker's and Duchenne's."

"Ugh. Those are both catastrophic diagnoses." Her voice was soft and there was a sadness he hadn't expected.

"Yes, they are." If anyone knew about catastrophic diagnoses, it was Santi. He remembered the moment he and Carmen had received her diagnosis: stage four breast cancer that had spread to her brain and left femur. She'd actually gone in for leg pain and after a slew of tests, they found it was metastatic cancer originating in her breast.

"Those are both caused by recessive genes. We don't have any history on the parents, if I remember right."

"No. The home said there's nothing other than the notes from his heart surgeries. There are normally some abnormalities on EKGs found on initial workup with Becker's, but since he's had the Fontan procedure for his hypoplastic left heart syndrome, his EKGs and echoes are abnormal, even on a good day. In other words, the findings might be so unremarkable they might not show up."

"Urine?" She glanced over at the wall. "Mind if I use that?"

He followed her gaze where a large whiteboard was hung. On it were a few notes from another meeting. "Feel free to erase all of that."

"Are you sure?"

He nodded, watching as she wheeled her way to the board. Realizing she wouldn't be able to reach the upper portion, he got up and erased it. "Do you want me to write at the top?"

Sasha stayed where she was, but lifted her head to look at them, tail thumping on the ground.

"No, I normally start at the very bottom. I work my way up as far as I can reach. I'll add more once we go see him. But I'd just like to know what to rule out when we head over there."

She wrote the two dystrophies on the lowest part of the board. "Do you have different colors?"

"Let me check." He didn't normally graph things out, but then again, he often referred complicated issues elsewhere. Except they didn't know which specialist Tomás needed. Not yet. He pulled out several of his desk drawers, giving a sigh of relief when an unopened pack of dry-erase pens came into sight.

He took them over and handed them to her. Their fingers accidentally touched, and they both froze for a second, and raw sensation spiraled up his arm and sizzled through his chest. He let go of the pack in a hurry. Unfortunately she chose to do the same and the box of markers dropped onto the ground.

"Demonio!" The swear word slipped out before he could stop it. He swooped down to pick up the box and his head collided with something on his way down.

"Ouch!" Elle's yelp caught him up short, and he almost bumped into her again.

Sasha leaped up and he had to reassure her, patting her silky head.

He was about to apologize to Elle, when the diagnostician suddenly giggled, hand going to cover her mouth. Then she laughed harder, her palm moving from her mouth to the back of her head, rubbing it.

Santi started to voice that apology, but there was something about those little chortles that were contagious. He found himself chuckling along with her.

It took an effort to shut his laughter down.

He looked at her. Really looked. Her cheeks were pink, eyes bright with mirth, and those lips were curved at a luscious angle that made him want to… Before he could stop himself, he leaned over and kissed her softly on the mouth before moving away again.

Some familiar emotion flooded his chest and flared outward, catching him off guard just as her eyes went wide.

"What was that for?" she asked.

He had no idea. It had been an impulsive move, almost as if it was muscle memory. Then he realized why, and he damned himself. He'd often done that with Carmen.

Santi swallowed and made something up. "I think I just needed a reason to laugh today. It's been a hard few shifts with Tomás's condition hanging over my head."

"Yes, it has. Speaking of hard and heads." She fingered Sasha's pink tutu, avoiding his eyes. "Has anyone told you that you have a very hard head?"

"Hmm, let's see… My mother, various teachers, my coworkers, a couple of friends—"

She held up a hand, smiling. "You can add me to your evidently very long list."

"You got it." He handed her the pack of pens, careful not to touch her this time. Having her here in his office was doing things to his libido that he didn't like. Especially since the moon was just starting to appear within sight of his window, reminding him that their meetings were almost always at night. Working these shifts was partly about not having to go to bed at night and tossing and turning at being there alone.

Somehow it was easier for him to sleep during the day. It also helped him manage any interactions with women, since they were normally sleeping when he was working and working when he was sleeping. No dinner dates. No movie nights. No complications. His job was perfect in that respect.

Except the one woman he'd kissed in ages now worked the exact same hours he did. In the same place. And it was getting harder and harder to not let his thoughts travel in that direction.

He glanced again at the darkening sky before turning his attention back to her.

She'd pulled out red and green felt tip pens and had added some of the diagnostic markers above each condition. Then listed the tests they needed to either confirm or rule out whether Tomás met those markers.

"What else?"

"We'd mentioned multiple sclerosis. He's young

but…no, scratch that. The CT scan didn't show any suspicious lesions."

"Right. Which rules out brain tumor as well, and some other problems."

Together they thought up and either ruled out or added other conditions to their board. He could have a problem with bone lesions in his legs, but to have those bilaterally would be as odd as bilateral blood clots.

Elle sighed. "Maybe the most important thing is figuring out how to get him to open up to us."

"I know. I'm hoping Sasha will be some help, but if not, we may need to pull in some reinforcements in the form of counselors who are trained to deal with this." Not that Santi had gone to anyone after his wife died, despite friends urging him to do just that. But opening up had never been one of his better traits.

Evidently it wasn't one of Tomás's, either.

"I'm hoping he'll just start to trust us."

Santi realized they were sitting with their heads close together. Too close. All he had to do was look over at her and their faces would be inches apart.

As if she were having similar thoughts, Elle suddenly capped the pens and put them back in the box. "Let's go see him."

She took out her phone and snapped a picture of the board for reference. "I assume Sasha's outfit is for Tomás's benefit."

"How do you know she doesn't just like to dress up?" He had no idea why he suddenly felt so carefree, especially when he was about to see a child who could have a life-threatening condition in addition to his rerouted circulatory system. But that quick kiss and the sense of intimacy being so close had engendered had somehow given him a burst of energy. For now, he was just going to sit back and enjoy it. He could worry about the ramifications later on.

And Elle hadn't seemed to mind the impulsive move. He almost wished she'd have shut him down immediately. Instead, she'd seemed almost bright. Almost as…

No. He wasn't happy. Wasn't glad. And that kiss wasn't happening again. He climbed to his feet.

"Come on, Sasha. Let's go." He clipped a lead onto the pink harness that matched the tulle around her waist, and they headed out the door and down the hall.

As they got closer to his room, Tomás's shrill voice echoed down the hallway, causing Sasha to balk.

Santi hurried ahead and found a representative of the group home in the room with the teen. "I'm sure you'll be getting out of the hospital soon," the woman said.

"I don't want to!" His face was beet red, a dangerous sign.

The woman tried to calm him down, but the more she cajoled and pleaded, the more agitated he seemed to become.

Before he could put a stop to the exchange, Elle moved forward and smiled at the woman. "Can I talk to you outside for a moment?"

"Of course." The poor woman looked relieved, her eyes skipping across Santi's dog. Elle gave him a very tiny nod, telling him to go for it.

He hadn't had much luck yesterday, but he was willing to try again. He moved inside with the Labrador retriever. "How are you doing today, Tomás?"

"Same as every day. I hurt." His voice still held a thread of anger, but his gaze was glued to Sasha. "Is that the dog you were telling me about?"

Rather than sullen, today the teen sounded resigned as if he didn't expect anything different now. "Yes, this is Sasha. Is it okay if she comes closer?"

The boy shrugged but swung his legs over the side of the bed, wincing as he did.

"Let me lower the bed a bit, so you can say hi to her." He stepped on a mechanism at the side of the frame and the hydraulics whispered as the bed moved downward.

"Why is she wearing a dress?"

He looked at his pup. "It's not really a dress. It's kind of that poufy part on a ballet costume."

Tomás blinked. "Does she dance?"

"No. She just tries to make people feel better."

The boy sat there for a minute. "Huh. People like me, you mean."

Santi didn't try to dodge the comment. "Yes, people just like you. And people like me." He held the dog away just a touch. "Do you feel strong enough to walk over here?"

Tomás licked his lips. "I don't know." Resting his feet on the ground, he stood, his gait a strange shuffling movement as he made his way toward Sasha. His posture was stooped as if anticipating pain.

"Does it hurt now?"

"Not as bad as it did a few minutes ago." He reached Sasha just as Elena came back into the room. Santi could feel her critical gaze as she watched Tomás's movements. He was pretty sure she was trying to read him.

"Can I pet her?"

"I think she would like that. Curl your fingers into your palm and hold your fist out to her so she can sniff you first."

Tomás did as he was told, and Sasha did her part by giving a perfunctory sniff before her tongue swiped across his hand.

The teen made a sound that was suspiciously like a squeaked laugh. "She's nice. I wish I could have a dog."

Santi did his best to hide his shock at the softer tones. Maybe this had been the right call after all. If only they could keep the boy like this, they might be able to get somewhere.

"I'm sure when you get a little older you'll be able to. We just have to help you feel better first."

The teen looked down at his feet. "My legs are tired."

Santi glanced as well, and sure enough the muscles in his thighs were shaking. "Let's go ahead and get you back in the bed."

Tomás leaned over to pet Sasha's neck again and all of a sudden cried out in pain, his legs almost crumpling before he caught himself. Sasha remained very still.

Whatever had happened had put him in agony.

"What is it?" Elena moved forward to help him back to the bed, careful to avoid bumping his legs with her chair. "Did it hurt when you stretched down like that?"

Tomás sank onto the bed, his relief evident in his

face. "Yes. Just like before when I leaned over to get my shoes."

"Stretch your arms out to the side."

He did as she asked. "Does it hurt now?"

"Not like it did."

She moved around in front of him, her face level with his. "I'm going to ask you to do something, Tomás. And it's very possible it might hurt. A lot."

His features went white, and he looked at Sasha with pleading eyes. He hadn't seemed this vulnerable any of the other times they'd met him. It had to be Sasha's doing.

Elle looked over her shoulder at him. "Can you bring her closer, if she won't be frightened of Tomás making a sound if something hurts."

"She's used to it." Santi didn't want to say that when Sasha was a puppy, she'd heard Carmen cry out in pain many times toward the end of her life.

He moved her closer, and Sasha laid her head on Tomás's knee.

"Okay, Tomás, I want you to curve your back and lean toward Sasha as if you're going to give her a hug. Do it very, very slowly and stop if it starts hurting at all."

He could almost see her brain picking at the problem as if the answer was right there, she just couldn't quite get to it. He liked that. Liked the way her analytical mind could take things apart and put them back together.

As long as she wasn't analyzing him. Because she could get a little too close to the truth, if she did.

Tomás placed his palm on the dog's head and slowly did what Elle had asked. In micromovements, he curved, bending until he was about a quarter of the way down before suddenly stopping. "It hurts really bad."

"Is the pain burning? Is it stabbing?"

"It burns, and it makes my legs feel funny. Like when they fall asleep."

"Okay, slowly sit back up and tell me if it feels better."

Tomás straightened, his eyes closing as if in relief. "Yes, it feels better, but my legs still hurt."

"Do you still have pins and needles in them?"

"It's kind of going away, but the pain is still pretty bad."

She looked over her shoulder at Santi. "I think I know what it is. And we're going to have to act fast if we're going to save function in his legs."

CHAPTER SEVEN

ELENA WAS 99 percent sure she was right, but they'd need an MRI to be sure.

She'd moved into the hallway with Santi, leaving Sasha in the room with Tomás, who was busy trying to seem like he didn't care, all the while petting the dog's head. Leaving the door open so she could keep an eye on the pair, she kept her voice low. "I think he has a tethered cord. It kind of hid itself while he was small and because of all of the difficulties with his heart, no one thought to look at anything else, especially since it wasn't causing symptoms at the time."

"A tethered cord." He glanced in the room. "It makes more sense than a dystrophy at this point. I think we can rule those out."

"I think so, too. He's hit a growth spurt and the trapped portion of his spinal cord is being stretched. Bending forward like that only stretches it more. It has to be near where the nerves to his legs are centered."

Strangely, Elena felt relief. A tethered cord was serious, no doubt about it. Tomás had been worried about ending up in a wheelchair like she was, and unless surgery was done to free the cord, he may very well be. Some of his impairment might be permanent, but if they could free it, there was a chance they could reverse some of the damage since he hadn't been symptomatic for long.

"Let's schedule an MRI to confirm, and I'll get a hold of the neurology department. Hopefully the cord is simply stuck, probably from a neural tube defect that closed and narrowed the space. If the cord itself is too short, surgery may be more complicated."

She nodded. "Osteotomy to shorten his spine. That would be tougher, but either way he has a great chance at recovery."

"All right. Do you mind staying here with Sasha and Tomás, while I make some calls?"

"I don't mind at all. Do I need to take Sasha's skirt off, or is she okay?"

"It's not tight. She kind of likes the attention she gets from it, I think."

She peered in the door to see the teen actually smiling. *Smiling!* He looked more at ease than she'd seen him in…well, ever.

"Can you call the home as well and let them know? The director was called back to help with something, so she's not here."

"I'll do it."

He went one way, while Elena went back into the room. "How are you doing?"

Glancing up, his smile faded, but so had the angry look he'd carried with him. "Am I going to die?"

"No. We think the problem is in your back and it's

causing the pain you're feeling. You'll need surgery, but I think it will help."

"Is that a promise?"

He probably hadn't had many of those that meant much, and Elena wasn't about to heap another one onto the pile.

"Let's not get ahead of ourselves. We need to give you an MRI, kind of like the scan you did a few days ago. We should be able to see on there if it is what I think it is."

"What is it?"

"Something called a tethered cord. Your spinal cord is trapped somewhere, I think, and we need to free it."

He nodded, appearing to be mulling over what that meant. "So leaning forward pulls on it?"

Her brows went up at how quickly he'd grasped what it meant.

"That's exactly right, Tomás. Surgery can either widen the canal and allow the cord to move freely like it should, or we'll need to help it a little more." She decided to leave the idea of osteotomy for another day. It might not even be necessary.

His head ducked for a minute before his eyes came up and met hers. "Thank you. Can you let Dr. McKenzie know? I... I wasn't very nice to her the last time I saw her."

"I will. It's hard when your body isn't acting like you expect it to. It can make you scared...or angry."

He stroked Sasha's head again. The dog was still sitting in front of the boy looking up at him with adoring eyes. Santi was right. The pup did like her job, and maybe even her costumes. Dressing her up probably signaled she was getting to go somewhere with Santi. She could see how that might make her happy.

Like Elena getting to go to the hippotherapy center with him? No, it was not like that at all.

She spoke again before she could dwell on those thoughts. "I'm sure Caitlin understands and from what she said to me, she was very worried about you. That's why she asked us to keep trying to figure it out. She got married you know."

"I know. She told me. Does it make you angry that you can't walk?"

The question came out of nowhere, startling her. She answered honestly. "Sometimes, yes. But it's been a long time and I'm happy for the things I can still do."

"Like figure out what's wrong with people?"

She smiled. "Yes, exactly like that."

He paused for a minute or two and glanced at Sasha before speaking again. "Do you think Bianca is mad at me?"

"Bianca?"

He nodded. "She's the *madre* of the home. I wasn't very nice to her, either."

"No, you weren't. But there's always time to tell her you're sorry."

"I will." He took an audible breath. "I'm ready for surgery. As long as Sasha can be there when I wake up."

She wheeled a little bit closer and placed her hand on his, the chilled skin telling her the state of his nerves. This kid had probably been terrified his whole life, using his sullenness as a cover. Actually, she knew he was. She could see it in the way he seemed to be trying to make things right with people before he had surgery. It was another indicator of how scared he was.

And now Tomás had his answer.

And so did she. She blinked as a realization hit her. Finding Tomás's problem meant she'd soon be moving up to the fifth floor, where her real office was. Where Dario Mileno was. She blew out a breath. It also meant she wouldn't be seeing Santi every day.

Did that bother her?

It did. And she wasn't sure why. She'd worked with lots of doctors in her career and had never had any problem moving on.

But those other doctors had never kissed her. He'd done so twice. Once at the wedding, and that kiss when they'd been laughing in his office. The first one had awoken her senses, trickling desire through her in an agonizing stream. But that second one... Well, it had awoken something far more dangerous than her body. It had stirred her emotions, making them long for something she'd given up on a long time ago: permanent companionship. The touch of lips had been short and playful, but she'd caught a glimpse of what life could look like. And she was having a harder time shaking that off.

She'd still work with him from time to time, once she moved, but probably not as closely as she was now, unless there was another case like this one.

Sasha nosed her hand as if understanding what she was thinking. She stroked the dog's warm soft fur and leaned close to her ear. "Shh, girl. This has to be our little secret."

"What's a secret?"

Tomás had evidently overheard her soft words.

"Yes, what's a secret?" The low gruff voice made her sit up quickly. Santi had walked up behind her with such stealth that she hadn't heard him. Neither had Sasha, evidently, as her head popped off Elena's leg, and she whirled toward her owner, tail wagging.

"That I'm going to put a dog cookie jar in your office and keep it stocked with pup treats." She had no idea how that fib had come out so quickly but was glad it had. Sasha was a great therapist, maybe too good. She'd helped break through some of the walls that Tomás had erected. But not only that, she seemed to see into Elena's deepest hopes. And fears. And she found they were one and the same. She wanted deeper relationships. Desperately. And yet she feared them. So much so that she tended to sabotage any possibility of having one.

"You are, are you?"

Maldición! Now that she'd said it, she was stuck with it. Which meant she would have to come down to his office periodically to fill the jar. Still, she decided to just go with it. "Is that okay? Unless she's on a special diet and can't have them."

"I'm sure she would appreciate having some when she's here."

His voice was slow and there was a hint of something in his tone that she didn't understand. A kind of softness that made her tummy go all wonky. And ignited that fear all over again.

She squashed the emotion, making a mental note to look for a doggy-themed cookie jar the next time she was out. And maybe some of those fancy home-baked treats they sometimes had at specialty cookie shops that were made with canines in mind.

The dog was currently sitting by Santi's side, but Sasha's soft brown eyes were on her, as if to say, "It's okay. Your secret really is safe with me."

It made her smile. "Tomás would like Sasha to be here when he wakes up from surgery, if that's possible—*if* the MRI shows a tethered cord."

"Yes, can she?" The teen's voice was soft, tentative, and it tugged at her heart. She hoped at least one of the foster homes he'd lived in had had a pet that he'd been able to bond with.

But that made it so much harder, didn't it? To bond with an animal—or person, for that matter—only to have them ripped away from you.

Like Santi's wife? There had been a sadness to his voice when he'd talked about her. It was obvious, despite the time that had elapsed since her passing, that he still loved her deeply. Maybe that's why he wasn't currently married, or even in a relationship from what she'd gathered. Some loves were irreplaceable.

She felt that way about Strato. She didn't see him as often as she would like or even as often as she should, but that horse was irreplaceable. He'd tried to move toward her after her fall, almost tugging the reins from her friend's hands. And whenever she'd visited the last couple of times, his majestic neck had curved, and he'd lowered his head to nuzzle her hair, warm breath blowing across her face. She'd held his head against hers and whispered an apology.

He was a talented boy, and he had always liked to work. Probably keeping him had been selfish on her part, but she just couldn't seem to give him up.

Her glance went to Santi.

No! Do not attach those kinds of feelings to him. To anyone. Hadn't Renato taught her that? Or the fact that she hadn't had a real relationship since then? People left. Her boyfriend from high school hadn't stuck around long once he realized her injuries were permanent. His sheepish expression the last time he visited had told her all she needed to know. The football jock had loved to brag that she was as good in her sport as he was in his. His sliding away had been awful and a terrible blow to her self-esteem on top of her other struggles. She'd gone through a depression that had taken months to work through. Renato not calling her after their failed lovemaking attempt had been just as much of a blow.

"Sasha won't be allowed in recovery or ICU, where you'll probably be when you first come out of surgery, but we can do a video chat with her on the line. How's that?"

Santi's voice jerked her back to reality.

She'd totally forgotten that she'd asked the question. Not good. Her thoughts were ricocheting around like those polo balls Santi probably batted when he was playing. Or did he even play here?

Glancing over, she noted the slight strain of muscles against his black polo shirt and the trim abs. He said he didn't ride as much as he'd like, but from the look of him, he found some way to exercise. He was strong and in shape.

Of course he jogged, as she'd seen that day in the park.

"That's okay." Tomás held his hand out, and Sasha immediately padded over to him in her pink tutu, soaking up the attention.

Yes, the dog deserved a treat jar. And a medal.

Maybe she should look into getting a dog.

"Did you get a hold of neurology?" she asked.

"Yes. They've had several emergency surgeries over the last forty-eight hours, so they're backed up a bit. But we'll get the MRI, and they'll take a look. If it confirms tethered cord syndrome, they'll work you in, Tomás, in the next couple of days."

Elena reached up to give the boy's shoulder a slight squeeze. "It won't be much longer, and you'll be feeling better."

The teen looked away for a long minute, before saying, "I really thought I was going to die."

Santi looked at her and she knew exactly what his thoughts were. That Tomás hadn't opened up this much the whole time they'd been working with them.

Tomás had probably faced dying many times in his life, with his heart. And he would probably face it again sometime in the future. The fortunate thing was that if the Fontan circulation started to fail, he was young and healthy enough to go on the transplant list.

"This is definitely a better scenario than some of the other possibilities," she said.

Surgery would be complicated by his heart problems, but it certainly wasn't an insurmountable obstacle.

"Okay, Sasha, time to say goodbye so Tomás can get prepped for his MRI," Santi said. He glanced at her

and the teen. "Neurology has already got you scheduled. They should be here soon to take you up. And I'll
check on you a little later in the evening."

Tomás nodded and started to lean over, arms
stretched wide, to hug Sasha, before stopping himself.
She knew why he'd hesitated, and her heart ached over
it. Soon, though, he wouldn't have to worry about pain
when reaching to give hugs to the dog...or to anyone.
She gave an inner sigh. And that was a very good thing.
It made everything, even her confusion about Santi,
worth it.

Santi fed Sasha her afternoon meal and took her for a
quick walk outside his apartment. Although he didn't
live in the hospital housing complex, he did run in the
park regularly after work. He still did. He hadn't come
across Elena while doing so since that first morning,
and he wondered if she'd chosen to run at another time
to avoid him, or if it was just his screwed-up mind in-
serting things that shouldn't be there. He couldn't believe he'd kissed her in his office. It was impulsive and
stupid, and while he might not always be the smartest
human alive, one thing he prided himself on was not
being impulsive.

And yet he had been.

So why Elena?

He didn't know, and he didn't care. But one thing he
didn't want to do was sit around and brood while eating
a meal in front of the television. Making a quick call
to Javier and Caitlin, he told them what Elena had figured out with Tomás. How quickly she'd figured it out

still amazed him. That woman's mind worked in ways he couldn't begin to fathom.

"A tethered cord? I never even thought of that," Javier said. They were on speakerphone so they both could hear and talk.

"I didn't, either. Elle did, though. You were right about her figuring the hard ones out, Caitlin."

"So it's Elle now, is it?" Her voice contained a hint of slyness that Santi didn't like. He didn't want anyone getting any ideas. "We all use first names at Aelina, you know that. It would be awkward to call her Dr. Solis and everyone else by their given names."

"I'm just teasing, Santi. Javier, how do you say 'take a chill pill' in Spanish?"

"Toma un tranquilizante."

Caitlin laughed. "Well, that certainly fits. What Javier said, Santi."

Take a tranquilizer? Seriously? In the background he could swear he heard them kissing, and it made his jaw set hard, a muscle pumping in his cheek. "Well, I won't hold you up. When are you coming back to Barcelona?"

"Grace and Diego are having a renewal ceremony coming up on the beach. We wouldn't miss it for the world."

Maldizion! Not another wedding. Technically Grace and Diego were already married, but they'd had some rocky times. He'd witnessed some of their frosty encounters firsthand. Evidently those days were over, something he'd missed. He forced himself to say something nice. "That's great. I'm glad they've worked out their problems."

"They have. Grace has already said she wants you there along with our other friends. She's going to ask Elena as well. You'll go, won't you? I think she'd be sad if you didn't."

"Since I haven't been invited yet, I'll cross that bridge when it comes."

Javier broke in. "I think our dinner reservations are soon, *querida*."

"Okay, I think he's telling me to get off the line, Santi. See you at the ceremony."

"See you when you get back." He left off anything that might hint at a promise on his part. If he could, he was going to make sure he had something scheduled whenever that beachfront ceremony was. Especially if Elena was going.

He shoved the phone in his pocket. He definitely didn't want to sit around the house until his shift started. So, Boomers it was. The place was fashioned after the American sports bar model, and he found he liked the noise the place afforded. There were large screens facing every direction and it would give him something to look at besides what was in his own head.

He gave his dog a quick rub, and when she whined, he shook his head. "Sorry, girl. You can't see Tomás tonight. But I promise, you will again soon."

He wondered if the diagnostician had already moved her things up to the fifth floor, or if she was still in her office in pediatrics. She wasn't even officially assigned to the night shift, they'd just put her there to help with Tomás, and since he worked nights, he assumed Letizia from HR had asked her to work during that time frame as well. Soon someone else would claim her as their own.

Okay, that was a weird way to put it, even for him. Maybe it was the memory of Dario's behavior around her. Or the veiled attempts at flirting in his texts to her.

Something about her being around him every single day just didn't sit right. *Maldizion!* He definitely needed to go somewhere besides his apartment.

Heading out the door, he went the short distance from his house to the sports eatery, which was located at about the halfway point to Aelina. He normally biked to work, only using his car when he took Sasha with him, to save her from having to walk on the burning pavement. And he'd drive on Friday as well, when he was taking a small group of kids to On Horses' Wings. And he'd invited Elle, too. Probably not a smart idea after all.

Caitlin was right. The shortened version of the diagnostician's name came to mind far too easily. But to suddenly switch to Elena now would draw attention, and that was the last thing he wanted or needed.

Pushing through the entrance to Boomers, he saw the place was already packed. Although Spaniards tended to eat dinner later than some of its neighboring countries, he needed to be at work, so he'd gotten into the habit of dining earlier. One of the wait staff asked how many were in his party and when he said one, he could swear the woman's smile contained more than a hint of pity.

Who cared? He'd eaten by himself lots of times.

As they walked between tables a voice called out to

him. His head turned toward the sound and his stomach dropped. It was Grace.

And Elena.

Great. Just what he didn't need tonight.

He nodded and gave half a wave, hoping to walk on by, but it wasn't to be.

"Join us!"

Glancing at Elena, he saw her head was down, and she was avoiding looking at him, almost as if she felt guilty about something. Had they been talking about him?

It didn't matter if they were. As long as she didn't develop some sort of crush on him. And by the looks of it, there was absolutely no chance of that.

He hesitated a minute, considering his options. If he declined the invitation, it would look odd. But he also wasn't in the mood for awkward, stilted conversation.

Would Elle think the refusal was because of her?

That made his mind up. He motioned toward the table and the server asked him what he wanted to drink. He gave his order and moved over to where the two women sat.

Grace smiled as he took his seat. "We were just talking about the renewal ceremony. You heard about it, didn't you? And of course we want you there."

"I actually called Javier and Caitlin to discuss a patient, and they mentioned that you and Diego were having one. Congratulations. I'll have to check my schedule."

Her head cocked. "I haven't even told you when it is yet."

"I realize that," he lied. "Can you tell me, and I'll look?"

She grinned. "Elena is coming, of course. It's on the twenty-third, two weeks from this coming Friday."

He took his phone out and put the date into it. How was it that he'd not only been stuck going to one wedding, but now it looked like it would be two? All in the course of a month.

A little voice whispered, *Two weddings for two kisses.*

And if there were a third wedding? Would there be another kiss?

He turned his head toward the diagnostician, who was finally looking at him. "Are we still on for this Friday?"

"I have it on my calendar."

Grace smiled. "The On Horses' Wings trip? Elle was just telling me about it. I've been meaning to go to one of the informational meetings and check it out. And now that things between me and Diego are settled, I can finally think about something else."

Elle's teeth came down on her lip and squeezed into it.

So they *had* been talking about him. And he understood exactly what Grace meant. He'd been having trouble thinking of much outside of a certain doctor. And that needed to change. And soon.

"Have you moved up to the fifth floor yet?" The question came totally out of left field, and he was pretty sure it was because of his thoughts about Dario.

Elena blinked. "Oh, um, not yet. I thought I would wait until Tomás was out of the woods in case there's a complication." She hesitated. "Unless you want me to make the move before then."

Maldicion! There was a weird look on her face. He hadn't meant to make her feel unwanted. She wasn't. The fact was, she was "wanted" far too much for his own good. With her dark wavy locks loose and free and looking far too touchable today, he'd needed to say something. Unfortunately it had been the wrong thing.

"No, of course not. I just know you've been working the night shift to help me with Tomás and didn't want you to feel stuck with our vampirish hours."

"I don't feel stuck. And I've actually come to like working at night." She smiled, her tongue coming forward to touch one of her canines. "Do these look longer to you?"

He laughed, despite his earlier thoughts. "Maybe just a touch."

A real smile appeared. He liked it.

"Anyway, if one of the day-shift doctors needed my help, I could swap over and work then instead. My specialty encompasses internal medicine, so I can see patients in my own right as well, so the hospital's money won't be wasted when there are no complicated cases. I just like those cases, which is why I traveled from hospital to hospital before."

"And if you find working so-called easy cases too dull, will you leave Aelina?"

Grace broke in. "We don't want you to leave. So we'll be sure to throw plenty of interesting stuff your way. Right, Santi?"

Hell, he'd done it again. Said the wrong thing. All

because *he* was the one who was uncomfortable. He wanted to pull out the sutures of conversation that were unraveling and start again, but unlike with a patient, he couldn't go back and rework things. He was stuck with what he'd said, unless he pulled her aside later and clarified. Which maybe he needed to do.

"Right. I'm sure we can find lots of reasons to keep her here."

When Elle's shoulders visibly relaxed, he knew he'd finally said the right thing.

He decided to add to that. "You are welcome to stay in your office in pediatrics for as long as you'd like. I'm sure our department will have patients you can work with. Or you can just have your base camp set up there and rove from floor to floor, rather than hospital to hospital."

"Thanks, I appreciate that."

Grace smiled. "Santi is head of pediatrics, so he calls the shots there. So if he says you stay, you stay."

"Good to know."

Santi added, "That doesn't mean I'm your boss, though."

He wasn't sure why he felt that additional bit of information was needed. Maybe because he didn't want her to think those kisses were from a superior and that she was expected to play along. If he kissed her, he wanted her to kiss him back because she wanted to, not because she felt her job was in jeopardy.

If he kissed her?

Santi needed to get control of himself and fast. He wasn't sure what was going on with him, but this train was beginning to pick up speed. And it wasn't just the normal city-to-city train that meandered along making plenty of stops. One where he could hop off at any time. No, this was a bullet train that didn't stop until it reached its final destination. Which was what? Sex? A relationship?

Carmen's death had almost destroyed him. He couldn't afford to let anyone else get under his skin again. Because losing someone else, either to death or something else, might just be the end of him.

CHAPTER EIGHT

FRIDAY CAME FAR too soon, and Elena was nervous. Really nervous. She hadn't been around horses other than Strato since her accident, and she was halfway afraid it would pull all those memories of pain and despair back to the surface. She remembered doctors telling her how lucky she was that her spinal cord wasn't completely severed.

Lucky. She hadn't thought so.

At first that news had given her a burst of hope that maybe her damaged nerves would find new pathways, and she'd be able to go about her life as she'd done before the accident. From her hospital bed, she read everything she could find on spinal cord injuries. But the more information she took in, and the more time that went by, the more despair she felt. She might have some feeling in her left leg, but once six months hit, she knew it was less and less likely she'd have any miraculous advances.

She tried her hardest during physical therapy, pushing herself beyond her limits, until her doctors talked to her parents, who in turn urged her to slow down, telling her she was going to do more damage to herself.

So with her extra time, she studied. And she studied. And she studied. The doctors on her case were amazed by the amount of information she had amassed in such a short time and the way her brain worked through and retained minute details. One of them suggested she might want to study medicine.

Somehow that resonated. She wanted to be involved in hard cases, cases like hers. The cases where patients needed hope. She might not be able to give it to them, but she would work her ass off trying to find answers. If there was a treatment, she wanted to be the one who helped figure it out.

It was why when Tomás stretched for Sasha and it hurt, her brain immediately tried to sift through the possible explanations.

Now that she was at a permanent location and would be dealing with patient exams on a regular basis, she'd been toying with adding a third wheelchair to her group. One that had the feature of a hydraulic system that would lock her legs and hips in and lift her to a standing position. With that, she could examine patients more efficiently. And since she'd retained some use of her left hip and leg, if her ankle and knee could be braced, she could manage it a little more easily, even though those chairs were designed for people who were fully paraplegic.

She purposely did not wear breeches today, opting for pants that would be totally unsuitable for riding, just so no one thought she was eager to get on. She wasn't.

Strato was her heart horse, and she couldn't imagine another equine taking his place. If she couldn't ride him… Well, she wasn't going to ride. And she knew that her lack of confidence would be transferred to any horse she was on, and horses—being a prey animal and living in a herd—needed a confident leader in order to feel safe.

They were taking the hospital's van, which was equipped with a chair lift, another of their attempts at accessibility. Santi was going to get the children and then swing by her apartment. Doing a last swoosh of mascara and checking her hair, she declared herself ready. Well, not ready, but as ready as she'd ever be.

Almost as soon as she exited the bathroom, her doorbell rang. She closed her eyes. Here it was. The moment of truth.

And if she couldn't hold it together?

She would somehow force herself to remain calm. The last thing she wanted anyone to find out was how very much she missed her horse. Missed riding. Missed her old life.

Making her way to the door, she opened it and found Santi there. He'd exchanged his normal khakis and polo shirt for dark washed jeans that hugged his frame and a rust T-shirt emblazoned with the name of the hippotherapy center. The color brought out the dark tan of his skin and made her struggle to normalize her breathing. And the thought of him volunteering to help people who needed it brought a lump to her throat.

He did that on a daily basis through his job, but this was different. This showed how deeply he loved kids. How much he wanted them to have a good life. This man would make an amazing father, if he'd allow himself to love again.

She had no idea why that thought had popped into her head.

"Hi," she said, her voice a little breathier than she would have liked.

"Hello, yourself. Are you ready?"

"I am."

They just stood there for a minute, neither of them talking, then Santi seemed to realize they should be moving. He stood aside so she could roll out.

Her purse was already slung across the back of her chair. She had her own wheelchair-accessible van, but since the hospital was so close, she rarely used it. There was even a small grocery store located a couple of blocks away, which made it nice. All in all, it was the ideal place to settle down.

If it weren't for her weird attraction to Santi that she just couldn't seem to shake. And thinking about him rocking a child in his arms? That was definitely off-limits.

She got in the van, and they were off. There was eager chatter all around her as three little girls were excitedly talking about seeing horses. She smiled when one of the kids, who was also in a wheelchair, craned her neck to look at her.

"Do you have any stickers on your chair?"

When Elena glanced at the girl's ride, she saw there were stickers from seemingly everywhere she'd been. From animal parks to amusement parks, her chair told a story of what the child liked and places she'd been. Her friend Letizia's chair was similar.

"I don't, but that's a good idea. I like yours a lot."

"Me, too. My mom helps me put them on."

Speaking of moms. There were no parents in the van, so they must trust Santi and the hospital quite a bit to let him take their kids on this outing. And he was comfortable enough around kids to not feel the need for extra support. Or maybe that's what she was here for. She didn't think so, though. It was more like he knew she'd ridden in the past and thought she might want to ride again someday.

She guessed she should have been clearer that she wasn't looking to reenter equestrian activities. Not yet.

If not now, then when? She wasn't getting any younger.

Thirty-two is hardly ancient, Elle.

No, but she wanted to do it on her own terms. Just like in the romance department. Trusting herself to anyone at this juncture was a scary prospect. If it turned out like Renato or her high school boyfriend… Yeah, not something she saw herself doing anytime soon.

It took about fifteen minutes to reach the center. It was beautiful. A big Spanish-style barn with clay roofing tiles and stuccoed block walls, it was geared to stay cool in the heat of the summer. On the front of the building was a hand-painted tile sign. At the top, it read En Alas de Caballo. Just below the name of the center was a watercolor depiction of a child in a wheelchair seated next to a horse, a currycomb in her hand. Next to that appeared the words *Healing Comes in Many Forms*.

She swallowed. It was true. There was physical healing, but there were also many other kinds. Her emotional and psychological healing had taken much longer than that of her physical injuries. And in some ways, it was an ongoing process, even now.

"Okay, everyone ready?"

That was her cue to say no she wasn't, right? There was no way she could do that in front of kids who were chattering about the opportunity to see actual horses. Instead of excitement, though, all she felt was dread.

"Do we get to see your horse?"

Santi smiled. "Actually yes, Billy will be the horse they'll bring in. You'll all get a turn to brush him and pet him. Sound good?"

A cheer went up.

So Santi had told these children about the horse he'd put into the therapy program?

Looking at him, he didn't seem tense about seeing the horse again. Of course, he did say he volunteered at the center, so he got to be with Billy on a regular basis.

Her heart cramped for a second, thinking of Strato and how few times she'd seen him. She made a note to fly to Mallorca the next vacation she had and see her old friend.

Santi got out along with two of the girls, went to the right side of the van and opened the door to the lift, sending it up. He called in to her. "Elle, do you mind helping Margarita get her chair locked into the lift and sending her down?"

She blinked. Not at his shortening her name—which she liked far too well—but at the simple request. She was so used to people being overly accommodating, trying to do things for her that she could do herself, that she was surprised he'd asked her to do anything.

A whoosh of emotion threatened to overwhelm her and their eyes locked for a second. Then two. She had to look away or risk being lost in the warm depths of his irises. It was on the tip of her tongue to thank him, but she didn't want to make things strange, so she smiled instead, forcing a lightness into her voice that she didn't feel. "I'll be happy to."

She went over and had to stretch to unlock the mechanism on the floor that held the girl's chair in place.

"You're very pretty." The girl's voice was quiet and shy, just like it had been when they'd talked about the stickers on her wheelchair.

"Why, thank you, Guida," she said, the nickname coming instinctively as she'd heard other girls call the child that. "I think you're very pretty, too."

Guida rolled over to the lift and expertly backed herself in. She'd been doing this for a while, if not her whole life. "Okay, I'm ready."

Elena locked her in and then pressed the button.

"See you at the bottom," the girl said.

That made her smile. Maybe this trip wouldn't be as terrible as she'd feared. After all, she could focus on the girls and their excitement and let it carry her through whatever horse stuff she'd be required to do.

Santi helped the girl out and sent the lift back up.

This van was slightly different from hers, but it was still fairly easy for her to reach everything. She got in and then pushed the button for it to move to ground level, even though Santi also had a set of controls on the side of the vehicle.

There was a slight bump as it reached the bottom, and he pulled the door open, waiting for her to wheel out. She smiled up at him and he gave her shoulder a slight squeeze that sent goose bumps over her.

His touch made her react in weird ways. Even as he walked beside her toward the door to the center, his hand grazing her upper arm from time to time, accidentally she was sure. But he didn't seem nearly as bothered by those soft brushes as she was.

He pushed a buzzer and identified himself to the voice that came through the speaker. "Hi, it's Santi here with my group."

A mechanism clicked, allowing the door to be opened. He reminded the kids that they couldn't yell or scream or run around the horse. "We have to be very calm, so we don't startle him."

Even though he'd said Billy was a very quiet horse, any equine could be startled and react in unexpected ways. She'd had Strato spook on her any number of times. But at least most of those times she'd kept her seat. And when she had fallen, she'd been able to leap up and continue her ride. Except for that last time.

The tension built again as they entered the building and reached a riding arena that contained a spectator area as well as the place where the actual interaction with the horses would take place.

"This is a little different from traditional hippotherapy, which involves one-on-one treatment of a patient using a horse. Here there are multiple clients in each class. Most of our center's instructors are certified physical therapists who are also certified in the equine portion of the spectrum. It's quite an involved process."

Since Elena knew almost nothing about equine therapy programs, what he'd said kind of went over her head, but she could understand that different programs had different affiliations. At least she assumed they did.

A woman came out of a side door, and she and Santi exchanged traditional Spanish air kisses. The woman was beautiful, with long dark hair, and unlike Elena, she was clad in skin-tight riding breeches that showed off the curve of her hips and backside.

She touched Santi's arm. "So good to see you outside of class time, Santi. And you brought quite the contingent along with you." Her eyes skimmed over the group, pausing on Elena for a moment. "A new student?"

Suddenly she felt ridiculous in her dress pants. She should have at least worn jeans, even if she didn't want to wear breeches. "No, I'm just here as a visitor." She wanted to head off any questions as to her interest in the program.

She only realized how sharply she'd answered when the woman apologized. Great. She was not only dressed inappropriately, she'd evidently turned into a mean girl as well. "It's okay," she said. "I was injured in a riding accident years ago."

"Well, I hope you enjoy your visit." Unlike Elena, the woman who'd been introduced as the program head was nice in a way that was genuine and not artificial. For some reason, it made Elena like her even less.

It's because of Santi. The thought flitted by before she had a chance to stop it.

She was pretty sure he didn't have a girlfriend. He didn't seem the type to kiss someone if he were involved with someone else. But Elena was also fairly certain that the center's program head had a soft spot for the pediatrician. And who could blame her? He was handsome and kind and caring and loved children. All of the things that most women would leap at.

But Elle wasn't even sure she wanted children, at this point. Not that it was something she dwelled on a lot. Oh, she liked kids. And Tomás's case had certainly tugged at her heartstrings, but to carry one inside her body? She pushed the thought away when something twinged inside her.

Her parents would certainly love grandkids, and since she was an only child...

She turned her attention back to the tall woman whose name was evidently Andrea. She was talking about horses and some safety precautions they needed to take. Like not walking behind the horse they were going to bring out in a few minutes.

"Every time a horse takes a step, it activates motor neurons in our bodies. And with each movement he makes, it shifts you, too, so that it's almost like *you're* walking and not the horse. Isn't that cool?"

The girls all nodded.

Great, she was not only gorgeous, she also had mad people skills. Why wouldn't Santi find her attractive? He'd be crazy not to.

Glancing at him, though, she found his eyes weren't on Andrea, they were on her.

Her face turned hot, and she quickly shifted her attention back to the woman in front of them who was demonstrating how to use different brushes and telling them why they were used in the order they were.

"Okay, so are we ready to meet Billy?"

A chorus of yeses went up from the three little girls.

So they really were going to use Santi's horse. What breed had he said he was? Criollo? Or was it just that the horse was similar to one? She couldn't remember.

Suddenly she was curious about Santi's life in Argentina and what his horse would look like.

Andrea sent a text to someone. A minute later, a man entered leading a horse that was shorter than she expected. Probably two hands shorter than her Strato.

But what the horse lacked in height, he made up for in muscle, judging from his wide body and broad chest area. She could see why they were popular with polo players. She assumed they were also used with cattle and livestock. Strato was tall, with long legs and a very sleek body. He was elegant and beautiful. What Billy lacked in elegance he made up for in his kind eyes and ears that were already seeking out the children in front of him. He liked his job. That much was obvious.

The man stopped with the horse toward the front of the arena, a gate standing between the girls and the animal.

Andrea again went over how they needed to approach Billy. "I'm going to let you curry him, one at a time. We'll go through all of the brushes, keeping our hands near the center of his barrel." The man stepped beside the horse and ran his hand over the area they would work on.

She nodded to Santi. "You can go ahead and bring everyone in. If you'll take one child over to Billy and help them brush, Elena and I will stand by the wall in the arena with the rest of the kids, until it's their turn to brush."

"Oh, but..." Her words trailed away. To refuse to participate would seem churlish and would set a terrible example for the kids who were so looking forward to this outing.

Andrea glanced at her as if waiting for her to finish her sentence, but Elena just shook her head.

"Okay, your chairs shouldn't have any problem rolling across the footing, which is shredded tire material. It's cushy on the horse's hooves and is a lot easier for mobility for us humans than moving through sand would be."

They got into the inner sanctum of the arena and Elena found that Andrea was right. It was surprisingly easy to push her chair through the rubber footing, which wasn't deep and was laid over a firm surface. She and Margarita were able to move to where Andrea and the other two girls were waiting.

Santi stood in front of them, legs braced apart, a lime green currycomb in his hand. The color was somehow incongruous with what she knew of him and made her smile. But it somehow just accentuated his strength. His masculinity. She forced herself to swallow. For the millionth time, the word *gorgeous* shimmied through her mind, perking up her nerve endings in a way that was similar to what Andrea had talked about earlier. Only this had nothing to do with the movements of a horse.

"Who wants to go first?" His low tones only threw gasoline onto the smoldering embers in her midsection.

Guida raised her hand more quickly than the other two.

"Okay, let's go. Remember to do everything slowly... quietly." His quick glance at Elena almost made the words sound like they were meant for her.

Fire flared up, licking at everything in its path. She could be pretty damn quiet when she needed to be.

Except he wasn't talking to her, and he certainly wasn't talking about *that*.

Guida was brushing Billy's side, while Santi stood next to the horse, blocking access to the animal's hind-quarters without making it obvious that's what he was doing. It was a smart move. He could still interact with the child, while being a physical barrier to anything that might be of danger to her.

Suddenly she wanted to be over there, having Santi standing next to her, pretending to show her what she already knew, his hand covering hers as he showed her how to stroke it across the animal.

Diablos! What was wrong with her? She almost never got like this around men. Not anymore. Not when she'd already seen what a disaster that could be.

Then it was the next girl's turn. She forced her thoughts back to what was happening, listening with half an ear as Guida excitedly told the third child what it was like to stand next to such a large animal, but that

Billy looked at her as if telling her that he loved her. "He wanted to help me."

And looking at the Criollo, she thought it might be true. The man at the front still held the horse's lead rope, but there was plenty of slack in its length. Billy was standing there quietly because he wanted to, not because he was forced to.

The last girl was a little more nervous but moved over to where Santi was standing. He explained to her what to do and watched carefully as she brushed the roan horse. And sure enough, Billy turned and looked at the child in a way that she remembered Strato looking at her. As if he could see through to her soul.

That would be a dangerous prospect right now. Because Elena wasn't sure what secrets her soul was carrying. Nothing good, she was sure.

Like the other two girls, he showed her how to use the currycomb, the hard-bristled brush and finally the soft brush that was used for that finishing touch and to flick away any dirt the other brushes might have left behind.

He sent the girl back and moved to the other side of the horse, motioning for Elena to come over.

She started to shake her head no, then remembered she needed to be an example to these girls. To show them that they couldn't let their challenges get the best of them.

Like she'd let them get the best of her in this particular area? Gritting her teeth, she rolled around the front of the horse until she sat beside Billy…and Santi.

Probably out of habit, he stood in the same spot he'd been with each child.

Out of a bucket he handed her the curry. "I don't suppose I have to tell you how to use this."

"I think I can remember that much."

She raised the brush and the second she laid her empty hand against Billy's warm side something magical happened. The horse's life and essence seemed to move through her palm and up her arm, carrying something with it.

Healing comes in many forms. The words on the center's sign came back to her. Maybe there really was healing through the touch of a horse.

She began the familiar circular motions of using the curry on Billy, and when she glanced over at him, she caught the wiggle of his bottom lip before he started licking and chewing, a sign of acceptance and understanding in the horse world. She could remember Strato doing the same thing many times as they moved together in the arena. Her horse who loved his work, who was now forced to be a pasture pet, except for the occasional ride that Sandra put on him.

She switched brushes before she was told to, using the hard brush to whisk away the dirt that the curry had raised to the surface. Was it fair to leave Strato in limbo, just because she couldn't ride anymore? The thought caused a pain that was almost unbearable to rise up inside her. She didn't want to give him up. Wasn't sure that she could. And yet he needed activity just like she did to be fulfilled. Maybe some horses were happy with a life of leisure, but she wasn't sure he was.

Billy had a purpose, and from what she saw, he was happy with it. It was there in the forward prick of his ears, the left one swiveling back as he listened for any direction she might give.

Dios, she'd missed this. Missed the touch, the scent of warm skin, the sensation as her finger trailed over shoulder, rib cage and beyond.

She gulped. Was she thinking about horses? Or men?

Santi was watching her, she could feel it, trying to gauge her reaction to Billy. Did she lie and pretend she couldn't stand being here, or did she tell the truth that her joy at being with a horse again was almost unbearable?

The truth. She'd done her best to live by it, no matter how hard that truth was.

She turned with the brush in her hand and looked at the pediatrician. There was an expectancy to his gaze, almost a kind of hope.

"Santi, thank you." She tried to put all the earnestness she could into the words. "I didn't want to come. But I'm so glad I did. I love Billy."

Before she could stop herself, she leaned her right cheek against the horse's side and breathed his scent. The equine's head turned, and warm, soft eyes regarded her with a knowledge that spanned the ages, seeming to know exactly what she'd suffered. Exactly how scared she was to care so much. About him? About Santi? As he blew out a breath, holding very still, she wondered if it even mattered which one. Because maybe… She cared about them both.

And right now—at a stage in her life where she'd

come to accept that things weren't going to change for her—that probably was the most terrifying and exhilarating thing she could imagine.

CHAPTER NINE

THE KIDS WERE dropped back off at the hospital and the only ones left in the van were Santi and Elle.

He hadn't been completely sure about pressuring her to go to En Alas de Caballo. But her reaction had blown him away. And when she'd pressed close to Billy's side as if she never wanted to leave, a wave of raw emotion had rolled over him, and for a second it had been hard to catch his breath or control his feelings. He'd started volunteering at the center not long after Carmen's death, afraid if he couldn't find a way to channel his grief into something useful, he would lose himself in a bottle, or worse.

But in all the time he'd been volunteering, nothing had ever moved him as much as Elle's reaction. To the horse. To him. For a second nothing had been hidden. His attraction to her wasn't one-sided. He saw it in her gaze as it moved over the horse. Over him.

But was it smart?

They sat in the van in silence, before he shifted so he could see her in the mirror. She was gazing at him with that same soft, hopeful look he'd seen at the center.

When she looked at him like that, he didn't care about smart. Or anything else.

He debated long and hard about just dropping her back off at her place. But something wouldn't let him.

So he decided to take the plunge and see if what he thought was true actually was.

"Elle, invite me back to your place."

Her teeth came down on her lip, and she hesitated. "Are—are you sure?"

Wasn't that supposed to be his line? But the fear and trepidation in her voice was the same fear she'd had when he'd first asked her to go with him and the kids. And look how that had turned out.

He got out of his seat and climbed back to where she was sitting in the van and squatted beside her chair. Taking her hands in his, he leaned forward and kissed her.

A sharp pang went through him as their lips lingered, as the kiss slowly deepened. His fingers burrowed into the hair at the back of her head, just as her mouth opened.

Dios! He accepted her unspoken invitation, his tongue sliding forward to explore the warm recesses of her mouth. Heat drilled into his chest and began a slow slide toward his lower regions. This van was plenty big to...

No. If this was going to happen, he wanted her in a bed, where he could touch and explore her to his heart's content.

He pulled back, his breathing not quite steady. "Would you like to ask me that question again?"

This time she smiled and leaned forward to kiss him again before saying, "No, I don't want to ask it. And yes, I'd like to invite you back to my apartment. Will you come?"

His thumb and forefinger curled around her chin as his mouth crooked sideways. "Why don't we go and find out. I'm pretty sure I will. Maybe even more than once."

That made her laugh. "Okay, that's not quite what I meant, and you know it."

"Oh, but I couldn't resist." He kissed her again. "I still can't."

"Me, either." She glanced out the window. "But I'd rather get out of the parking lot before someone sees us necking here like two schoolkids."

A quick shadow of something went through him, before he chased it away with a laugh. "Do you want me to drive over to your place?"

"Let's just go through the park, if that's okay? It's not far, and I'd rather the van not be seen parked in front of my apartment."

That was the second time she'd indicated she was worried about them being seen together. Shouldn't he be feeling the same thing?

He surely should. But for the first time in a long time, he didn't really care about anything except getting this woman where he could kiss her some more.

"Okay. The park it is." He forced a smile. "You don't plan on racing me, do you?"

"Afraid you'll lose?"

He was. And it had nothing to do with a race. But that wasn't something he was going to think about right now. He'd been with a couple of women since Carmen had died and had come through the experience pretty much unscathed.

But something was different about this woman. Or was that just his libido talking? He climbed out of the driver's side door and waited for her to use the lift to let herself out. Then he locked up the van and left the keys in the drop box just inside the door of Aelina. He caught up with her just as she was starting on the running path. The sun shone down on her head, making her hair gleam with auburn highlights, and the tip of her nose was pink, probably from her time running her chair up and down the jogging paths in the mornings.

She was gorgeous, but with a vulnerability that he hadn't really noticed until today. She was good at her job, and she knew it. But she had some fears that were probably deep-seated. He'd seen that today at the riding center.

Well, that was okay, because he had some fears, too.

It took about five minutes to get to her apartment, which was the last one in the row of energy-efficient residences. She unlocked the door and pushed it open, motioning for him to go on in. He did, waiting for her to join him and shut the door.

"Do you want anything? A drink?"

No, he didn't. He didn't want anything right now, but her. "I don't. But if you want one, then go ahead."

"No, I don't, either." She seemed to take a deep breath. "I need you to know the last time I tried this with someone, it was a disaster."

He frowned, he had visions of someone hurting her

either intentionally or unintentionally and a fire lit in his belly. "Hey, you call all the shots here. If something isn't the way you need it to be, you tell me, okay? If you want me to stop, all you have to do is say the word."

Because by God, he was not going to be the reason she told the next man in her life that their time together had been a disaster. He wanted to make this as good for her as it was going to be for him.

And he already knew it would be good. No matter how it happened, or how this played out. If there was some physical limitation besides her paralysis, they would work it out…find another way. He could think of any number of ways that they could both gain pleasure.

"I don't want to stop. It's just that my legs…"

"Your legs, your arms, your face—everything about you is beautiful and perfect and makes me want you more than I should."

She smiled. "Same."

"I have beautiful legs?" His brows went up.

"Well, I don't know yet, but I'm pretty certain that everything about you is perfect, too." She grinned. "And just for the record, you look really hot in those jeans."

"I do, do I?" He didn't know about hot, but there was a certain amount of heat that was beginning to settle in areas that were going to make themselves known pretty quickly. "Do you need to do anything before I carry you off to bed?"

"You don't have to carry me. I've been getting myself in and out of bed all by myself for a long time."

"This isn't about what you can or can't do. I know you're very capable. But what if I *want* to carry you in there and toss you onto the bed? And kiss you until you can't breathe?"

Her eyes heated. "I think I might like that. I think I might like that very much."

"In that case." He reached down and scooped her into his arms as she gave a little shriek of surprise.

Her arms went around his neck, and she leaned forward to kiss him, planting her lips on his mouth, his chin, nibbling at his jawline. Maybe she'd be the one kissing him until he couldn't breathe, because right now she was doing a pretty good job of lighting his nerve endings on fire.

"Bedroom?"

"Down the hallway, last door on the right."

He carried her, loving the way her fingers toyed with the hair at his nape. Hair that was still a little too long at the moment, but she didn't seem to mind. Those little brushes of warmth against the back of his neck were causing gooseflesh to break out over his arms, his chest. He tightened his grip, finding the door and pushing it open with his shoulder.

Despite his threat of tossing her onto the bed, he instead leaned over and peeled back the covers before setting her down with infinite care, making sure her head was nestled in her pillows. "Okay?"

She shook her head, and a jolt went through him.

"Did I hurt you?"

"No, you're acting like I'm going to break. I won't, you know."

He sat on the edge of the bed and looked down at her, before his finger trailed a course from just under her chin, down her throat, over the swell of one of her breasts.

She gasped, arching up into him in a way that made his cock clench. He wasn't sure exactly where that line of sensation ended, but he intended to find out by the end of their session. But for now... His fingers tunneled under her blouse and bra, finding a nipple, which was already tight and hard. Her eyes closed reflexively before opening again.

As he watched her, his fingers tickled along her rib cage, making her squirm. He liked that: watching her react. He stroked down her belly, ending where her waistband stopped his exploration. "Tell me what you like, *querida*."

"I like everything. Everything you're doing."

He leaned over and kissed her, letting his lips trail over her features as he unbuttoned her pants and tugged the zipper down. "Wait right there," he whispered against her mouth.

"I'm not going anywhere."

Her breath washed across him, warm and moist and so, so sexy.

As a doctor, he knew all the clinical stuff about paralysis, but every person was different, and he needed to approach things with care. "Anything special that I should know?"

He worked on sliding her pants, admiring her lacy undergarments before hooking his fingers under the elastic and inching those down her legs as well. He felt her shiver when his hand slid down her left thigh.

She waited until he'd gotten her pants off before

answering. "I might need some lubrication. It's in the drawer of my nightstand." She hesitated. "And I—I can't sit on you."

His head tilted. Why had she said that? Of course he knew that she couldn't. "I don't expect you to."

"You might not now, but if later you wanted me to try... I—I couldn't."

He got it in an instant. The reason she'd said her last encounter had been a disaster, and he cursed inwardly at the idiot who'd even thought to ask. "I don't need you to, Elle. I just want to love you. This is about both our pleasure, not just mine."

He got the lubricant out of the drawer and laid it on the bed. He then tugged off his jeans, getting a condom out and setting it next to the lubricant.

Her eyes on him were eager, with a hungry look in them that made his insides squeeze together. He recognized that look and it made him swallow back a memory or two of his own. He was not going to let that ruin things for him. For her.

Pulling his shirt over his head, he threw it to the side.

"I was right," she whispered.

His head tilted. "What?"

"You're perfect."

That made him smile. Not so perfect. He stretched out on the bed next to her, still in his briefs. Her shirt had ridden up her smooth belly, laying it bare to his gaze.

He put his palm on it, letting the warmth of her skin seep into him. "You're so incredibly soft." His hand trailed across her, his finger dipping into her belly button. "Can you feel this?"

"Yes." Her voice was breathy with a current of desire that made his body react.

He moved to her right thigh… "Here?"

Her eyes closed. "No, but I can imagine it."

"Where do you want me to touch you?"

"Everywhere. It doesn't matter where I can feel or not feel. I like seeing your fingers running over my body."

"I like that too."

He sat up and slid her shirt up her torso, and she pushed herself up with her arms so he could pull it over her head. Then he reached behind her and undid the clasp on her bra, letting it slide down her forearms.

Unable to resist, he leaned down to take one of her nipples into his mouth, the sweet scent of her skin acting as an aphrodisiac. He pulled, hearing her gasp as she arched into him.

He liked that. Far too much. Moving to the other side, he repeated the action, loving the low moan she made, one hand coming off the bed to hold him against her.

"*Dios*, that feels so, so good."

He took his time, laying her back on the bed and kissing her. Shoulders, breasts, belly, before licking his way up to her chin. He took his time, swallowing each reaction, every sound she made.

"Tell me when you're ready, *querida*."

"Now, I'm ready now."

He kissed her mouth, tongue plunging in. She closed around him, and they remained like that for what sccmcd like an eternity, before he couldn't stand it any longer. Getting up, he kicked off his briefs, then sheathing himself and using the lubricant, he climbed back onto the bed and gently separated her thighs and levered himself on top of her, balancing on his forearms. Looking down at her, while trying his best to control his needs, he sought her eyes and looked into them. "Are you okay?"

"Yes. I'm more than okay."

The press of his pelvis against hers, the solid steadiness of his weight, was almost more than she could stand. He'd already built her up to a fever pitch that she hadn't felt since her accident.

She knew the second he entered her, not by feel, but by the way her back moved against the soft sheets.

Heaven. She was in heaven.

He set up a slow, steady pace, leaning down to whisper to her. Nonsensical things that had no meaning in and of themselves but added to the friction of his body against hers, the shivery need in the touch of his lips against her ear. It served as a pathway that connected her brain to her nerve endings.

That steady push and pull against her body was like waves of the ocean that tugged her back and then pushed her again to shore. It caused a spiraling need in her belly. Her nipples, every area of her body that could feel, and even those that could not, were being nudged toward something.

He wasn't asking her to do anything she couldn't do.

He was helping her. Helping her feel. Helping her know that sex was still so very good.

Her arms wound around his neck after her fingernails trailed up his back in a soft scrape that was rewarded with a rough groan.

"What you do to me, *querida*."

What she did to him? Oh, man, what he was doing to her was the issue. He was bewitching her. Using some kind of sorcery to ratchet her to heights she hadn't achieved in a long, long time.

His rhythm changed and she used the muscles of her torso to move along with him, the scrape of the dusting of his chest hair over her nipples driving her crazy. Making her reach toward something.

She wanted…she wanted…

Dios! Some kind of lightning struck her, deleting her thoughts in an instant, until all there was, was a blast of sensation.

Her body couldn't be still, her arms tightening, head arching back into the pillow.

Santi gave a shout, the muscles in his neck straining under her fingers, and she knew he'd reached his own climax.

And heavens, it was every bit as good as it used to be when she could feel her orgasm. Every bit as fulfilling.

His body slowly relaxed against hers, lips nuzzling her neck in a way that tickled, making her giggle.

"You okay?"

"Mmm, sorry. Can't talk right now."

When he stiffened against her, she realized her words could have been taken more than one way, so she was quick to add, "Yes, I'm okay. Just trying to find my way back down that mountain. I—I'd forgotten just how good…"

A weird emotion went through her, and she had to stop talking.

Don't, Elle. God, please don't fall in love with him.

Why not? The voice whispered in the darkest recesses of her being. *You are worthy of love. Don't settle for anything less.*

Santi rolled off her and for a panicked second she thought he might try to pull her on top of him, but he didn't. He just lay there with his hands behind his head. He didn't say anything for a minute or two, then his hand touched hers and squeezed, causing her to relax and take a deep breath. Her muscles went slack with a deep sense of contentment. It was okay. There was no rejection here. She was safe.

Before she realized what was happening, her lids slid closed and that same sense of relaxation spread over her, causing blank spots in her brain that slowly moved to take over the parts that were responsible for thinking. When her muscles jerked, she realized she was falling asleep, and she made an effort to open her eyes again, finding him leaning over her.

He kissed her forehead. "Go to sleep. It's okay."

"You'll still be here when I wake up?"

There seemed to be a hesitation in his voice, but she was so drowsy and comfortable, she must have been mistaken, because the last thing she heard before unconsciousness took control of her was his deep voice.

"Yes. I'll be here."

CHAPTER TEN

HOURS WENT BY. Watching her sleep, Santi felt something kick him in the gut. A deep wrenching sense of guilt.

How often had he watched Carmen sleep just like this, unable to get enough of it? So many times. Times he could never get back again.

Carmen. He swallowed.

And now he was lapping this up like…

Diablos. There was no room for anyone else in his life. No room for another possibility of loss. This was why he didn't sleep with women on a regular basis. He'd always been afraid of finding himself in a spot just like this one: where emotions slid in and played games with his psyche, making him think things were possible that weren't.

He'd vowed he wasn't getting involved with anyone ever again. The pain when Carmen had died had been debilitating. That was why he'd put his emotional energy into his work and volunteering rather than a relationship, not that he'd ever come this close to that familiar precipice.

And hell, he didn't want to go over it. Not again.

He needed to get out of here. But he'd promised her he would stay.

What an idiot. Sex was one thing. Making promises of any kind was another thing entirely.

But she looked so sweet. So totally at ease, all of her defenses lowered.

He had a feeling that more than one of his defenses had caved in as well, and he had to get home to rebuild them, before it was too late.

It's already too late.

Maldicion! Maybe it was. But that didn't mean he couldn't pull back and push Reset on everything. But in a way that wouldn't hurt her.

At least he hoped it wouldn't. Better to do it now than later, though.

And maybe it wasn't even an issue. Maybe she wasn't interested in anything permanent, either. The other two women he'd been with hadn't been.

A murmur came from beside him and a hand reached out, touching the bed before finding his arm. Her eyes slowly slid open, squinting against the light that poured through the window, the warm brown of them threatening to do terrible things to his insides. He wanted to forget everything and roll over and spend another hour or two with her, drowning out his thoughts. His regrets.

But to do so would only make what he had to do harder.

Softening it with a smile, he pulled from her touch and hurriedly slid out of bed. Hauling on his briefs before facing her again, he tried to squelch the rush of desire that had poured over him. "I need to get back home. My housekeeper is used to my weird hours and will have taken care of Sasha, but it's not fair to leave her to do all of it while I…"

What could he say? While I fall in love? While I rip apart everything that was once Carmen's and hand it to someone else?

Elena pushed herself up with her arms, the blankets falling to her waist, baring her torso.

Don't look.

He didn't, but he already knew every inch of her. It had somehow been burned into his brain.

Into his soul.

Her chin went up, but there was a suspicious tremble to her lower lip that told him he'd hurt her, despite everything. "I understand. I'll see you back at the hospital."

He sat on the bed and touched her cheek. "Elle, I want you to know—"

"Don't. I knew what this was when I invited you here. It's fine." She angled away from his touch. "But just so we're clear, this isn't going to happen again."

Those were the words he should have said. Instead, he'd been about to say something that would have put paid to all of his efforts to walk away.

Instead, Elena had saved him from himself. And for that he was grateful. He yanked on the rest of his clothes without looking back at her. Then his phone on the nightstand rang before he could get out of there. The ringtone said it was the hospital.

Then Elena's went off, too. A sense of foreboding

went over him that had nothing to do with what had happened in that bed.

They both picked them up at the same time and answered.

Her eyes met his as he heard words he'd hoped not to hear.

It was Tomás. He'd taken a turn for the worse.

He hung up, and before he could say anything, she said, "Go. I'll meet you over there."

"Are you sure?"

A tiny thread of anger burned in her eyes. "I've been doing this for a very long time. I think I can manage without you."

The spear thrust deep and hit its mark. She was right. She had. And she would continue to long after the memories of last night had faded.

"I'll see you over there."

When Santi arrived at the hospital, rushing up to the third floor, he could hear Tomás's loud, pain-filled voice before he even got there. "They promised! They said I would be all right. That I wouldn't need a wheelchair."

He entered the room to find a nurse, trying to hold him in bed.

"Tomás, stop it." He laid his hand on the boy's shoulder, and he quieted almost immediately. "Tell me what's wrong."

"My legs. They have those pins and needles things, and this time it's not going away. And I can't feel my feet anymore. At all."

Hell. His surgery was supposed to be later today. "Lie back, so I can examine you."

Tears streaked the teen's face, and Santi knew what it had cost Tomás to let that emotion through. The sullenness of those first several meetings had given way to fear. The pain had to be unbearable. Santi didn't need to ask him what his pain levels were. He already knew. They were every bit as high as Santi's emotional pain was right now.

Being with Elle had brought everything roaring back, and the waves of it were still crashing over him despite leaving her house. And soon he would have to face her all over again.

Five minutes later, she wheeled into the room and took in the scene, her face showing nothing of the turmoil Santi was experiencing.

"His legs," she said.

"Yes. There's no sensation in his feet and the numbness is working its way up his legs."

"Did you call neuro?"

"Yes. Dr. Avario is en route now, and they're going to prep him for surgery now rather than wait."

"I agree." She wheeled over to the head of the bed, where Tomás was staring at the ceiling, his tears drying into white salty tracts, his face set in lines of resignation.

"You told me this wouldn't happen. That they could fix me." His voice was softer than Santi had ever heard it.

"They're going to take you to surgery as soon as Dr. Avario gets here. Your body is still growing and stretching your spinal cord. So we need to get it untethered."

"I can't feel my feet anymore. I can't even walk. I tried and fell."

"I know. I'm hoping surgery will return feeling to them."

His head turned on its pillow, fixing them both with a look that Santi would never forget. A quiet accusation that wound around him, squeezing the breath from him. "You promised. Just like all the others."

He had. He'd promised so many things.

To Tomás. To Carmen.

He couldn't make promises to anyone else. Not right now.

Where the hell was Avario?

Almost as if summoned, the man appeared in the doorway, his cool, unruffled manner in place, just as it always was.

"Well, young man, it sounds like we need to get you in and fix your back." He repeated the physical exam that Santi had just done, but it didn't bother him. He was the same way. He wanted to see for himself what the progression was.

He glanced at Santi. "Surgical suite prepped?"

"It's ready, there's a team waiting to get started."

Dr. Avario motioned him over to the side before asking, "Perfusionist?"

"Yes. He's ready in case you need to put him on bypass."

Tomás's Fontan circulation presented a big challenge for any type of surgery. And this one would be tricky, and it was hard to tell how long Tomás would need to be under anesthesia. Or exactly what they'd find once they got in there. Or if there would be more surgeries down the road.

"Okay, let's get him in there. Thanks for coming in." His gaze swept to include Elena. "Both of you. Without your diagnosis, we might not have found this in time."

Elena smiled, and there was still no sign of what had transpired in her bedroom before he left. "That's what I'm here for. Working on the hard cases."

Was that a reminder that he was one of the hardest cases yet? Or that she was here for the patients and not for him?

Well, of course she was. They hadn't even known who the other was when they met at Caitlin and Javier's wedding. At the time he'd been glad of that. Hadn't wanted to know her name.

Dios, that seemed like so long ago. But in reality it had been less than a month. A month in which so much had happened.

"What about Sasha?" Tomás was still looking daggers at him. "You said she'd be here when I got out of surgery."

Those daggers weren't nearly as sharp as the ones he was using on himself. He'd been such a fool in so many ways. To think that he could walk away from Elle like he had the two women before her. Somehow this wasn't going to be nearly that easy. Or as painless.

"I know I did. And she will be. As soon as they wheel you out, I'm going to go pick her up and bring her back here."

It would give him a reason to get out of here and not have to face Elena's chilly silence.

Despite his best efforts, despite his saying she was in charge, he feared he'd broken that promise as well. In the end, he hadn't been able to be vulnerable and lay himself emotionally bare the way she had. Not once he'd come back to his senses.

He couldn't allow anything like that to happen again. Because he already knew a truth that his heart was keeping tucked in a quiet corner. Away from his mind. Away from anything that might try to crush it and stop it from growing.

In spite of all of his efforts and wrangling and arguments. He'd fallen in love. Again. And Santi had no idea what to do about it.

While Santi went to pick up his dog, Elena hurriedly packed up the stuff in her temporary office.

Temporary. Just like last night with Santi had been.

She ached in a way that had nothing to do with a physical sense of pain, but something that was lodged deep inside her. If she didn't deal with it, it would fester and turn something that had been beautifully fulfilling into something dark and ugly. Something like she'd experienced with Renato years ago.

It could turn her bitter.

But only if she let it.

Instead, she needed to accept it for what it was. A one-night stand that had blown her expectations out of the water.

She slumped in her chair for a moment as a wave of anguish went through her. Why did it have to be Santi who awoke those feelings in her? Why not some random man in some random place. Other than her bed.

She frowned. Except Santi was some random man. Wasn't he?

No. He was a man who was still in love with his dead wife. She'd seen it in his eyes as she'd reached for him. He'd almost recoiled away. And the sadness and fear she'd seen in him had crushed any hope she might have of a meaningful relationship with him.

Was that what she'd expected when she invited him home? Despite her words to the contrary?

She didn't know. All she knew was he hadn't been able to get away from her fast enough when they'd been prepping for Tomás's surgery. She knew he had to get Sasha, but his attitude matched what she'd seen in her apartment. He didn't want to be near her. And she shouldn't want to be near him.

Because right now her emotions were so tangled up that she couldn't separate truth from fantasy.

And that's what their encounter had been right? A fantasy? One where the handsome prince carried her over the threshold and promised to love her forever? Or rode off into the sunset to live happily ever after.

Santi had already had that happy ending with one person and it looked like he wasn't going to be able to have it with anyone else besides his late wife.

So she would just put that from her mind and pull herself back to reality.

With that in mind, she finished putting her laptop in her bag and the few other items she'd accumulated onto her desk. It would take her a few trips to get things up there. But from what Dr. Avario had said, surgery would take a couple of hours at least. She dreaded seeing Santi again. But that was the reality of it. She was going to have to see him. For as long as she remained at Aelina.

What if she didn't stay? What if she went back to rotating from hospital to hospital? Or went back to the island where she grew up.

Yes, running looked very attractive right now. Too attractive.

She wasn't going to make any decisions now, though. Not until she'd had time to sit back and think about everything that had happened. To decide if she could move past it, or if it was going to continually cause her pain.

But for now, she would do what she had to do to keep functioning. And that began with removing herself from his realm.

With that, she headed for the elevator with her first load of items. Pressing the button for the fifth floor, and watching the doors as they closed, she felt like she was also closing the door on that episode in her bedroom and entering a new space mentally. One that she hoped was devoid of anything involving the handsome pediatrician. If that didn't help, then she was going to make a decision every bit as hard as the one she'd made when she quit trying to regain the use of her legs. She would turn the page on this chapter and start her story all over again. A story that had no place for Santi or the idea of a forever love.

An hour later, Elena was in a waiting room. One where Santi and Sasha sat a few feet from her. Neither of them said much, although she greeted Sasha with a quick hug. Santi was right to have picked up the pup. Right now, Tomás and his well-being were far more important than heart-to-heart conversations or talks about where she and Santi went from here.

She said nothing about clearing out her office. And if she was honest with herself, she didn't think she could bear to see the relief in Santi's eyes when he found out she was no longer housed on the third floor. She only hoped she would be long out of sight when he realized. But right now, all she was going to do was think about Tomás. At least that was her hope.

Dios. She hoped the teen regained use of his legs. It would be agonizing for him to have to face one more crisis in his life after he'd suffered so much already.

Letizia came in, saving her from sitting in awkward silence. "How's he doing?"

"No word yet, but it's only been an hour."

"That is one brave kid."

Elle lifted a shoulder. "I think he's one scared kid. He doesn't have a choice of whether to be brave or not. And he certainly doesn't deserve this."

"Do any of us deserve the suffering we go through?"

She was keenly aware that her friend had parked herself to include Santi in the conversation.

Santi was someone else who had endured something no one deserved to go through. His wife had suffered and died. And she was pretty sure a piece of Santi had died with her. Like the part of his heart that might have allowed him to fall in love again. Or to have a relationship like the one he'd had with his late wife. If so, she couldn't imagine anything sadder. Her brief relationship with her professor had soured her, but it hadn't killed anything inside her. Maybe that wasn't so with Santi.

Last night certainly seemed to bear that out. Not that she thought she'd be the one to prove to him that life could still be good after surviving a trauma like that. But she hoped he could find someone who could.

Her heart cramped at the thought of him with someone else. With anyone else.

Not good, Elle. Not good.

"No. No one deserves to suffer," she murmured. "But I hope Tomás can get through this. Not only that. I hope he can get his own family. One who won't return him, saying that the challenge of having him in their home was too much for them."

Like her finding someone who didn't think the challenges of loving her were too much for them?

"I've been thinking about Tomás. A lot."

Elena hadn't been aware that her friend knew that much about the teen. But there was something in her eyes.

"You have?"

Santi hadn't said anything, but she could tell he was listening to every word Letizia said.

"He deserves a better chance than the one he's getting." Her friend clasped her hands in her lap. "I'm thinking of applying to be a foster parent. Actually, I've been toying with the idea for a long time. Every time the group home brings a kid to the hospital, my mind returns there. Would either of you be willing to serve as a reference, if I decide to move forward?"

This was why she'd come down to sit with them. A prickling began deep in her eyes and radiated outward. "Of course I will. I'd be honored, Leti."

"I would, too."

The deep baritone tones came from beside her, causing that wrenching sensation in her heart to happen all over again. So he'd serve as a reference as long as he didn't have to commit his heart.

Stop it!

"Thank you both." Her mentor looked from one to the other. "Do you mind if I sit here with you until Tomás is out of surgery?"

"Of course not." It would be a relief actually to have a buffer. To have someone who could keep hard subjects from coming up. Who could keep Santi from trying to issue another awful apology that cut deeper than any scalpel known to man.

And who could keep her from thinking or saying things she might someday come to regret.

Like *I love you*?

Oh, God. Please, no. Please don't fall in love with a man who seems incapable of loving you back.

That voice was inside her, whispering that it was already too late. That the care and sensual way he'd made love to her last night had caused her to hope for something she'd long thought was beyond her reach. Like riding Strato.

But was it? She'd seen firsthand at On Horses' Wings that it wasn't out of the realm of possibility. It was just her fear that had allowed her to believe it was.

Maybe it was easier that way. Easier not to hope for something that might cause disappointment or anguish.

She glanced over at Santi to see that he was reading something on his phone. And she was shocked to realize his proud profile was already burned into her brain.

The man was the whole package. He loved his work. Loved the kids he worked with. Loved his dog.

The only thing he didn't love, evidently, was her.

Those words turned over and over in her head until she couldn't stand it anymore. "I'm going to get some coffee. Does anyone else want some?"

"Nothing for me," said Letizia.

"A coffee sounds great. But I can get them."

"Nope, I need to move, so I'll go. How do you want it?"

Too late she realized that last question could be misconstrued. It was there in the narrowing of his eyes. In the way his fingers tightened on his phone.

"Black."

"Okay." He liked his coffee unadorned. Like his life? Devoid of anything that might add flavor or color to it? *Diablos.* She was reading way too much into everything.

When he tried to hand her money, she shook her head. "I have a machine that uses pods in my office. I'll just make the coffees there."

Except she'd forgotten that she'd already packed her office up and hauled her stuff to the fifth floor. She hadn't set her coffee machine up yet. But she wasn't about to retract her words. So she wheeled down to the cafeteria and picked up two coffees. Hers a skinny vanilla latte and his a dark, opaque brew that made her shiver. Light didn't always vanquish the night. Her optimism on most days couldn't always erase someone else's pain, and it shouldn't. But, oh, how she wished it could.

What she did know, however, was that she couldn't let whatever dark currents that swirled inside Santi quench the joy she'd found in living life to the fullest.

Even if it meant steering clear of him now and for the rest of her life.

CHAPTER ELEVEN

HER OFFICE HAD been cleared out.

He'd gone to see her when Letizia had contacted him again for a reference after their talk yesterday.

A moment of panic went through him, and he pulled out the chair she'd replaced under the desk and sat in it for a minute. As far as he knew she'd been in here yesterday. She'd certainly stayed in the waiting room for the rest of the time, until they'd gotten word on Tomás.

Had she lied to him about staying at Aelina? Had his attitude done something to make her decide to leave the hospital?

It made him think of the professor from her past who had treated her with such insensitivity.

And really, had Santi done any better by her?

Probably not. His head hadn't been in the best of places after waking up in her bed. It still wasn't. There was a lot of junk in there that needed to be separated and sorted, but he just didn't have the emotional energy or desire to do it right now.

And if he never did?

Honestly, it might be easier if he didn't. Life had

moved along pretty damn smoothly for the last couple of years. Until Elle had come along and made him feel things he hadn't felt in a very long time. Hadn't *wanted* to feel in a very long time.

Tomás had come out of surgery with flying colors and as soon as he woke up, he said the pain in his legs was gone. And his toes and feet were tingling in a way that said the nerve endings were reviving. He hadn't needed to go on bypass, which was another good thing.

And he'd been so happy to see Sasha when he woke up. Said that she was good luck for him.

He didn't know about good luck, but Letizia seemed to be following through with what she'd said in the waiting room. And if it panned out, that boy would be with one of the best, most competent people he knew. And she had a dog of her own. A big Labradoodle that would be the answer to his desire to have a dog. The stars certainly seemed to be lining up in the teen's favor. Finally.

If only they could line up that way for him.

He decided to call Letizia under the guise of telling her he'd received the document and see if she volunteered any information on Elena.

Maldizion! If he'd somehow hurt her...

Before he could, however, his phone rang, sending his heart into overdrive. When he looked at the readout, however, he saw that the caller was Grace.

"Hello?"

"Hi, Santi. It's Grace."

Despite his earlier thoughts, he smiled. "I can see that from my caller ID."

"Smart ass! I hadn't heard back from you about my

and Diego's renewal ceremony on Friday and wanted to make sure you were coming."

Hell, he'd totally forgotten about that. "Sorry. It slipped my mind. Of course I'll be there."

He could have made up an excuse, but Grace was pretty intuitive. She'd know if he were lying. But right now, the last thing he wanted to go through was witnessing yet another set of vows.

You're not "going through" anything. This is about Grace and Diego. Not you.

"Great. Do you want me to seat you and Elena together?"

His brain froze for a few seconds before he was able to figure out an answer. "Why would you do that?"

"Uh… I don't know. I thought maybe…" There was a pause. "Never mind. Forget I asked that."

"Okay. I didn't realize seats were assigned."

"They're not really, but we're not having a huge contingent of guests, so I was trying to organize things a bit. But that's probably not a good idea. Sit wherever you'd like. Gotta go. See you Friday, if not before."

"Sounds good."

With that the line went dead, leaving him to wonder if Elena had told her about what happened between them. The women seemed to have become friends, but hell, he didn't want their night together making the rounds.

He could call the diagnostician and ask her outright, but right now he didn't want to hear her voice. Didn't want to ask her if she was still at Aelina or if she were out of his life forever.

His chest constricted until it was hard to breathe.

So he called Letizia, like he'd planned to do.

She answered on the first ring. "Hi, Santi. I take it you got the request for a reference form. Did you change your mind?"

"About?"

"About giving me a reference. What else would I mean?"

"Nothing." He needed to get more rest or something. He hadn't felt himself since sleeping with Elena, and he didn't know why.

Well… He knew. He just didn't want to examine the reasons or do anything about them. Even if he'd gotten emotionally entangled with her, it didn't mean he had to act on it or allow it to drag him to the bottom of that particular pool. Maybe it would even be easier if she really had moved on to another place of employment. Out of sight, out of mind, wasn't that what they said?

Except, that hadn't been true about Carmen, had it? And he had a feeling it wouldn't be true of Elena, either.

What a huge, huge mess he'd made. Of everything.

"Are you okay, Santi?"

"Yes, why wouldn't I be?"

"I don't know, you just seemed out of sorts yesterday in the waiting room."

He knew he had. He'd caught several of Elena's sideways glances. He'd pretended to be enthralled by something on his phone. Which was a big fat nothing. His screen had been blank. Just like the screen on his heart. For six long years it had been a dark hole that he'd stared down into instead of looking up at the life going on around him.

"I was just worried about Tomás." He needed to bring up Elena's empty office but had no idea how to word it without giving her some of the same ideas that Grace evidently had.

"I know you were. I bet it's a lot quieter down in pediatrics since Elena left."

His whole being seemed to ice over, making it hard to move his lips. "She left?"

"Of course. You didn't know? Her office down there was only temporary, remember? She's up on the fifth floor now. I'm surprised she didn't say something."

The sense of relief came out of nowhere, weighing him down and pinning him in place. "I didn't. But yes, I did remember her permanent office was going to be up there."

With Dario. The flirt.

The fact that a move to the fifth floor hadn't been what had popped into his head when he'd first arrived to find her gone was telling. He expected the worst out of situations many times, even though he'd denied it time and time again to those who cared about him. This was another of those cases, where he'd assumed the worst, even when it hadn't happened.

But her leaving wouldn't be the worst thing. Wasn't that what he'd just finished convincing himself of?

Maybe she'd even be better off with someone like Dario than with him.

"So the reference. You're going to fill it out for me? I've spoken to the group home's director and told her

I was going to apply for guardianship of Tomás at the very least, but I asked her to keep it between us for the moment. I don't want to get his hopes up, just to have them crushed if my application isn't approved."

"Anyone who knows you knows how competent you are. In every area. I can't imagine this being any different."

"Thanks, Santi. *De tus labios a los oídos de Dios.*"

From his lips to God's ears. That saying was pretty ironic, since his lips had murmured prayers during Carmen's sickness that had never seemed to reach the ears of any deity. But that hadn't meant he hadn't tried. Time and time again, only to be met with stony silence. And suffering. And, in the end, death.

"I wouldn't count on me for that, Letizia."

After a few more minutes of conversation involving Tomás and the medical needs and challenges the boy had, they said goodbye. And Santi found himself murmuring the first quiet words to God that he'd uttered in over six years. And this time, it wasn't for himself or for Carmen. Or for Elena. It was for a teenage boy who'd gotten so few breaks in his life.

He and Carmen had at least had three years of happiness before her death. And if she were up there looking down at him, she probably wasn't thrilled with what she saw of his life. His days had been spent working harder than he should. And of being far less happy than most people were.

And yet, what could he do about it?

Maybe for a start he could go to Grace and Diego's vow renewal ceremony and be genuinely happy for them, rather than wallowing in his own self-pity. He could start looking outside and enjoying some sunrises and spend his jogging time being thankful for the good things in his life.

Like Elena?

No, she wasn't in his life in a real way. Maybe because he hadn't allowed her to be. But what he did know was that he wasn't going to impulsively jump into something that might bring both of them grief. What if they weren't compatible?

From what he'd seen, he didn't think that was a real issue. But he couldn't afford to hurt her by trying to move on from Carmen and failing. So what he had to do was spend some time really thinking about what he wanted and didn't want out of life.

And then he needed to act, or he needed to put it out of his mind and his heart. Once and for all.

"Hey, you." Grace popped her head around the door of Elena's office. "Are you busy?"

"Not right now, come in." The truth was, she hadn't been nearly as busy as she'd expected to be, and it gave her far too much time to think and mope around about things she couldn't change.

Grace dropped into one of the chairs. "I meant to come by yesterday after talking to Santi but got too busy."

She'd spoken to Santi? About what?

"Okay…"

"I wanted to make sure our plans to make the ceremony accessible are on target. We're planning to construct a kind of wooden boardwalk that goes from the parking area across the beach and widens as it goes between the rows of seating, so that wheelchairs can park next to the seats without hindering the flow of traffic."

Elena smiled. "That sounds perfect. Thank you for doing that. I would have made it to the ceremony even if I had to stay on the asphalt of the parking area."

"That would make me incredibly sad. I want you there with everyone else." She hesitated. "Speaking of which, I asked Santi if he wanted me to seat you together, and he got kind of weirded out. I'm sorry if I stepped out of line. I don't want to pry, I just thought you guys were getting along really well. I'd even hoped…"

Grace's brows went up in question and Elena shook her head.

"I actually did, too. But you know, love is one of those things I've never been able to figure out."

She and Grace stared at each other for a long minute as she realized she'd let the cat out of the bag. But keeping that word to herself had been killing her over the last couple of days.

Grace reached across and grabbed her hand. "Give him a chance, Elle. Santi has fought against his feelings for so long that, well…" She took a visible breath. "After Carmen died, we were all worried about him. Really worried. We even thought he might have a breakdown of some sort. He shut off his feelings just like a water spigot. He threw himself into work, but he wasn't the same."

"You don't have to—"

"I want you to understand. He's not fighting you.

He's in a battle against himself. If he'd gone to counseling like so many of us advised, he might have been able to accept the idea of falling in love and remarrying, but as it is…" Grace tipped up a shoulder. "I guess I can understand to a certain extent. When Diego and I fell in love I tried to tell myself it wasn't happening. That it couldn't happen. Not to me. Not when I'd fought so hard not to be one of those statistics. But you can't always choose who you love, or when. That's why I said to give him a chance. He might just need some time to figure it all out."

"And if he doesn't? I don't think I can stand to stay at Aelina if I have to see him day in and day out."

"Please don't tell me you're thinking of leaving."

She realized she had been. The idea had sprung up out of the ashes of their night together, and she'd been unconsciously watering it. Right now the stalk and first leaves were growing steadily and pretty soon she'd be forced to make a decision.

"I haven't decided anything yet."

"I'm so sorry for making things worse."

She squeezed her friend's hand before releasing it. "You haven't. In fact, maybe you've helped me face some pretty hard truths. And maybe Santi, too."

"Face them, yes. But don't make any hard-and-fast decisions while you're in pain. If I'd done that, Diego and I would probably be going our own separate ways. Just give it a few weeks. Or maybe even a few months. I promise everything will become clear in time. Don't make a decision about forever that you may come to regret. Promise?"

She nodded. "I promise." She forced a smile. "And thanks. For the ramp. And...for everything."

"That's what friends are for, *querida*." With that, Grace rose to her feet. "I'll see you on Friday."

"Okay, see you there." As soon as she said it, she realized that her avoidance tactics were doomed to fail. Despite moving to the fifth floor and doing her best to not stop on the third floor for anything, she and Santi were bound to run into each other from time to time. The renewal ceremony was proof of that.

All she could do was go and see how she felt. She wheeled herself around to face the large picture window behind her desk and looked out over the city of Barcelona. The sun was a mere speck on the horizon, red shafts of light painting the clouds and the city beneath it with a glorious glow. As she sat there thinking about all that had happened since she'd moved there these last couple of weeks, lights began flickering on, one by one all across the area. The beauty in that was unmistakable. Building after building, street after street became illuminated against the deepening shadows. And she couldn't help but hope that a light very much like these would pop on in Santi's head and banish his own darkness. And that he would realize that life wasn't over for him. He could find happiness and a whole new beginning, if only he'd allow himself to.

And if he couldn't?

Then she was going to have a very hard decision to make. Grace was right. She didn't have to make it right now. But she also couldn't put off the inevitable forever.

* * *

Friday came far too soon. Hell, he'd been stupid to nix Grace's idea of seating him and Elena together. Maybe it would have forced him to muster up the courage to talk to her. As it was, he hadn't caught sight of her since the day of Tomás's surgery almost a week ago.

It was almost as if she were avoiding him.

Like he was avoiding her?

Of course she was. He hadn't given her any reason to do otherwise.

He walked down the boardwalk, his thoughts again on Carmen. The truth of how unhappy she'd be with how he was dealing with her loss had been weighing on his mind more and more. It was a hard realization to come to. He'd been given the wonderful opportunity of a second chance, and he'd been willing to throw it all away, all over a misguided sense of guilt.

Would he have wanted Carmen to do the same if their situations had been reversed? Hell no. He would have found a way to haunt her for the rest of her life if she had.

There were so many coincidences attached to his and Elena's first and second meetings that it made him wonder if the diagnostician had somehow been sent to him. Maybe his prayers hadn't been completely unheard after all. They just hadn't been answered in the way he'd expected them to be.

On impulse, he'd made a weird purchase yesterday on a rare trip into Barcelona, surprised when he'd seen the item in a storefront window.

Coincidences. It was what finally made him decide to face whatever it was he felt for Elena head-on. He was going to do it after the ceremony. If she even came.

The waves lapped against the shore in front of them and the scent of salt on the breeze was thick and warm and bracing. He breathed it in, glad to be alive in a way he hadn't been for a long time. He dragged his hand through his hair and found a seat near the back just off the boardwalk.

Where Elle could see him? Probably.

He'd arrived twenty minutes before the ceremony, maybe unconsciously hoping to find her and pull her his way.

And if she rejected him? Hell, he couldn't blame her if she did. He'd certainly rejected her. The look on her face after she'd reached for him only to have him step away had haunted him. If he was right, she cared for him, or at least she had in that moment.

And now?

Demonio. He was so confused about his own feelings that he hadn't really stopped to think about what he might have done to her, beyond the superficial worry about hurting her.

What if he'd done permanent damage, the way that goon of a professor had? What if it stayed with her for years?

What if she went out with Dario and he did the same?

He swallowed. Yes, whether or not they were able to work this out, he needed to talk to her and set the record straight. Those stupid words "It's not you, it's me" were all too true in this case. It had been wholly about him and had nothing to do with what he'd been beginning to feel for her.

Diego came alongside him, stopping to shake his hand and give him a lopsided grin. The Spaniard looked cool and confident in light khakis and a loose shirt, a perfect combination for the beach, which is what Grace had asked her guests to wear.

Santi had opted for dark jeans and a white linen shirt with rolled-up sleeves. He hoped it met with Grace's approval.

"Have you seen my bride yet?"

"Not yet." The man didn't look worried about being stood up; it was more of a simple question. Or maybe he was just anxious to get this show on the road. "And congratulations. I'm glad things worked out for you two."

"Me, too. I'm just glad I didn't blow my chances with her."

Grace glided up to meet them in a loose white dress that floated just above her knees, revealing tanned legs and sandals that looked to have a million crisscrossed straps. She smiled. "You didn't." She didn't ask what they were talking about, seeming to already know.

Maybe that's what love was.

He and Carmen had had that. And so had he and Elle that day at the estate where Caitlin and Javier's wedding had been. Coincidence? He was beginning to think more and more that it hadn't been. He just hadn't recognized it at the time. And now?

Yes, he thought he finally did. And like Diego, he hoped it wasn't too late.

Diego bent to kiss her. "Are you ready to make this official?"

"It already is, silly. We're just telling the world we're sticking with each other. I'm glad Caitlin and her new hubby made it back in time for the ceremony."

Santi spotted the pair on the other side of the aisle. Javier's arm was around Caitlin's shoulders and the pair looked relaxed and very much in love. There were a couple of other faces he recognized. Diego's sister Isabella was there with Carlos Martinez. The couple was expecting their first child in about four months.

It seemed love was definitely in the air.

Diego made his way to the front, where his best man and the hospital's minister were waiting. Grace turned back and hovered at the start of the aisle, waiting for the violins to cue her walk to the front. Santi caught a flurry of movement behind him and turned to see Grace laughing as she hugged an older woman before the music started up and they walked arm in arm to where Diego was waiting.

All of the pair's family and friends were there, with very few chairs left open. Except for Elle, who still hadn't made it.

Maybe she wasn't coming. What if she'd decided to leave Aelina after all, the way he'd feared on Monday when he found her office vacated.

What was he going to do if that were the case?

He would do what he should have done a week ago. He was going to hunt her down and talk to her. Tell her what he'd discovered about himself and ask her if she felt the same way.

Dios! And if she didn't? Or if unlike Diego, he really had screwed up his chances with her?

Well, at least he'd know he'd tried and not buried his head in the sand and attempted to pretend life would move on by, unseen and unfelt. Except life around him was pretty dull and gray, despite the beauty of today's setting. And he realized it was all due to Elena's absence.

Hand in hand, Diego and Grace renewed their vows, their eyes never leaving each other. And the farther into the service they got, the more uneasy he felt about his own prospects. It wasn't like Elena to be late for anything. She was one of the most organized people he'd ever met. It was one of the reasons she was so good at what she did.

Just as he was thinking about getting up in the middle of the ceremony and going to find her, she appeared beside him, stopping her chair and setting the brake.

He swallowed back a huge ball of emotion, letting go of the fear he'd felt moments earlier that he'd lost her completely.

She wouldn't have chosen to sit beside him if that were the case, would she?

Man, he didn't deserve her. Didn't deserve a second chance to be with her, but here it was, as if handed to him. He wasn't going to turn his back on it again.

He leaned closer. "I was afraid you weren't going to come."

"Tomás wanted to speak with me. That's why I'm late."

She didn't seem angry or upset. She just seemed like… Elle. The one he'd grown to know and love.

He frowned. "All okay?"

"He's fine. I'll tell you about it once the ceremony is done."

Elle's hand was resting on the arm of her chair, and before he could stop himself, he covered it with his own, entwining his fingers with hers. He waited for her to pull away or make some sign that she didn't want this. Or him.

Instead she seemed to sigh, her digits closing around his own. Her eyes met his and a sort of silent communication passed between them before they turned their attention back to the front.

A sense of hope rose in his chest, as his heart grew lighter and lighter with each moment that passed. And when Diego pulled Grace into an embrace and kissed her with a fervor that was unmistakable, he tightened his grip until he was sure Elle would notice. And she did. But she didn't ask him to release her. Instead she laid her right hand over their joined ones and whispered, "I know."

He believed it. If Grace had been able to read him so easily, then why wouldn't Elena?

The couple at the front finally broke apart to much laughter as Grace's hand went to cover her heart and she then put her palm to Diego's lips. Then they turned to face their loved ones, hands raised high in the air for all to see. This was one union that was going to stand the test of time. The way he hoped his and Elena's one day would.

As the happy couple made their way back down the walkway, Grace found Santi's eyes and gave him a wink and a quick thumbs-up. Then they were gone, off to a reception before sweeping away to their long-overdue honeymoon.

As the guests began to make their way down the aisle heading toward the festivities, Santi and Elena stayed where they were, until they were the only ones left on the sand.

"Tomás is okay?"

"He's doing great. He told me that Letizia broke the news that she's trying to become his foster parent and that they've been spending a lot of time getting to know each other this week."

He smiled. "She told me she was going to try to wait to tell him until things were more certain."

"Evidently they are. Tomás has been so unhappy at the group home that the director petitioned the courts to fast-track Letizia's application, and the process is very nearly finished. No one sees any reason why it can't or shouldn't happen."

"That's wonderful."

"Yes."

They sat there in silence for a few seconds before they both tried to speak. They laughed and then Elena told him to go ahead.

"I need to apologize for something—" He stopped at her stricken look and then realized what she thought he was going to say. "No. Not for what happened that night between us, but for my behavior afterward. I felt things I hadn't felt in a very long time, and frankly, it scared the hell out of me."

"I know. Me, too."

He lifted her hand and kissed it. "I'm sorry for walking out like I did. It was cowardly, and I hope you can forgive me. Because I love you."

"And Carmen?"

He frowned. "What about her?"

He hoped she wasn't going to ask him to compare them because he couldn't. He couldn't explain how he could love his late wife and still feel this piercing, uncontrollable love for the woman seated next to him. The one he hoped felt the same thing for him. But it was there. And he wasn't going to deny it any longer.

"Grace told me a little bit about what happened after her death. I know I'm not her but—"

"I know you're not. And I love *you*. Not because you're anything like her. You're not. And that's a good thing, Elle. You're not someone to take her place. You're someone I love because… Well, I just can't stop myself. Believe me, I tried. It's there, despite every effort I've made to stop it from happening."

She laughed. "That describes what's happened to me in a nutshell. You make me happy. That's all there is to it. And the thought of you not feeling the same way was gutting. I love you, too, Santi. I love the way you try your best to help your patients, the way you give to kids at the center. The way you love horses. And your reaction to that silly painting at the Maravilla estate."

He tipped her chin and looked into her eyes. "Do you believe in coincidences?"

"What?"

"I need to show you something. Will you come with me?"

"Where?"

"Back to my house." He grinned. "I rode my bike here, though, so…"

"I'll drive. I'm right back there in the parking lot."

He drew a deep breath, the crush of the past finally beginning to loosen its grip. He kissed her. Softly. Deeply. Trying to infuse everything he felt for her into that act.

They loaded his bike into the van and Santi told her how to get to his house. They stopped outside and she stared at the white stucco house with his clay-tiled roof. "Your home is beautiful."

He tried to see it through her eyes, but all he saw was the house he'd lived in for the last six years. And he realized he'd never made it a home. Not really. But he hoped that was going to change very soon.

He opened the door, and he called out to Maria, his housekeeper, who was following Sasha as she rushed to greet him. After a few yips and turning circles of happiness, the dog turned her attention to Elle, whom she also greeted just as enthusiastically. Then Santi smiled at Maria.

"This is Elena Solis. She's my…" His words trailed away as he realized they hadn't made anything official. Fortunately, his housekeeper saved him from his blunder.

"I already know," she said. "I've been hoping to meet you."

Hell, did everyone know what he felt before he did? Probably. He'd just been too stubborn to let his heart tell his brain what was what. At least until now.

Maria went on, "I have some things to do in my cottage, so if you'll excuse me."

She turned and exited the room.

Elle looked at him. "Does that seem weird to you? Grace came to my office this past week and already knew that I was in love with you."

"I was just thinking the same thing. Like I said, there are so many coincidences about us that it makes me think…never mind." He wasn't going to say that he wondered if Carmen had ordered God to send him someone to love. He didn't want to ruin what was happening here. "Which brings up what I was going to show you. I happened to be walking past an art gallery and saw something."

Santi drew her into the next room, Sasha hard on their heels. In the drawing room was a framed print, facing the wall. Elle looked at it, her head tilted. "What is that?"

"It's one of the biggest coincidences of all. And I can tell you that I finally understand its meaning."

He went over to the painting and slowly turned it around to face her.

Elle's hand went to her mouth. "That was at an art gallery?"

"It's not the original, of course, but it's a print of the original."

The framed image was a replica of the one that hung on the wall at the Maravilla estate. It was a man and a woman sitting sidesaddle on a horse that was racing across the countryside.

"Wow. I don't know what to say."

He set the picture against the wall as he watched her study it. "I hoped it might help 'sell' me to you."

"You don't need to sell yourself to me. That auction ended the moment I watched your head tilt in confusion at that painting."

"Me, too. I just didn't realize it at the time." He glanced at the print. "I'd like to hang that in our bedroom, if you're in agreement."

"*Our* bedroom?"

"Is that so hard to imagine?"

She shook her head, her hand buried in Sasha's fur. "No. Actually it's not. It's like a dream. Something so unimaginable that I'm having trouble believing it."

"Kind of like that painting?"

"Yes, it's exactly like that painting. And having a reminder is a good thing. To remember that what might seem impossible is actually very possible. Especially when you're talking about love."

"De tus labios a los oídos de Dios." He found himself repeating the words that Letizia had said to him over the phone less than a week ago. From your lips to God's ears. The prayers he once thought went unanswered hadn't been. And he was so very grateful.

"Let's change that to from *our* lips to God's ears. Because we're in this together, Santi. You and me. And I wouldn't have it any other way."

"Me, either, sweetheart. Me, either."

EPILOGUE

Six months later

STRATO AND BILLY stood side by side in the arena of On Horses' Wings. The place had been transformed into a garden oasis with draped lighting, and flowers and plants of every kind imaginable.

Elena could barely believe this was possible. And if Santi hadn't thought it was, he never would have let this happen. The horse that had once stood over her, trying to make sure she was okay after her accident, had been sent to a trainer who specialized in equines whose owners were differently abled.

He told her Strato had taken to the training so easily, it was almost as if he'd been waiting for this his whole life. And maybe he had been. The man's words had made her cry, partly for all the time she'd wasted but mostly for the opportunity to sit astride her beautiful horse once again.

She glanced at Santi, wondering if he was thinking the same thing. That the very thing that had helped her sit her horse had given her an idea of ways she could sit on him with a little extra support.

The results had been…very, very satisfying, for them both.

When he winked at her, her face heated.

Seated in chairs that had been draped in white fabric were both sets of parents and family and friends. Sandra was her maid of honor and stood next to Strato, holding a bouquet of red roses. Every once in a while her horse eyed that bouquet in a way that made her smile. He still had a mischievous streak to him, but when it came to riding, he'd learned to listen to her hand cues rather than those from her legs.

And Santi's best "man" was Tomás, who had been officially adopted by Letizia last week and was doing so very well. It was meant to be, they all agreed.

Just like her and Santi.

When she'd asked him if they could be married at the center on their horses rather than at some beautiful but unfamiliar venue, he'd agreed instantly. And On Horse's Wings became the place of her dreams.

They gripped hands as their horses stood in the midst of loved ones, and when Santi stood in his stirrups and leaned over to kiss her, she shivered. There was nowhere she'd rather be than with this man and these two horses.

She was now volunteering at the center as well, learning a different way to interact and care for the animals she loved so much.

The flash of a phone's camera made Strato snort for a second, but he stood stone-still as if he were carrying a piece of porcelain. The way Santi had carried her to bed that first time. And she understood. It wasn't because they were afraid of hurting her, although that might have been part of it, but because they cared about her.

And she was grateful. Grateful for Santi. Grateful for her work. Grateful for life.

And full of more love than she ever thought possible.

When the minister invited them to kiss once again, they did. With the promise of a bright future and the hope that forever truly was possible.

* * * * *

COMING SOON!

We really hope you enjoyed reading this book. If you're looking for more romance, be sure to head to the shops when new books are available on

Thursday 18th August

To see which titles are coming soon, please visit

millsandboon.co.uk/nextmonth

MILLS & BOON®

Coming next month

HER SECRET RIO BABY
Luana DaRosa

The door opened, interrupting their conversation, and Dr Salvador strode back into the room. The fierce protectiveness in Diego's eyes vanished, leaving his face unreadable.

Eliana's eyes were drawn to the emergency doctor, who stepped closer. She was wearing an expression of medical professionalism on her face that quickened her pulse. She knew that look. She had given it to patients herself.

She whipped her head around, looking at Diego, and whatever he saw written in her face was enough to make him get off his chair and step closer to her side. A similar look of protectiveness to the one he'd had a few moments ago was etched into his features.

'Would you mind giving us some privacy?' Sophia asked him, and a tremble shook Eliana's body.

The nausea came rushing back, her head suddenly felt light, and Eliana reacted before she could think, her hand reaching for Diego's and crushing it in a vice-like grip.

'It's okay if he stays,' she said, in a voice that sounded so unlike her own.

Something deep within her told her she needed him to stay. Whether it was premonition or just a primal fear gripping at her heart, she didn't know.

Diego stopped, giving her a questioning look, but he stayed, and his hand did not fight her touch.

'Well, it looks like it's not a stomach bug, but morning sickness. Or, in your case, late-afternoon sickness.' She paused for a moment, before confirming the absurd thought that was rattling around in Eliana's head. 'You're pregnant.'

Eliana opened her mouth to speak, but no words crossed the threshold of her lips. Pregnant? How was she pregnant? Her head snapped around to Diego, and whatever expression she was wearing on her face seemed to convey to him all the words she didn't want to say in front of the doctor.

The baby was his. They were pregnant.

His hand slipped from her grasp as he took a step back. The shock she felt at the revelation was written on his face.

'How long?' she asked, even though she knew it didn't matter.

Eliana had only slept with one person in the last six months, and that was the man standing here in the room with her.

Continue reading
HER SECRET RIO BABY
Luana DaRosa

Available next month
www.millsandboon.co.uk

MILLS & BOON

THE HEART OF ROMANCE

A ROMANCE FOR EVERY READER

MODERN

Prepare to be swept off your feet by sophisticated, sexy and seductive heroes, in some of the world's most glamourous and romantic locations, where power and passion collide.

HISTORICAL

Escape with historical heroes from time gone by. Whether your passion for wicked Regency Rakes, muscled Vikings or rugged Highlanders, aw the romance of the past.

MEDICAL

Set your pulse racing with dedicated, delectable doctors in the high-pre sure world of medicine, where emotions run high and passion, comfort love are the best medicine.

True Love

Celebrate true love with tender stories of heartfelt romance, from the rush of falling in love to the joy a new baby can bring, and a focus on t emotional heart of a relationship.

Desire

Indulge in secrets and scandal, intense drama and plenty of sizzling ho action with powerful and passionate heroes who have it all: wealth, stat good looks…everything but the right woman.

HEROES

Experience all the excitement of a gripping thriller, with an intense ro mance at its heart. Resourceful, true-to-life women and strong, fearless face danger and desire - a killer combination!

To see which titles are coming soon, please visit

millsandboon.co.uk/nextmonth

JOIN US ON SOCIAL MEDIA!

Stay up to date with our latest releases, author news and gossip, special offers and discounts, and all the behind-the-scenes action from Mills & Boon...

 @millsandboon

 @millsandboonuk

 facebook.com/millsandboon

 @millsandboonuk

It might just be true love...

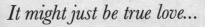